WALK LIKE YOU

LINDA COLES

PROLOGUE

There was no going back now. He'd be on his own from this point on, he knew, and he deserved to be so. Too coward to tell her what he'd done, that he'd betrayed her trust in him, again; he couldn't bear it, couldn't deal with it. And after all the tears she'd shed, they'd both shed, promises that he'd try harder, get some help. Promises that she'd wait for him, but not for an eternity, she'd made that part clear. He'd eventually managed to abstain from the devil. But temptation had long, gnarly fingers that pulled at him like a fly dragged to a spider's web. And like a fly, he'd fought hard to set himself free.

Not hard enough.

He was weak, he knew that. And he despised himself for being so, for what he'd done, and for the upset to come, for her. The pity he'd see reflecting back at him from her eyes. Or would it be hatred now, this final time? Maybe that would be easier to deal with. The thought sparked resignation and he lifted his chin slightly as a tear rolled over his three-day-old stubble. He watched it land on his thigh, a tiny wet stain spreading as another fell and added to it, widening the dampness on the trousers of his uniform. There'd been so many tears from them both. There could be no more.

The idea was born.

It would dissolve the anguish in each of them, set them free. Wiping his face with the flat palm of his hand, the driver sniffed loudly to clear his sinuses and force an energy into his lungs. The idea had caught him by surprise, but he was instantly comfortable with it all the same. There was no other choice. He sniffed again, loudly, his nose flaring like a racehorse's, then wrinkling in determination. He lifted his eyes and dragged them into focus, shaking his head slightly in an attempt to clear them. A shot of determination coursed through every muscle, every sinew, every tendon. He sat up straighter in his seat, feeling cocky almost as he edged the accelerator on another ten. He heard the engine change slightly as it processed the request for further power and he listened to the increase in tempo like he might an orchestra. Another ten, and another subtle change in sound. It was likely not audible to anyone sat in the carriages further back, but he was tuned in, he knew what to listen for. He was the conductor though of a rather different kind of orchestra. There were no music instruments on his dashboard. No triangle to chime when the time came, no drum to beat, no bugle to blow.

It wouldn't be hard to hear the next acceleration, and his passengers would certainly feel it. The driver knew the tracks well, knew every signal, every bend, every station platform. Even faces, though not their names. The train hurtled through the Kent countryside – the vivid yellow of rapeseed topping fields on both sides of the tracks like runny egg yolk resting on soldiers of toast – as the long string of carriages headed south then on to France. They wouldn't be getting that far, not today. He was sorry, though he couldn't tell them all. Or explain why.

And still the orchestra played on in his head, cymbals crashing, double bass bellowing.

His timing, once his decision had been made, was crucial. He was in control, his actions clear in his mind. The bend he needed was rapidly looming in the distance and he forced another shot of determination into his veins, wrinkling and flaring his nose once more as he added the final instalment of electric power to the engine. The train could go no faster. Idly, he wondered if anyone further back had noticed the shift in acceleration. Were they concerned at all? Frightened, possibly? It was too late to think of them now. He knew his plan would work; the corner would make sure of that. Then the steel arc was upon them, and he sounded his horn, though not in warning, there was no point in that. The scream that descended was his own anguished cry of pain, the engine vocalising for him what he felt in his core so deep down inside.

He'd done it.

Peace at last. The torment deserted him, the betrayal extinguished, the noose around his neck slackened. The darkness was a blessing. His own orchestra quiet.

CHAPTER 1

'An adventure for one' is what her own internal doctor had ordered. A little celebratory excitement consumed on her own time with no one to be concerned about but herself. Since her husband Marcus was away working in Hong Kong again, Susan Smith had made the decision to go alone. And enjoy herself. He'd been distracted when they'd spoken by phone the night before, and so she wasn't actually sure he even knew she was planning her little awayday or two. But then they weren't as close as they had once been. Susan had already come to terms with that, though she doubted Marcus had even thought about it.

A woman further up in the same Business Premier carriage caught Susan's eye as she stood, presumably headed for the toilet. Watching her move gracefully away down the aisle, Susan was intrigued by the woman's hair colour and style – they were identical to her own. She wondered what the woman looked like, if her face was similar too. Absent-mindedly, she touched her own strawberry blonde hair that just brushed her jawline in a shaggy bob. She'd have to wait and see when the woman returned. Not feeling like reading the newspaper that was resting in her lap, Susan fixated on a building in the distance and let her empty thoughts drift a while, dissecting nothing in particular. A few moments passed then her mind caught on the sound of the doors opening up ahead. The woman was returning to her seat. Susan gasped quietly to herself as she noticed her facial resemblance. Though a little older than Susan, the woman could have passed for her older sister. Not that she had an older sister. Her doppelgänger? She could well have been Susan's. She watched the woman check on something in her handbag, which was balanced on the table in front of her, then satisfied, move it away to the side again. The simple action reminded her to check the money belt she'd added before leaving the house earlier in the morning. Cash was required for this particular trip, though her credit card was along for the ride, just in case. Patting her stomach, she traced the thick line around her waist – it was still in place. The familiar webbing was there, its two pouches firmly closed. Happy all was safe, Susan resumed her fascination with the building approaching in the distance. A large, decrepit house maybe, it was hard to tell from where she was, but it was certainly in need of repair. Parts of the roof were missing, the tiles long gone, leaving glaring holes for the elements to wreak havoc with. A gable end looked like it would buckle at any minute and, as they drew closer, she could finally see the building had once been a home of some sort, or possibly a pub. So many had closed down over the years but that was progress. As the building vanished behind her, Susan felt the subtle shift of the carriage as it appeared to pick up speed. Or did she imagine it? Idly, she picked her newspaper up and scanned the front page, the carriage rocking her from side to side slightly, the sound of the rails clacking as the wheels passed over the joints – it was almost therapeutic. But another shift in speed caught her attention and she glanced over her paper at the handful of other passengers. Had they noticed it too? Was she imagining it? Nobody appeared to give the subtle shift any attention, they were concentrating in their own worlds, and so Susan went back to her paper and tried to settle. But she was a perceptive woman and so when she felt the third shift, and looked intently out of the window at the horizon flying by, she instinctively knew something was wrong.

Standing, she pondered what to do or say – anything? Susan made her way towards the doors and the luggage rack that was filled with cases much like her own; she wasn't the only person heading away on a break, work or otherwise. The red emergency lever was right there in front of her, daring her to pull it as she held on to the overhead rail to keep herself steady. She felt the train increase in speed one more time. Frightened now, she called out to her fellow passengers for what to do.

"Something's not right!" she yelled, sounding like a demented woman. "We keep increasing speed!" she explained as eight blank faces tried to focus on what she was saying and decide for themselves if there was anything to concern them. A couple went back to their laptops, passing her off as a deranged individual no doubt. Susan looked on in disbelief, anxiety building in her chest – something was about to happen. But not everyone dismissed her. A man in a navy suit eventually called out to her, "I thought it was me!" he said, panic evident in his voice as he too stood, holding on to the headrest in front to steady himself. That was all it took for the remaining passengers to once again look up from what they were doing and take notice. Two people had sensed it.

But they were all too late.

Then, all hell let loose.

CHAPTER 2

There was no stopping the catastrophe that was to unfold. As the train entered the bend at nearly double the speed limit, the rear of the first carriage left its tracks and twisted back on itself awkwardly before it collided with a concrete wall that formed part of a bridge. Only momentum dragged the remaining carriages on. They screamed and groaned like a metal dinosaur in distress before, eventually, each one slammed down on its side. Glass windows were ripped out and loose gravel sprayed into the air like machine-gun fire. The deep, anguished screeching and bellowing filled the late morning air as metal mangled and grated where it slid, the dregs of the train's energy propelling it forward. Concrete from the bridge collapsed and fell, adding grey dust to the mayhem. The impact was catastrophic. Smoke and fumes seeped out of giant tears and crevices in the train's carcass, rising into the air in pungent, billowing clouds. Carriages were tossed far and wide, most lay on their sides as they'd come to a grinding, piercing standstill. The front ones now a mangled mess and unrecognisable from what they had been only moments before. It took seconds for the whole event to unravel, catapulting its internal cargo of human life across nearby

tracks and grass banking. The stench of ammonia from damaged
capacitors drifted along like low cloud. And then it went quiet.

Susan was on her back, flung from her seat unceremoniously
and, like other passengers in her carriage, lay quiet and still.
Minutes passed until sirens filled the air as emergency services
approached the scene. Maybe it was these sounds that brought
Susan out of unconsciousness. Maybe the smell. As she opened her
eyes and tried to fathom what had happened, what was going on,
panic hit her chest with a heavy thump as realisation grabbed her.
The speeding train had derailed and crashed. She listened as
passengers in nearby carriages came around to the enormity of what
had happened. Crying, wailing and sobbing added to the steam and
smoke, filling the air with an acrid horror and grief. With calls and
cries from passengers trapped within their metal confinements, the
birds stayed silent.

As her sticky eyes did their best to focus, Susan registered the
sheet of protective steel above and almost covering her. Miracu-
lously, a large part of the carriage ceiling had fallen down and
covered her protectively from other mangled debris that had been
pushed skywards or flung across the chaotic space. She had to – no,
needed to – get out. In one frantic, claustrophobic moment, she
somehow found the energy to shimmy her way out of the dark grey
mass, not stopping to think she may be in further danger, or to see
if she'd been badly hurt. It was on impulse. Once out of the metal
confines that had undoubtedly saved her life, she stopped briefly to
catch her breath and steady her heartrate. Then the severity of
what she was now in the midst of hit her. Her carriage was wedged
upside down and she was sitting on the inside of the old roof.
Luggage had been tossed across the space, shards of broken glass
littered the new 'floor', seats dangled above her head. Thank goodness for their bolts.

She held her hand to her mouth in horror as she took in the
other passengers. They were strewn awkwardly as she had been but
without the lifesaving protection of a metal sheet covering them.
There were no sounds from anyone, no whimpering, no screaming –

not in her carriage. On her hands and knees, she carefully made her way over to each person, checking for a pulse, any sign they were still alive, hoping. Many were heavily soaked in their own blood. One man had lost most of his arm, severed at the elbow. Another had been impaled through his thigh by a jagged piece of metal. Susan diligently checked them all for signs of life anyway. When she reached the only other woman, Susan could see by the awkward angle of her neck that it was broken. There was no pulse. Sitting back on her haunches, Susan gave in to the despair and shock and began to silently cry.

There were no other survivors in her carriage. Susan Smith was the only one.

Blood streamed down her nose, mixing with salty tears as she sat stunned by the carnage and loss of life around her. Debris was everywhere, luggage and laptops and briefcases landed on the floor with her, anything that had been loose now resting haphazardly among the mangled chaos. The harsh stench of ammonia assaulted her nostrils. Susan leaned forward and began to cry in earnest, arms wrapped around her body, consoling herself since no one else could. She reached out and grabbed a soft bag. It was something to cling on to, like a child might hold on to a teddy bear in a time of need, the soft leather object giving her a modicum of comfort. Holding it tightly to her chest, she sobbed harder, letting the emotion, stress and horror vent from her being until she finally calmed a little. Her own case was somewhere in the wreckage, though she'd no idea where. Susan again glanced over at the dead woman, then looked down at the bag she was holding. She'd seen the woman carrying it only minutes earlier. Unfastening the zip, she peered inside, pulled out the woman's wallet and opened it. The name on the driver's licence was Tabitha Child. Susan quickly slipped it back inside, feeling like she'd pried on something immensely private. The dead woman lay only a few feet away from herself.

"I'll say a prayer for you, Tabitha Child," she said gently, wiping at tears with the back of her hand.

A noise nearby, a voice calling, brought Susan back to reality and she listened. A rescuer, she surmised.

The voice called out again, "Hello! Anyone?"

Scrambling to her feet, being mindful not to add to her injuries, she stood on wobbly legs and inched herself forward, straining to look through smashed windows for what was happening on the outside of the wreckage. She spotted an older man, wearing a high-viz vest, who was the source of the calling. As he approached the carriage, Susan yelled back.

"In here!"

The man smiled, likely relieved to have found someone alive in the mangled wreckage.

"Stay there, I'll help you," he called back, but Susan wasn't listening. Now more stable on her feet, she carried on towards an open gash in the carriage's wall and forced herself through it, still holding on to the comfort of the soft bag. The man was by her side in an instant, helping her down from the twisted mess. In the distance, Susan could see people moving in all directions, some obviously passengers, some rescue workers, each with a safer destination in mind. The air smelled metallic. Debris littered the tracks as far as she could see.

"They're all dead," she said to her rescuer, pointing back towards her carriage. "I couldn't find a pulse on anyone." The man looked at her, sadness and anguish evident on his face at the news.

"Come with me," he said gently. "We need to get you to the hospital. What's your name, love?"

But Susan was elsewhere, her mind as jagged as the gashed wreckage behind her. When the words finally made their way to her lips, she replied.

"Tabitha. Tabitha Child."

CHAPTER 3

Since her father had died, and following an unavoidable falling out with her mother, Chrissy Livingstone had become a little closer to her younger sister, Julie. Even though there was only a year between them, with the amount of Botox and the copious amounts of time Julie spent on spa days, she looked a good ten years younger. Money bought youth for Julie Stokes and she had plenty of it to play with. On the other side of the sister spectrum, Chrissy generally opted for the more natural look. Max Factor didn't cling to her face in the same quantity, or with the same regularity, as it did her sibling, but as a naturally striking blonde herself, she didn't lose out on admiring glances. Polar opposites, men gawped at one or the other depending on their own personal taste. Both women were at the start of their forties and in good shape, though Julie needed a good hot meal or two in Chrissy's view, she was on the thin side and it concerned her. Recently, Julie had gone back to work, setting up a boutique shoe store in Richmond, The Quadrant main street no less, one of the most affluent areas in greater London. The unit on its own had cost a King's ransom never mind the eclectic stock she'd purchased. Chrissy had kept her judgement to herself, hoping that her sister would take the investment and the workload seriously, and not rely on Richard to bail her out if she screwed things up. She had to admit, Julie was pulling things off beautifully. One skill Julie had in bucket loads was an eye and a sense for a person's ability and work ethic. The three women she'd employed were excellent characters as well as creative marketers, leaving Julie to hover over them like a mother hummingbird as they reaped the rewards together. The life that Julie now led was doing her good, and Chrissy was pleased she'd finally found a use for her talent. Getting out into the real world and discussing more than gossip-magazine material was broadening her horizons. Chrissy had always detested the fact that Julie had lived off Richard's money all their married life, and with their girls at boarding school there wasn't even that excuse for being a home bird. But that was Chrissy's opinion, her own ethic. Now, Julie was blossoming with the success of Jooles, Jooles and there was talk of another boutique opening closer to home in Egham. 'Jooles, Jooles'? The name said it all.

Richard, her long-suffering husband, worked in the city. Though the man was as dull as dishwater, Chrissy knew he was silently impressed with how the business was performing. One day he might say so out loud.

The two women were sitting in Julie's conservatory enjoying a little down time together with the help of a glass of ginger beer each. It was almost lunchtime and the room was so bright from the overhead sun that Chrissy wished she hadn't left her shades in the car out front.

"I could do with a spa day this week, but I can't see where I can squeeze one in," said Julie dreamily. She looked nearly asleep, head resting back on the soft cushion of the wicker recliner.

Chrissy rolled her eyes, knowing Julie couldn't see since hers were closed. Julie's pale skin looked almost porcelain, like one of those dolls with a pot head that wore frilly dresses.

"Stop doing that."

"What?"

"You know what, rolling your eyes. Like you stick your tongue out when you think Richard can't see you." Julie lifted her head off the back of the lounger and glanced across at Chrissy, a smile forcing its way through chemical filler. There was no malice, and Chrissy met her smile with one of her own.

"Has he ever said anything?"

"Not to you, he won't. He ignores you largely; he likes a more mature woman."

Chrissy raised herself upright. "Eh?"

"In nature, not in looks, silly. You're too flighty, too 'gung-ho' for him, whereas I am demure, ladylike." Julie's mouth creased a little at her own words. She was having fun bugging her sister.

"Heavens above! Really? He said that?" Chrissy settled back down and closed her own eyes, trying not to let her smile break into a full-on giggle. Richard had her down pat, Chrissy could indeed be described as gung-ho. If only he knew the half of it. But then only Adam, her own husband, knew the full story. Having worked for MI5 for most of their marriage, she told everyone she worked in human resources and that generally dried the conversation up. Nobody ever felt like delving further, it was hardly scintillating. They still shared the secret, one that Julie would never know the full truth of. Her past was never mentioned.

"I should come with you on one of your spa days. It could be fun."

"Darling, you'd be too disruptive; you couldn't sit still long enough to enjoy relaxing. Too much energy, you should drink less coffee. It stains your teeth anyway."

Chrissy rubbed her tongue over her front upper row self-consciously. Did they need bleaching, were they stained? Maybe Julie had a point.

"What are you working on at the moment?" Julie asked, enjoying the tranquillity of the sunroom. It was her afternoon off.

"Interesting you should ask," quipped Chrissy. "It's a little perplexing actually."

"Then tell me, I might be able to help."

"I'll tell you what I can, client confidentiality and all, but I'm working with a college, a rather important and well-known one."

"And?"

"They suspect there's something going on in that the students are doing things on behalf of somebody else. Does that make sense?"

"Kind of. Do you mean like doing each other's homework? Because that's old news."

"No. A lot more sinister than that. They'd hardly need a PI for a homework issue, now, would they?" Chrissy rolled her eyes a little in exasperation. No doubt Julie felt the gesture. "I mean, for instance, odd and potentially dangerous pranks carried out on behalf of another, usually a student. But more recently there's been an instance where outside involvement is suspected too, so coming in from outside the school gates."

"Oh, that sounds creepy," added Julie. "And how far have you got?"

"Not far enough. But I will. I've a digital forensics guy involved now so it's good to have his input. Anyway," she said, anxious to change the subject from a client, "why do you ask? Need my services?"

"Not that I know of, and taking an interest in my sister's business, nothing more."

"And on that same subject, any news on your next shop, have you found a location yet?"

"Looks promising actually, but I'll not tempt fate and say, not quite yet."

"Meany," Chrissy added petulantly like they were ten years old again. She glanced at her watch. It was past 12.30 pm.

"Damn! Look at the time," she said suddenly, struggling to get up off her lounger without toppling back down. "I've things to do, people to see."

"Like who?" Julie asked, sounding intrigued and reaching for her glass.

"Figure of speech. I'd better get going. But I'm serious about the spa, I can be still and relax if I put my mind to it. Maybe for a couple of hours? It could be fun. Let me know next time you're going, or we can plan to go together. You only just said you needed one, and you sure do deserve one."

"I'll let you know." Julie's eyes were still closed as Chrissy said goodbye to a hand lightly waving her off Marilyn-Monroe style. Chrissy pulled her tongue out.

"I saw that."

CHAPTER 4

She'd been swept away with her own actions immediately after the crash and now it was too late to change it. She wasn't sure why she'd even contemplated it, never mind actually done it. But something had triggered her actions. The woman's bag, Tabitha Child's bag, had been a lifeline at that moment, a soft pillow to hang on to in the mayhem, but now, as she sat in a wheelchair among other walking wounded at the hospital, Susan wondered quite why she'd done it.

While she hadn't planned to take the woman's name, events had unfolded that felt like a sign from some higher power, an opportunity had presented itself to run. And the odour that had lingered reminded her of times past. The sole survivor of the carriage, protected by a piece of warped, fallen ceiling metal, the lookalike woman on the same train, the same carriage even. There were too many signs, too many events lined up, too many instances that, when you put them all together, pointed a direct line to one action: if you want it, take it and make it your own. So she had.

Dazed, glazed over and looking at nothing in particular, Susan, or Tabitha as she was now assuming, sat alone in A & E, silently, with her thoughts. Her fingers ran over the gold bracelet on her wrist and contemplated the clasp. Had it been part of the reason she'd run? Subconsciously even? Instinctively, knowing each word of the inscription on its inside, she slipped it off and placed it in a pocket of her purse for safe keeping. It would be secure there. Until she could put it back on.

She'd been at the hospital for an hour, medical staff busy with more pressing cases than her own. She wasn't badly wounded, nothing physical except for a bloody nose, a black eye, and superficial cuts and scratches. The emergency room was a riot of activity, doctors and nurses struggling to cope with the influx of passengers all needing assistance of varying degrees. She was taking up a wheelchair and felt like a fraud.

The bag she'd been clinging to was in her lap, its soft leather soothing, and she fiddled with the strap to keep her hands occupied. Orderlies pushed makeshift beds and trolleys with heavily blood-soiled people on them, orders and directions were shouted, and confusion hung in the air like a wet cloud. The familiar smell of hospital disinfectant was now tinged with a sooty odour. Dirty faces of survivors were all around her. She was lucky; so many hadn't been. A vibrating phone dragged at her attention. It was in the bag still on her lap. Slowly, she unfastened the zip and glanced at the screen. The word 'Dominic', along with a photograph of a handsome and dark-haired man looked back at her. She assumed it was the woman's partner, maybe husband, maybe lover. Though it could have been her boss, perhaps. She'd been on a work trip after all, her laptop had been on the table in front of her for most of the journey. Whoever it was, he'd rung six times previously, though she'd not noticed amid the mayhem. Someone would be worried no doubt, probably heard of the crash on the news, and would be looking for her. She let it ring.

Nobody would be looking for Susan, not for some time anyway. Marcus would be hard at work and though lunchtime approached for her, he was hours ahead with the time difference. If he heard of the crash later, it likely wouldn't register she had even been aboard. The phone stopped buzzing and she wondered about Tabitha.

Would the authorities assume the dead lookalike was not Tabitha but her? Would they match her bag that she'd left somewhere on the train with the woman, perhaps using her driver's licence for ID? How did these things work? The man's face looked back at her. He obviously knew the woman; it would only be a matter of time before things got awkward. If she was going to carry on with someone else's identity, she had to get out of the hospital, and fast, before Dominic figured things out and came running to her bedside. God, he could already be on his way to the hospital, could be parking his car even, could be organising childcare. Did they have children? The thought instantly saddened her, what if they did?

It was time to cement an important decision – move on right now with her new identity or carry on being Susan Smith and put her stupidity down to a bump on the head. Stepping out of the wheelchair, she casually made her way down the long corridor and out towards the front entrance and bright sunshine. She had until she reached the double doors to decide.

CHAPTER 5

She was on autopilot, someone making decisions for her and sending them to her brain to action. Still she clutched the bag; it contained her new and only possessions as Tabitha Child, such as they were. Where would she go? How much time, realistically, did she have before she was found out? Before Marcus found out? Before Dominic found out? The thought of him drove her forward towards a taxi rank and she slipped inside a waiting car. There was little point heading for the train station, the rail system would still be in the same turmoil as the inside of the A & E behind her.

"Where to, love?" the driver asked, part way turning his head towards her. He must have noticed the bloodstain on her face. "Hey, are you all right, love?" She caught his eye in the rear-view mirror as he glanced at her. They were as dark as Ghanaian cocoa beans and they held hers for a moment.

"Yes, thanks. A bad nosebleed. Sorry, I thought I'd cleaned up better than I have," she said and opened the bag on her lap looking for a tissue.

"My daughter gets them all the time. You should see the state of the pillow on her bed," he said, smiling. "So, where can I take you then?"

She really had no idea. But if she needed more cash, the bank was as good a place to start as any. She reached inside for the woman's wallet and looked at her credit card.

"HSBC. Is there one nearby?"

"Not far," he said and started the engine.

She sat back and studied the credit card in her hand as he drove. She needed a PIN number, which she hadn't got, and she couldn't get a replacement quickly. Flipping the plastic over, she saw the signature would be fairly simple to recreate, a capital T, then Ch and a fairly straight but lumpy line. And she had Tabitha Child's passport so at least she could draw some money out. It would have to do. She pulled out a small compact mirror and studied her face. Blood was still evident under her nostrils and with the help of a moist wipe, she did her best to get rid of it. A bruise was beginning to form over her right eye; it would be a shiner by the morning. There was a small amount of make-up in the side pocket where she'd found the mirror and so she applied lipstick then a little blusher to her pale cheeks. With colour back in her face, she looked and felt a little better. A quick comb of her shaggy hair and she was ready to test the acting lessons she'd had one summer break over fifteen years ago. It was fair to say she'd be rusty.

A few minutes later, they pulled up outside the bank.

"I won't be long. Can you wait, please?"

"Will do. If I get moved on, I'll pull back around, okay?"

"Great," she said, climbing out. The fewer transactions she performed with her newfound credit card the better – someone could already be looking for the real Tabitha Child.

Once inside the bank, she headed for a short queue and hoped for a teller that was bored and wasn't too observant. Rummaging inside her bag again, she pulled out the wallet and passport and quickly checked the date of birth and last place visited, ready for any inquisition to indeed 'confirm' her identity. Her story was simple, she couldn't remember her PIN and needed some cash. She was such an airhead at times. It was a plausible story and if she demonstrated enough conviction, she felt sure it would work. A teller became free and she recited her dilemma.

"Your passport should cover it," the teller said breezily, opening it and looking at the picture and then her. "You look younger today than when this was taken," she said, smiling, "I should ask what brand of face cream you use."

"Thank you," she gushed lightly. "Nothing expensive, but I use it religiously morning and night, no excuses." She managed a smile. Keeping the subject on the mundane side kept the conversation away from the formalities of what was actually happening. And helped with her nerves. She watched as the woman hit keys on her keyboard then waited while she counted out £500 in cash. She'd no idea what was going to happen from this moment on but getting some extra cash seemed sensible. While she still could. Transaction completed, she headed back to the waiting taxi and breathed a deep sigh of relief, closing her eyes for a moment before climbing into the back seat.

"What is the quickest way to France from here, do you think? What with the train disruptions? Gatwick?" she asked the dark-eyed driver.

"I'd say south towards a ferry. It's a good ninety minutes, if we're lucky, getting across to Gatwick, though it depends on what part of France you want to get to. Flights from there will take you straight to Paris almost. If you get to Calais via the ferry, a quicker journey from here, you've still a long trek on to Paris. Your call."

The driver had a point. Either journey gave her thinking time, but she wanted to leave the country as soon as humanly possible. And she didn't have a flight booked or even know how often they went. A long stay hanging around at the airport was not on the cards. Europe was the obvious choice, almost borderless now and the thought of moving freely was enticing. She'd been heading to Paris when all this started, hadn't she?

"Let's go south then. To the ferry. Can you take me all the way?"

"It'll cost you, but yeah, I'd be happy to," he said, smiling.

"You'll take my credit card? Only I've forgotten my PIN so it's signature only. I'm guessing it'll be more than thirty pounds." She held his eyes, hoping he wouldn't see the lie.

From the way he glanced back at her, she could see he wasn't too keen. "What the hell. I could do with the fare actually. It's been a bit slow of recent and I've not much to hurry back to tonight." She sensed sadness in the dark chocolate eyes that looked back from his mirror and she wondered what was going on behind them.

Perhaps she wasn't the only one with problems.

"Then I'm glad I can help."

CHAPTER 6

Chrissy had been out all afternoon working on a case. Several miles out from her home in leafy Englefield Green, an old-fashioned bike horn sounded, an incoming text from Adam. Each of her family had allocated tones, giving Chrissy the heads up who wanted her when she wasn't right by her phone. Any other incoming text wasn't so important, not compared to the three men in her life. Harry and Thomas still had to become fully grown men, but at fifteen and fourteen they were as tall as her already. A dash of fine fuzz across each of their chins, they were all hormones grunting and thumping music when they weren't playing rugby. Their bedrooms smelled and looked like gym changing rooms. One day they'd become men, and their hygiene would improve.

The horn blared again, and she asked Siri to read the message while she waited behind a cautious learner driver at an intersection.

Trains delayed, I could be late back. The smash earlier causing disruption all over. Eat without me. Xxx

"What smash is that?" she said and turned the radio on low ready for a news update. The learner driver hadn't moved forward and, as best she could see, the passenger was showing their frustration. Judging by the haphazard 'L' plate in the back window, it was a friend or relative that had taken on the task rather than a driving school. The learner had now stalled. A driver further behind Chrissy blasted their horn. Everyone wanted to get home. She asked Siri to reply to the text.

No problem, can't be helped. Not heard about the crash, I guess it'll be on the news. See you when I see you. Xx

Siri read it back to her and Chrissy accepted it. As the radio announced its 5 pm news update, the learner finally pulled away, in the opposite direction to Chrissy. She breathed a sigh of relief. The smash was the lead story and Chrissy listened intently as the newsreader described the disaster that had occurred several miles outside Ashford earlier in the day. With the death toll currently around thirty, A & E departments across the county were dealing with over two hundred injured passengers, many of whom had broken bones or needed stitches. Several were in a critical condition, with those in the front carriages having taken the full force of the smash. Thankfully, the highspeed engines were not diesel but electric so fire hadn't been such a big issue. It would be some time before the line could be reopened and passengers were being ferried from surrounding rail stations on coaches that had been brought in. An emergency number was given out for relatives to call. An inquiry as to how the train had derailed on the tight bend would be undertaken, but an eyewitness out for a run suggested the train was going way too fast into the corner. As was often the case, reporters and opposition party leaders speculated whether budget cuts were to blame. Either way, speed or money, thirty people had been killed, and the repercussions for their families were horrific. Chrissy switched it off before the reporter hashed it out or repeated the account yet again.

Adam caught the train, not that particular line, but he caught the train daily into London. A shiver shimmied down her spine as she was reminded of the Ladbroke Grove crash nearly twenty years ago. She'd been dating Adam back then, and a similar number of fatalities had arisen in what was then termed one of the worst rail accidents in Britain. Inside her head, she said a short prayer that her Adam would be safe, though a little late home tonight. Home. That was the important thing. That he got home.

Turning in to their driveway, she could see the front door open and two bikes propped up against the wall at the side. Her boys were home. Two of her three, present and correct. Two pairs of evil-looking trainers lay on the front door mat; it looked like a flying visit, a food stop.

"Hello," she called through, assuming they were in the kitchen at the back, and headed down herself. Dropping her bag on the kitchen countertop, she was greeted by two ruffled-looking youths on a mission to fill their stomachs, each with a roughly made jam sandwich in hand. It amazed her quite how much food two teenage boys could consume in one day, and seemingly without an ounce of fat added. Harry did his best to say hello with a full mouth of bread.

"Could you not get any more in there, Harry? I'm sure there must be an atom-sized space you could fill."

His reply was barely a grunt tinged with a slight smile.

"Did you both hear there's been a train crash?" she asked.

Two heads shook from side to side. No, they hadn't.

"It wasn't your father's line, but he'll be home when he can, the trains are backed up all over the place. Are you boys off out?"

Swallowing the last of his mouthful, Harry said, "Gary's place. Will you be cooking if Dad's late?" The glance from brother to brother wasn't lost on Chrissy. She knew what they were thinking.

"I get the hint. Here," she said getting cash from her bag and handing it over. "If Gary's mum is fine with it, buy dinner for you three."

Any excuse not to eat Chrissy's cooking was taken, though the speed they ate she doubted it touched the sides of their mouths as it went down anyway.

Her phone began to ring. It was Julie.

"Hey sis, what's up since I left not an hour ago?" She said breezily. Sniffles greeted her ears and Chrissy immediately tuned in, sensing her upset. "What's wrong, hun?"

"It's my friend Susan. She was on her way to Paris today, on that train that crashed." Chrissy immediately picked up on her sister's tone, she was obviously worried.

"Oh, Julie, have you heard from her at all?"

"That's just it. I've tried her phone but she'd not answering. I don't know what to think," she said, her voice wavering as if tears were imminent.

"If she was on that particular train, it'll be chaos over there, so try not to worry just yet. Are you sure she was going away today? Maybe she's elsewhere and can't get to her phone." Chrissy wasn't one for dramatics, but Julie was. Just because her friend wasn't answering didn't mean she was lying in a mortuary somewhere.

"Definitely today. I spoke to her yesterday so I know she was on it." The words wobbled a little as she fought the urge to cry no doubt.

"Is Richard home?"

"No, not yet. He texted to say he'll be late, the trains..."

Chrissy broke in, "Yeah, same with Adam. Look, do you want me to come back over?"

"No, don't worry. I'll see what else I can find out. I just needed to tell someone, but you're right, there could be a perfectly reasonable explanation. It will be chaos."

"Well, let me know when you hear, or if you want me to come over, okay?"

"Thanks, I feel a bit better now. Call you later."

Chrissy turned back to her boys, not that they showed any concern if they'd caught her side of the story.

"It's all right. Julie had a friend on the train that crashed earlier and she can't get hold of her."

"Probably dead then," Harry said unhelpfully.

CHAPTER 7

The view from Marcus Smith's room was dazzling, quite literally, but nothing compared to the woman that lay between the sheets on the bed behind him. The reflecting light from Hong Kong's Victoria Harbour below filled the room, twinkling like a dance-hall glass ball, tiny bubbles of light tangoing across the walls. Her body was as firm and sculptured as the marble table in the dining room of the suite – and just as useful. The woman was a regular in his life when work returned him to Hong Kong. She understood him, though that was what he paid her for. And generously. Her petit body and dark head of silky long hair was a far cry from the woman he lived with at home who was not nearly so big on giving. As he finished tying his Windsor knot and admired his reflection in the floor-to-ceiling mirror, he heard the woman behind him stirring and, remembering the pleasure he'd taken the previous night, a smile crept to his mouth. He took his special interests and desires from women like the one lying in his bed right now. Enthusiasm was an important ingredient.

The stark difference between this woman and his wife back in England was immeasurable. The two were worlds apart, both in their lives physically and attitudes in general.

Hot and cold. Open and closed. Spicy and bland.

He should give Susan a call. Not that he desperately wanted to, but the little conscience he had left told him he should. 'Should' always meant something you didn't want to do but would do under sufferance. While he had a soft spot for Susan, he knew he no longer loved her, though he had once. She had been there at the perfect time and so he'd been happy with the arrangement back then. But that was years ago, he'd changed. Lots of things had changed. And it was old ground, and he knew his marriage was all but over save for the documentation of it finally dissolved, like a bad business contract ready to be ripped up.

The woman slipped from between the sheets and wordlessly made her way to the bathroom. Water ran from taps, a toilet flushed. They rarely spoke, there was no need for conversation, they weren't lovers; it was merely a transaction, she filled his needs. And she knew the procedure, to be out of his room before he left for the day, and why it wasn't an affair. It kept it simple, no ties just pleasure. He watched her dress and gather her belongings silently, and he marvelled at her body once more before the suite door closed behind her without another word. Maybe he'd call her back again tonight. If today's deal worked out as planned, he'd reward himself. He deserved such indulgencies.

Ten minutes later Marcus Smith was on his way to the International Finance Centre and the walkway leading to the ferry pier. A constant breeze blew in gusts across the water allowing various pungent smells of Hong Kong to fill his nostrils. It reminded him of New York a little, a place that never rested no matter the time of day or night. The short walk persuaded him to call Susan, call home and check in, the dutiful husband for a while longer.

It rang. It rang again. Then went to voicemail.

That's odd, he thought, Susan always answered his calls. It was one thing he insisted on and she carried her phone wherever she went. Maybe she was in the bathroom? He slipped the phone inside his jacket pocket and watched the view across the water while he waited for the ferry to arrive. After two minutes she hadn't returned his call and so he tried again, but as previously her phone rang out, eventually going to voicemail. He left a brief message saying simply he was checking in and would call back later.

By the time the ferry finally arrived Marcus had tried Susan three more times to no avail, though he didn't bother leaving any more messages. What the hell was she playing at? He checked the private app he'd installed on her phone some time ago, an app that showed her current location. The blob glowed somewhere south of Ashford in Kent. His wife was clearly not home. Thinking back, he didn't remember her mentioning anything when he last spoke to her, did he?

"What are you up to, Susan? Another dull day shopping, doing nothing? God you bore me," he said under his breath.

Boarding the ferry, Marcus Smith returned his thoughts to something a little more important.

CHAPTER 8

The taxi journey down to Dover Ferry Port had been a good idea as it turned out. It gave Susan time to run through what had happened so far and what she was now going to do moving forward. Somebody was going to be looking for Tabitha Child no doubt and no one would be looking for Susan Smith quite yet. While she'd been planning her trip for a while, she could only recall telling one of her friends, Julie, about it. But that had been ages ago and she doubted Julie would even remember let alone figure she'd been involved in the accident. Although there was still the small matter of Marcus, he probably wouldn't realise that she was even gone for a couple more days yet. It had been convenient his being in Hong Kong, and even more convenient the train had crashed at all, giving her an opportunity that she'd snatched and ran with. While she'd planned an adventure in Paris, the trip was turning out to be one all on its own. She figured she had a couple of days clear and no more before someone missed her. Europe was easy to get lost in with most countries having open borders. And she had a passport if need be, one she'd have to use to get into France in the first place.

There was £1,000 in her money belt and another £500 in her wallet along with Tabitha's passport and credit cards so she was going to have to be careful how and where she used her resources. If some bright-spark detective caught on to the identity switch early on, they'd be looking at Tabitha's movements too so the trail would have to go cold when she reached Calais. She had no plans to use the cards or passport from there but had decided to keep them in case she absolutely had to use them. Life or death situation only. She hoped she never would. Susan pulled out Tabitha's phone and tried all the common passcode numbers that she could think of – 999999, 123456, all zeros – but nothing worked. The woman obviously had more intelligence than lackadaisical owners who relied on such common ones.

"Dammit," she said, showing her frustration. It would be handy to get inside the phone, find out more about the woman's life, find out who this Dominic person was even. If she was going to be Tabitha Child, there was a good deal more she needed to know. Phones contained people's whole lives, offering up a plethora of personal information once unlocked. The phone aspect of the device was often the least used. A voice broke into her tired and now throbbing head. She wondered if she had concussion.

"What's up, love, forgot your password?" he said, chocolate-brown eyes looking through his rear-view mirror at her again. "I used to stick with a simple one, all zeros," he said, laughing.

I rest my case, thought Susan.

"But my son said I was stupid and set me up with another number and I'm always getting locked out of mine. So he showed me a couple of tricks to get back in. What sort of phone is it?"

"An iPhone," she said, waving it in the air.

"Well, there's a couple of things you can do until you remember your password or get home to retrieve your backup. You can still get access to your messages and you can still send emails. Really useful I can tell you. I don't know how I'd operate without texting. And when my phone is locked because I forgot the password again... Mayhem!" His arms gesticulated like a passionate Italian.

"Really?" enquired Susan. "How do you do that from a locked screen?"

"Trust me, it's easy, I'll show you when we stop. Best I show you rather than trying to explain it. It's useful having a techie son. Like I say, I'm always getting locked out. Can't remember my own date of birth half the time."

"If I could just send a couple of messages that would be great, thanks."

"No problem, like I like say, I'll show you when we stop. Not much further now."

Susan sat back again and closed her eyes for a while, trying to work through what she still needed to do, where to head even, when she got over into France. It was getting late in the day. Her stomach growled, she needed sustenance. With all the stress and concern, and generally being tossed around like a pair of jeans in a tumble drier, it wasn't long before her eyes closed, and she slipped off into a deep sleep. How long for she wasn't sure, but she was aware of the driver calling her. Glancing at Tabitha's phone, it told her she'd been asleep for about half an hour.

"We're here, missy," he said gently. "Sorry to wake you, but I don't want to hang around too long. Now, let me quickly show you how to sort your phone before you go. Susan felt a little bleary eyed. Thirty minutes sleep was not enough, not after her day. Since she intended to use the woman's passport here and probably in Calais too, the credit card was still a viable option and made sense. But nothing past Calais. She wished she could get more cash out. Susan handed the card over and waited for the payment to be confirmed. When the transaction was finalised, he took the locked phone from Susan and pressed the home button, waking Siri up, then showed her what to do.

"Wow, I can't believe you can do that from a locked screen! And the same for email messages?"

"Yes, simple enough. Now you'll be fine until you get back into it properly. Safe travels, now, eh?"

Susan shuffled across the rear seat and thanked the driver once more as she got out. It had chilled down a little since she'd set off in the taxi and she wished she'd a coat, but there was no point in wishing, she'd have to make do with what little she had. There'd be a blanket she could wrap herself in on board somewhere, maybe in the first-aid room.

Now she had to get through passport control for the second time in the day, though this one would be a little more stressful and she hoped any nerves didn't show. And surely the name of Tabitha Child wouldn't ping anything up just yet, the woman was hardly a wanted criminal. She certainly hoped not anyway.

But she was a dead woman.

She shook her head to dislodge the rampant negative thoughts that were clambering around like monkeys on a climbing gym and headed inside the terminal building to buy a one-way ticket to Calais. It couldn't have gone any easier. With her ticket purchased, passport control was a breeze, almost pointless but at least it was out of the way, a non-event. Tabitha Child had now officially left the country.

Paperwork all taken care of, she headed over to a Burger King and ordered much needed fuel. Breakfast had been a hell of a long time ago.

Her head throbbed.

In a quiet corner of the ferry building, Susan wondered about Dominic again. Who the hell was he? He'd called a couple more times since her hospital stop and now, thanks to the taxi driver, she'd be able to hear his messages.

They didn't make pleasant listening. Tomorrow she would have to move quickly. But for now she sat patiently and waited to board.

CHAPTER 9

The last voicemail Dominic had left Tabitha had been a little over an hour ago and simply said *"I'm getting worried now. Where are you? Call me."* The last text message he'd sent had been an hour before that and read *I hope you're not avoiding me*, which could have meant anything, depending on how you read it and the context it was sent in. And that was something Susan had no clue about. Was this man Tabitha's partner, boyfriend or what? Someone she couldn't shake off, a loan shark even? There could be so many reasons for his text, but without knowing Tabitha and her life it was impossible to know. Whoever he was, "getting worried" sounded like he cared for her in some way. She asked Siri to read the last email Tabitha had received from Dominic.

There wasn't one.

Just text and voicemail. So he likely wasn't a work colleague or connection as email would be the obvious way to communicate if they were. That narrowed it down – a little. But she needed to get him off her case, or at least put his mind at rest since he was obviously concerned. And buy herself some space until she could figure out just how he fitted into her new life as Tabitha. But there wasn't time right now, the ferry was boarding, so she grabbed her bag and joined the queue.

The ferry was packed with a mixture of holidaymakers, tourists and shoppers, the latter heading for the cheap booze on the other side. Judging by the state of them, it seemed most had already had a skin-full on their way to purchasing shopping trolley loads more at the hypermarkets. A grating laugh caught Susan's attention as she sat quietly in the small café with a cup of coffee. A fake-tanned and badly bleached blonde woman with a group of identical-looking friends had parked themselves at one end of the bar, the end nearest her. The woman gave a raspy laugh as rough as sandpaper, likely from far too many unfiltered cigarettes, as another of the group got to the punchline of a joke and shared it. Heads turned from all directions at the noise and Susan noticed the disapproving looks as the women's combined laughter increased in volume. But they were on a trip with every right to enjoy themselves as they simultaneously pickled their livers. Still, Susan hadn't the desire to pay the women any further attention and did her best to block them out of her head.

Since the air outside had cooled, and she hadn't got a jacket, a stroll up on deck was out of the question as the ferry sailed away from the chalky white cliffs of Dover and into the open waters of the English Channel. She'd have much rather preferred to be outdoors, taking in the salty sea air away from the diesel engines and watching the birdlife come and go on the ferry's railings. But she'd be frozen stiff. The windows from the warm bar area would have to suffice for a sea view for the next ninety minutes or so.

She composed a message for Dominic. Figuring if he dug deep enough, he'd see Tabitha had travelled to France and so there was no sense in deviating from that truth. Letting him know where she was would hopefully satisfy his angst. Surely he'd leave her to travel for a while. The text read:

I'm fine, decided to go to France for a couple of days. Talk when I get back.

It went with a whoosh, and she hoped it would do the trick. By keeping it vague, she hoped it would read like something Tabitha herself might send. No doubt Dominic would reply and maybe it would tell her more about their relationship, whatever that was. She didn't have to wait long. The phone in her hands rang almost immediately – it was him. There was no way she could answer it, so she let it go to voicemail, again. The guy was obviously keen. When the message alert came through, she asked Siri to retrieve it. And listened. He didn't sound pleased at her actions:

"Well, I'm glad you're all right Tabitha, but have you gone mad? Have you thought this through? What you're doing is crazy stupid, not to mention bloody dangerous! And since you won't pick up, I'm guessing you're not going to return my call either!" There was a pause, and Susan heard him take a deep breath before he changed tack and spoke in a nearer normal way. He was obviously upset at the news of her departure. *"Look, if you're intent on doing this, I can't do much about it. But send me text updates? Until you come back? Then we can perhaps sort something better out. Just ..... just stay safe. And watch your back."*

And then he was gone. Susan sat open-mouthed at the man's response, the content of his message, and his obvious exasperation and concern at the woman's choosing to leave. It didn't make any sense on the surface, though the initial tone of his message rang bells from her own life. The domineering opening, the "crazy stupid", "have you gone mad?" They were all terms and words she herself was used to hearing and they sent tiny prickles up her spine that each dissolved and floated away.

Like she was doing now. Floating away from a life she no longer wanted and the controlling husband she'd come to dislike immensely. Cackling laughter from the rowdy group of women turned her head in their direction once more. When had Susan Smith last thrown her head back and laughed so heartily? Had such fun? Had drinks with a friend?

She couldn't remember how long it had been.

CHAPTER 10

Around ten million passengers passed through Calais Ferry
Terminal each year, making it the busiest car ferry port on mainland
Europe. Susan wished she had a car as she stood on the deck
watching vehicles set out on their way. With the motorways right
nearby, driving into France was an easy and cheap option for many.
But, without a vehicle, Susan would follow the other passengers
travelling by foot and jump on the shuttle bus to the heart of Calais
town centre. Her plan then was to eat again, buy some toiletries,
and find a cheap bed for the night. There would be time tomorrow
to find a change of clothes or two from an outlet store nearby
before she made her way south. With limited funds after she left
Calais – the end of the trail for anyone looking – she had to make
sure she'd enough supplies but was still be able to carry everything.
And that she still had a reasonable amount of cash tucked away.

She was almost the last passenger on the shuttle bus, save for a
couple of stragglers that smelled as if they had spent half a lifetime
propped up in a bar with a beer in hand. His and hers beer bellies
complemented the look. They jumped on at the last moment.

"Sorry, everyone," the man yelled with laughter. "Got caught
short!"

"And when you've got to go, you've got to go," added his companion, her raucous laughter and sour breath almost as bad as her partner's. Susan tried not to wince as her eardrums caught the lion's share of noise bellowed in her direction. All the couple needed was a large straw hat each and a stuffed donkey and the whole 'Brits on holiday' look would be complete. Susan held on to a vertical pole as the doors closed behind her and the bus lurched forward, causing the backpack of the young man in front of her to hit her flat in the face as he corrected his footing at the sudden movement. He glanced back over his shoulder.

"Pardon."

Susan shook her head in a 'no problem' way, smiling slightly and winning a small one in return from the young man. He looked in his early twenties, no doubt taking some time out to see the world before life moved on without him. Dirty blond curls touched his T-shirt collar. They looked soft.

A few minutes later, the shuttle pulled up in the town centre of Calais. As everyone stepped off the bus and went their separate ways, Susan saw that the town was much bigger than she'd thought. Even though she could see from her spot on the pavement it wasn't the small village she had somehow envisaged, its busyness made her feel welcome, a little safer even. Her job now was to get immediate supplies and a much-needed bed for the night.

Tomorrow was another day.

CHAPTER 11

It was almost 8 pm by the time Adam entered the house, tired and weary from his aggravated and disrupted journey home from work.

"Hi, I'm home," he called, slamming the front door behind him.

Chrissy had been watching TV in the lounge and had heard his car pull into the driveway. By the time Adam had entered the house she'd already fixed him a drink.

"In here," she called from the kitchen. "I bet you're exhausted."

"Glad to be home," he said. "I can't say that was the best journey of my life. It won't be long until it's time to go to back out to work again." He dropped his briefcase on the floor by the door. Even exhausted he looked like a GQ model. Chrissy planted a peck on his cheek and handed him a glass of red wine, which he took like a thirsty man in a desert.

"Have you eaten?"

"No and I'm famished." He slipped his jacket off and Chrissy flung it on to a nearby chair while Adam kicked each shoe off in turn and let them land somewhere away from his feet. He wiggled his toes as if to set them free. His socks were damp from sweat.

"I don't know whether to eat or have a shower first," he said, wearily, with his eyes closed for a moment. "But tell me, what's been going on in your world today?"

"Nothing too exciting, although I do have a bit of news."

"Oh? What's happened?"

"Well, I'm not entirely sure yet, but do you remember a friend of Julie's, Susan Smith? We met her and her husband at a dinner one night. Julie organised it and we all ate in the garden. She hired a marquee, do you remember?"

"How could I forget that night? The rain soaked everything," he said, almost smiling. In the end they'd had to abandon the evening and retire inside. He and Chrissy had called for a burger on the way home. "What about her?"

"Julie seemed to think she was on the train that crashed this morning, going to Paris. And she's tried calling and texting but there's no answer. It doesn't sound good, does it?"

"No. Has she tried calling the hospitals? There must be a list generated by now."

"Not sure, but the thing is, if she's not been admitted to hospital − you know, if she's dead − there might not actually be a list yet."

"I see what you're saying. No, I doubt there's a list as yet, not for the dead. They're not going to release names until they are a hundred per cent sure of who they are and that means formal identification or even autopsy, I'd bet."

"Could you imagine if they got it wrong?"

"Well, I feel for Julie, really I do." Adam said, standing, "But right now I'm going to have a quick shower then something to eat." He moved off to head upstairs. "How well did she know her?"

"I only know they occasionally went to the spa together. I don't really know from there. I'll give her a call in the morning and see if she's heard anything, see how she is. She seemed upset earlier and apparently the woman's husband is working away overseas somewhere so he might not even know she was on the train in the first place."

Adam yawned so wide his tonsil scar was almost visible.

Chrissy could hear the tiredness in Adam's voice and felt sorry for him. Picking up his wine and jacket, she kicked his two shoes to a spot by the table, out of harm's way, and said, "You'll feel better if you have a soak for a while. Perhaps a bath would be better?"

"Perhaps you're right."

Adam felt better after a soak in a hot, Radox bath, the remains of the red wine softening his tired nerve endings and relaxing his shoulders as if he'd had an hour-long massage. Wine did that, gave a rewarding smoothness to a hard day's hustle. He slipped into his robe and headed back downstairs where Chrissy had put a plate of sandwiches together. She joined him at the small table, just the two of them, the boys still engrossed in whatever they were doing in their rooms. Probably *Fortnite*. She slid the plate in front of him and he took one.

"You know," he said, talking through a mouthful of bread. "As I lay in the bath, I wondered what it would be like if you didn't come home one night, you know, like Julie's friend. She might never come home. Because something's wrong, isn't it? Otherwise she'd be answering her phone."

"I guess so," said Chrissy, "but when Julie calls and tells you her friend is sort of missing, you want to be the positive one, give her a modicum of hope, don't you? Even though deep down you're wondering what's going on yourself. Anyway, what would you think if I didn't come home one day?"

"How sad it would be. How our lives would change so dramatically and unexpectedly overnight. It would take a lot of emotion to deal with that, particularly helping the boys deal with it at the same time, almost putting my own grief on hold." Both of them sat in silence as Adam's words were digested. Then Adam spoke again, breaking into their thoughts. "I can't imagine trying to find another life partner again either. Could you imagine dating now? At our age? With modern-day ways of finding love? Could you imagine joining the masses on Tinder, for example? Swiping this way and that?"

"So, what, you've killed me off and already you're worrying

about where you're going to get your next lay from?" she said, laughing.

"No, course not," he said. "I'm just saying, that's all. I guess my brain jumped ahead a bit, but the time would come when you would have to start dating again. Neither of us would stay single forever, we're both still young. I just couldn't imagine doing it, that's all." He bit into another sandwich while she answered.

"But you're right, if you didn't come home one night I couldn't begin to comprehend how I would cope, what I would do and how I'd get through it." She leaned in and gave Adam a peck on the soft side of his neck, nuzzling in with affection, and was tempted to swipe a piece of his sandwich. "So don't be going anywhere because I love you, Adam Livingstone," she said, pulling him closer.

And with a mouthful of chicken-salad sandwich Adam said, "Ditto, Mrs Livingstone."

CHAPTER 12

There was little chance of Julie getting any sleep. She'd lain in bed for over an hour, wide awake, staring at the ceiling, tossing and turning, and counting sheep. But nothing worked, not counting backwards, not reciting the alphabet, not counting woolly animals, nothing. Richard had rather grumpily suggested that she get up, make herself something to drink and try again later. "Go and read a book downstairs," he'd said, "or just go in the other room so I can get some sleep. I've got work tomorrow." Like she hadn't? Julie knew something was terribly wrong, she just didn't know the severity of it, and so she decided that first thing in the morning she'd call the hospitals. Surely somebody would know whether Susan Smith had been admitted? But what if she was on a different list, a mortuary list? Did they even have one yet? How long did that kind of thing take? Oh God, then she'd have to tell Marcus.

Not a task she would relish.

Julie threw the quilt back, grabbed her Kindle from the side of the bed and, pulling on her robe, padded back downstairs, figuring she may as well try and read herself to sleep in the conservatory. She was not doing any good tossing and turning where she lay.

Finally, sometime during the early hours, she'd slipped off into a fitful sleep.

As dawn broke, pale-pink sky filtered through the trees outside decorating the room with its delicate pattern. Julie was exhausted having dozed on and off. She knew her eyes would be puffy; they felt sore already, full of grit though without a visit from the sandman. She pushed the Angora blanket off and wandered from her makeshift bed into the kitchen, quietly, so as not to wake Richard. It too had a pink hue from the reflection of the sky streaming in through the floor to ceiling windows. Everything appeared watermelon pink, a bad sign on the weather front but pretty to look at. Today it was going to rain: 'red sky in the morning, shepherd's warning' as the saying went. She put water in the coffee-machine tank and ground fresh beans to make her first latte of the day. But as soon as she'd pressed the grinder button she knew it had been the wrong thing to do. The noise reverberated around the kitchen and probably the front bedroom upstairs. Where Richard was sleeping. But Julie needed coffee, she needed something to get her going, because she could sense already it was going to be a heavy day. Creaking above told her Richard was indeed awake and he wouldn't be pleased at the disturbance. In the hope of pacifying him, she took him her own coffee. An apology for breaking into his sleep. She met Richard on the stairs, the mug in her hand a peace offering.

"It's a bit late now," said Richard, rather grumpy and somewhat sleepy.

"Why don't you drink it in bed, you don't have to get up just yet. I'm sorry to have woken you."

Richard accepted the coffee mug, grunted and turned back to their room. Wispy greying hairs on the top of his head floated around like tiny apparitions. He favoured a comb-over, but his hair wasn't currently combed. Julie headed back down and ground more beans to make another mug for herself then went back to the conservatory to watch the world wake up around her.

It was still too early to call the hospitals. She grabbed her iPhone and entered Hong Kong in the clock app to see how the time differed from London. They were seven hours ahead. It was coming up to 5 am, which meant 12 pm in Hong Kong. She'd make the call now – maybe Marcus had heard something, maybe all this worry was for nothing. She found his contact details and waited for the call to connect. Knowing Marcus was a busy man she wasn't sure he'd even pick up. Some time ago Susan had given her Marcus's number and although Julie couldn't quite recall why she was grateful for it now. Maybe it had been at that weird dinner party. On the fourth ring it went to voicemail. He must be in a meeting, Julie surmised. She couldn't leave a message, or could she? Undecided, at the sound of Marcus's recorded greeting ending she garbled a few words asking him to give her a call as soon as he could and hung up. Her own mug of coffee finished, she was about to head upstairs for a shower when her phone vibrated in her hand. Looking down she could see it was Marcus – he must be screening his calls. She stared at it for a moment and then allowed herself to answer.

"Hello Marcus," she said.

"Hello? Yes, this is Marcus. Who is this, please?" he asked questioningly.

"Marcus, it's Julie Stokes here. I'm a friend of Susan's."

"Yes Julie, what can I do for you, is everything all right?"

"Well, I don't want to worry you Marcus, I don't quite know what's going on," she said, fumbling for words.

"What do you mean? Is Susan okay?"

"Have you heard from Susan at all?" Julie said, gathering strength and trying to sound as if she were in control, knew what was going on even.

"No, I haven't. Should I have? Look, what's going on?"

"I'm sorry, Marcus," she said. "I don't want to worry you, but I can't get hold of her. And it's not like her. Only she was going on a trip yesterday, taking herself off shopping to Paris. Only there was a train crash." Julie gulped the last words out, her strength fading.

Neither of them said a word while it registered with Marcus what Julie was trying to say.

"What was Susan doing on the train to Paris? Shopping, you say?" His tone seemed to deepen somehow, and Julie caught the tingle it sent across her shoulders. It was icy cold.

Marcus thought back to checking the tracking app: she'd been near Ashford, a town on the Paris route.

"She said she was going to take off for a couple of days. Only the train that crashed was the London to Paris one and I'm rather worried." Julie couldn't hold it any longer and began to cry as Marcus waited patiently until she'd calmed down.

Taking charge, he said, "Leave it with me. I'll see what I can find out. And if you hear anything let me know. I'll make some calls from this end." He sounded all business, like he was conducting a deal not wondering where Susan was, the woman he'd married.

"Marcus, I'm so terribly worried," said Julie. "Please keep in touch. You've got my number and I'll call you if I hear anything."

But Marcus had already gone – the line was dead.

CHAPTER 13

Had Julie known the process of what happens after a disaster she wouldn't have needed to wait for the hospitals, because in reality they couldn't help, not yet. There was a disaster victim identification process to be followed and they'd given her the emergency number to call for further information. So Julie had contacted the emergency team and basically been told the same thing, and that it was going to take time. It was a huge disaster, and since she was a friend, and not a relative, they wouldn't be able to divulge information to her anyway. But what she had been asked to do was provide a description of her friend to help the forensics team and others who were part of the identification process. That would give them prior knowledge of someone they were searching for. Having found out what the procedure was to be, Julie had then called Marcus back and left a message on his voicemail. Maybe he'd have better luck since he was related, though neither of them knew what Susan was wearing when she left for the train that morning. Marcus would have access to a toothbrush for any DNA comparison. Julie doubted that Susan would have fingerprints on file for comparison and identification. It was going to take days before they'd finally know anything and, as each hour passed with not a call nor a whisper from Susan, it looked increasingly unlikely that she'd see her friend again.

Julie had then called the hospitals to check again, but no, they didn't have Susan Smith recovering in a nice, warm bed. The thought of her lying in a cold mortuary made Julie's blood run cold. She'd phoned as many of Susan's friends as she knew of, but, like most people, she and Richard had replaced the little black book kept in the dresser with their own phones. And without Susan's phone, who else could Julie call to ask if they'd heard from her?

It was mid-morning when Julie got a call back from Marcus. He asked if she could go around to their house and retrieve a toothbrush or hairbrush, something with Susan's DNA on it, and courier it down to the forensics team that was working on the incident. He gave her the front-door code and alarm code to gain entry. In the meantime, Marcus would be on his way back from Hong Kong to see what else he could do. Julie doubted Susan's toothbrush or hairbrush would be still at home if she'd gone away for a few days, but there'd be something of use, surely. She didn't relish rummaging through her friend's belongings in her absence, but there was no choice in the matter.

"Why can't they just match her driver's licence from her handbag with her picture on it, why can't they just match her that way?" Julie asked Richard, who was paying little interest, an article in the *Financial Times* holding his attention. "It just seems it's going to take forever, and I can't see why when they know who they are looking for. Surely her handbag must be there as well?"

A grunt from behind the newspaper, nothing more.

"Richard, are you even paying attention at all?" Julie asked, her voice rising in annoyance. His newspaper rustled noisily as he dropped it down on to his lap and stared over his half-moon glasses at her like she was a child that had disrupted his train of thought. He was working from home for the day, supposedly.

"They have a process to follow. They can't just do what they feel like to appease relatives," he said. "They have to follow procedure because if they didn't and a family member identified a body incorrectly – because the person lying in front of them looked a bit like them – imagine the stress that would cause. Not to mention they'd be a bit banged up having gone through an accident and all, and with the family member somewhat stressed, maybe not thinking or seeing too clearly," he said, rolling his eyes. "Can you imagine how stressful that would be, that the body was identified wrongly?"

"I understand that it just seems kind of pointless really. I mean they've got a description of Susan. They must have people lined up that can say 'yes' or 'no', she looks or doesn't look like the missing person we are searching for."

"Yes, but as I said, could you imagine if someone's got blood on their face or has been cut or worse? Imagine if somebody identified me wrongly, what would you do then? It's a bit late when I'm part of some other family's funeral procession to get my body back."

Richard had a point, Julie knew. "I guess we'll have to wait for the process, but it could take days, maybe weeks even. If they have to rely on DNA, it won't happen overnight."

"No, but if they think that they have a victim they are looking for, dental records will be readily available so it will only be a matter of comparing the two. And still we're assuming Susan is a part of this mess. She might not be."

"What other explanation can there be?"

"I'm just saying maybe you're jumping ahead a little. Maybe she has gone off to a retreat, has not listened to the news, and has no idea that people are looking for her. Remember that last retreat you went to? You had to hand your mobile in at reception so that you could have complete tranquillity. Maybe she's done something similar."

It was a possibility though Julie wasn't convinced. "Marcus is on his way back. I can't do much more, I'm not next of kin. It'll be up to Marcus now."

"Then let him deal with it. Look, Julie," Richard said, "I know she is your friend, but this could literally take days before you get an answer. Can I suggest you find something else to focus on? Work maybe? Because you didn't get any sleep last night, and you're not much further forward today apart from alerting Marcus, who's on his way back. Keep your mind busy."

"But I feel so helpless. Susan's my friend."

"I know she is, and I feel for you, really I do. But like I said earlier, there may be some perfectly obvious explanation, she may well be sat at a retreat unaware that everyone's worrying about her."

Newspaper rustled as he picked it back up again, the conversation over. Julie could see why Chrissy often pulled her tongue out when Richard wasn't looking. She felt like doing it herself. Conversation over, move on, don't be part of it. That was the message Richard was sending loud and clear. Then Julie had a brainwave – the passenger list. There had to be a record of who had gone through passport control.

But would they tell Julie if Susan Smith was even on it?

CHAPTER 14

Julie wasn't about to sit around all day. She had things to do. And since Marcus had asked for her help, she intended to help. She dialled Chrissy to fill her in on events so far.

"So I'm going over to their house. And I could do with some moral support since I'm not looking forward to going through her things. Fancy coming?"

Chrissy was in her attic office working when Julie called. She checked her screen for the time.

"Where does she live?" she asked.

"Richmond. Not too far from the shop. Do you have time?"

"If you think it will help, okay. I'll set off in a couple of minutes. Shall I pick you up or make my own way?"

"Perhaps make your own way, I'll text the address to you. I might nip to the shop afterwards and I don't want to hold you up."

"Sounds like a plan. I'll get my things and go. Meet you outside, I guess?"

"Perfect. And thanks, I know you've got things of your own going on. I do appreciate it you know."

Chrissy smiled at her sister's consideration. The two of them had mellowed in each other's company so much since the death of their father. It seemed they were finally growing up. It had taken forty years.

Julie jumped in her car and headed over to Susan's place, which was about a thirty-minute drive north of where she lived. Richmond was an old town teeming with affluent people and beautiful homes, though it had been some time since she'd last been to Susan's place. They tended to meet at a neutral venue somewhere and go on from there. Or meet at the shop. Julie had never given it another thought as to why that might be. When she finally pulled up outside, she was first to arrive. Chrissy wouldn't be far away.

It was a huge, white detached property sitting back from the road with smart black-wrought iron fencing interspersed with a tall, red brick wall around the front. Leaving her car, she headed through the small pedestrian gate which was nestled under a stone archway. It squeaked a little as she entered. She clicked it shut behind her and made her way to the front door to wait for Chrissy. It would be weird going inside without her friend being there but there was little choice. The sound of another car pulling up caught her attention and she waved at her sister as she made her way to the front door.

"Wow, nice place," Chrissy said and reached out to give Julie a quick hug. "How are you feeling?"

"Tired. I didn't sleep much."

"Well, you look great as always," she said chirpily, trying to be positive for her sister's sake.

Julie pulled out the scrap of paper where she had jotted down the security code and let them both in, the shrill beep-beep sounding of the alarm in the hallway to her left. She punched the numbers into the keypad and the noise stopped. Julie took a moment to stand in the hallway and feel the coldness of the place. It didn't appear to have any personality and certainly didn't feel welcoming, feeling more like a museum almost.

"Chilly in here," Chrissy added as they moved on down the passageway towards the living room, taking it all in. Huge double wooden doors, beech presumably, led through to the main lounge.

Big swathes of gold fabric adorned the windows, giving the room a rather formal regal style. It was immaculate – not a thing out of place. Each highly polished surface shone brilliantly. Photographs, decanters and other odds and ends were displayed around the room. But it wasn't the living room they were after, it was the bathroom or the bedroom, so they made their way up the stairs.

The bathroom itself felt as cold as the rest of the house, unlived in, nobody home, and again it was spotless. Not a hair in the bathtub, not a speck of fluff on the windowsill.

And not a toothbrush in the toothbrush holder.

"Well, just as I thought. If you're going away for the weekend you generally take your toothbrush with you," Julie said, confirming what she'd already suspected.

"Is it me or is the whole place cold and a bit weird?" asked Chrissy.

"Not particularly comfortable, is it," Julie agreed as she opened a drawer to see if there was a hairbrush, a comb or even a spare toothbrush. There was very little inside; Susan would have her toiletries with her. Satisfied there wasn't much in the bathroom that would be of use, they went through to the bedroom, which was decorated similarly to the rest of the house though a little bit more modern. A giant bed almost filled the room. While the decor was a bit more modern and informal, it reminded Chrissy of a hotel room – clinical, functional and not much more. She wandered over to a tallboy and opened the top drawer, but it was filled with Marcus's things, as were the second and the third.

"This is all Marcus's things. How about over your side?" Chrissy asked, pointing to another set of drawers. Julie opened the top one on the left. Again, there didn't seem to be anything of Susan's.

"Strange, Marcus's things again," she said, closing the last drawer. She checked the bedside cabinet and opened the top drawer – Marcus's side. Moving round the bed to the other side, Julie opened the top drawer and found a few belongings of Susan's. Face cream, hand cream, a book and some other odds and sods, but nothing of any use from a DNA point of view.

Chrissy opened the wardrobe. It was filled with beautiful clothes, many of which looked like they hadn't been worn, some still had their price tags dangling from the cuffs, but Julie flicked through them to see if there was anything of use. Chrissy watched on.

"My goodness! What does a woman need quite so many clothes for? There's got to be thousands and thousands of pounds' worth in here!" she said, reaching in and looking at a price tag. "This dress is over a grand on its own."

Julie turned and smiled, her sister really didn't *get* fashion and the importance of looking great all the time. "And the shoe boxes, how many do you think there are?" Awe coated her words.

"She's been a good customer of mine of recent," Julie said, opening a familiar box, one of her own. Would a pair of shoes carry DNA? Surely from sweat they could pick something up? She took out a pair of simple, neutral pumps. They had been worn.

"These should work, don't you think?"

"I'd think so. But that looks like a laundry basket in the corner?"

"Good thinking." She lifted the lid. "Damn, it's empty." It seemed that Susan Smith was a very tidy person, everything just in its place, even the dirty laundry had been dealt with.

"Maybe there's a mug still in the dishwasher?" Chrissy offered as they made their way back downstairs. But it seemed Susan had taken care of everything. The kitchen was as spotless as the rest of the house. Then Julie spotted something of interest. Looking out at the long garden from the kitchen window, she saw two small buildings, one on either side of the path, though one looked a bit more substantial than a place where you might pot plants. A bunch of keys hanging on a small rack nearby caught her attention and Julie wondered if one would work. Chrissy read her thoughts. "It's worth a look," she said and the two headed off down the bowling-green-striped lawn to the little brick building at the bottom. There were no blinds or curtains pulled across the windows so they were able to see in as soon as they reached it. It looked like some sort of studio, a reading room, perhaps, and wonderfully feminine, though why

Susan would need such a place with the many rooms in the large house was puzzling. And with Marcus away half the time it didn't make sense. But still, Julie slipped a key in the lock and turned it.

The click told her she was in. The morning sun had warmed it, the interior quite toasty, and they scanned the room that was no bigger than a double garage. It was tastefully kitted out with a rather different look and feel than the rest of the house; it was feminine and stylish.

"What is this place?"

A studio, a personal space of some kind, perhaps. In any case, it was obvious Susan spent time there. Books filled shelves almost floor to ceiling on one wall. The woman obviously liked to read. A coffee machine and a small fridge made a tiny kitchen area, and the sofa looked large and soft enough to sleep on. The little space that Susan quite obviously frequented wasn't as clinical as the rest of the house and on the table next to the comfy chair was a mug – complete with smeared lipstick mark. They'd be able to get DNA from that for sure. They had to assume it was Susan's. Julie picked it up gingerly by the handle, checked the contents had gone and slipped it into her bag on top of the pumps, careful not to smudge anything.

"Well, that's a result. Shoes and a mug should be enough," Chrissy offered as they both did a final glance round.

"I hope so. Time to go," said Julie. "Thanks for coming. I feel much better now I am helping. And this lot should help with ID so we may hear something sooner than later." Her weak smile wasn't fooling Chrissy, but Chrissy was powerless to make her feel any better. Satisfied they had what they needed, they both made their way back up to the mausoleum of a house, locked up and headed out to their cars.

"Strange," Julie said as they stood looking back from the pavement. "Just strange." The whole set-up seemed quite unlike the Susan Smith she knew. Apart from the one studio room down at the bottom of the garden. Maybe that was why Susan always insisted on meeting up elsewhere.

"You can't do any more now, sis, so try and take your mind off worrying. Go to the shops for a few hours."

"I think I will. Thanks again."

Chrissy waved and watched Julie pull away before getting in her own car. It was her turn to wonder about the missing woman. The room at the bottom of the garden spoke volumes about Susan.

CHAPTER 15

As a new day broke, Susan was up with the larks and walked down to the beach to blow her cobwebs off and just enjoy five minutes' peace before she headed off. What appeared to be white-painted sheds lined the shore and stared off into the sea. Two rows deep, they looked out on to the ocean like square white birds waiting for the tide to come in and take them. She assumed they were old-fashioned changing sheds left over from the Victorian era, but trendy to have now as a kind of poor man's beach house. There were plenty of them along the British coastline and people that owned them generally stored their deckchairs, blankets and picnic equipment in them. Many sat with their flask of tea and a book, taking in the sea air with a blanket across their knees. The morning breeze was welcome on her face, the squawk of seagulls high in the sky sounded cheery, and the sea air deposited tiny salty particles on her lips. She licked them, enjoying the taste of the sea.

Susan hadn't planned on being on the beach this morning. She'd planned on waking up in Paris, but life threw curveballs and she'd chosen to take this particular one and roll with it, not entirely sure where she was going to end up.

But now it was time for her to move on. The shops would be open shortly and so she made her way towards the town centre to wait. If there was a 24-hour supermarket that sold cheap clothing and the few bits and pieces she needed she could be on her way sooner, but not knowing the town, not knowing the brands, she was clueless. She need not have worried.

Within the hour she had purchased a small backpack, two changes of clothes to take with her, another set she changed into in the fitting room, and other basic necessities. She used the credit card again, reasoning that if anybody was looking for Tabitha Child, they'd already know that she'd landed in Calais. Thank goodness for PINless technology. It would be the last time she'd use it. Susan debated cutting the card up, but reasoned if there *was* an emergency later on, she'd be thankful she'd kept it. With everything she now owned strapped to her back, she set off towards the main trunk road in search of a suitable prospect to give her a lift further south. At least that way she wouldn't leave a trail. It was less than twenty-four hours ago that she'd been sat in the same carriage as the now deceased Tabitha Child, heading off on an adventure, one so polar opposite to the one she was on now it was almost comical. Up ahead, she could see a petrol station and figured it would be the easiest place to get a lift from. There would be folks starting out on their journeys after leaving the ferry, hopefully a family with room to spare for her to travel with. She stuck her thumb out anyway. That's how you caught a lift, wasn't it? Susan would never have had the balls to do something so reckless in her old life, but Tabitha Child found herself smirking at the adventure ahead. If Marcus could see her now, he'd have a hissy fit of nuclear proportions. The thought of his beet-red face screaming at her 'stupidity' made her shudder. He was ugly when he shouted.

As a lorry blew past, forcing her blonde hair to stick comically across her face, she found herself laughing out loud. The wide-open world lay straight ahead and with spirits lifted after a good night's sleep, Susan felt like the woman she'd been some years ago.

Carefree. It was as if something inside of her had been released, like a tight elastic band had been broken. It was the only way she could think of to describe it.

CHAPTER 16

She didn't have long to wait before the deep grumbling sound of air brakes as a lorry pulled up nearby. The cab lurched a little as it came to a complete stop and diesel fumes filled her nostrils. Air seeped out with a loud hiss. Susan wasn't entirely sure of the etiquette, having never asked for a lift with a stranger before. Should she climb up to the passenger side? Should she go around to the driver's side and speak to the driver? The thought amused her. She was so far out of her comfort zone it was laughable, and this was something else to add to her repertoire as a free woman. While it was only a small action, it was the start of doing new things. In the end she climbed up the passenger side and stuck her head through the window, hoping when she got up there the guy wouldn't be a creep.

He looked quite normal.

"Any chance of a lift?" she asked with a smile.

"Where you headed?" he questioned. Susan took a moment to glance him over before answering. He had messy brown hair along with three- or four-days' beard growth, and he looked like a stereo-typical lorry driver that hadn't had a great deal of sleep, probably having just got off the ferry. A chequered shirt with the sleeves rolled up and jeans completed his ensemble, though he didn't appear to have a beer belly hanging over his trousers. In an instant Susan decided he'd do. What was she looking for exactly? A good-looking chauffeur at the wheel of a limo that was never going to come? Chequered-shirt man had a friendly face.

"I'm headed south towards Paris. Can you help?"

"Sure can, jump in," he said casually. "I could do with the company. I've been on my own too long."

Susan wasn't sure whether the guy was simply tired of driving on his own or advertising his relationship status. Not one to ask, she opened the door and climbed inside. It was high up compared to a car, but then she was at the equivalent level of sitting on a car roof, and the view from the cab looked quite different to that from down on the gravel. Like being in an aeroplane's cockpit almost but with fewer instruments. As the lorry pulled out, she fastened her seat belt and settled in, again wondering about etiquette. Was she meant to talk or stay quiet? Either way introductions probably needed to be made.

"Thanks for the lift," she said by way of something to say.

"No problem, glad of the company like I say. I'm John. What's your name?"

She thought for a moment before answering. Not Susan. "Tabby," she said, figuring the casualness of the name suited her better than Tabitha. Perhaps it would be best to keep away from Tabitha anyway, just in case.

"That's unusual name for a human, Tabby. My daughter has a cat called Tabby." His smile was warm and held no offence.

Not feeling insulted, she let a smile spread, which was becoming easier as she relaxed. "That's nice. How long is it to Paris?" she asked, avoiding more about Tabby the name.

"About four hours from here so you might as well sit back and relax and enjoy the view. I don't intend stopping, but if you need a pee, let me know. We should be on the outskirts of the city by lunchtime." He turned to her and gave her an easy smile; she noted his bright-white, even teeth. The guy had standards while out on the road; he looked after his dental.

They quickly caught up to speed. The warmth of the sun shining through the window relaxed her, and even though she'd had a good night's sleep, it wouldn't be long before she dropped off again. The stress and strain had caught up with her, but inside she vowed to stay awake, after all she'd no idea who this John character was, where he was from or even where he was going. Except south. He could have been in prison until last week for all she knew.

"So, Tabby," he said, "where are you travelling to? Going on holiday? I can tell you're English just like me."

"Yes, and yes, you could say that I'm taking a break, a bit impromptu actually."

"I find that those are the best type of trip – no plans, free as a bird, go where the spirit takes you."

"It's the first time I've done it actually, you're my first hitchhike lift."

He turned to her and smiled again and said, "I'm honoured to be your first." Then, "How did you get the shiner?" he asked, pointing to her eye.

Tabby instinctively touched her forehead and remembered how it had got there, how this whole escapade had started only yesterday. Had it really been only yesterday?

John must have picked up on her change in mood and added, "None of my business. Sorry, I shouldn't have asked."

"No problem," she said, trying to pick up her mood again. There was no sense in being maudlin over past events.

"Shall we put some music on or would you prefer quiet?" he asked.

"Whatever, you're the driver, you choose."

John reached for his smartphone and handed it over. "Here, pick a playlist, find something you like and if it's too young and hip for me I'll tell you."

She took his phone and searched through his Spotify playlists to see what music he'd listened to in the past and found 'singalong through the decades'. A moment later and Aretha Franklin filled the cab singing about saying a prayer, which was apt under the circumstances.

"Good choice," he said and began to hum along to the song, filling in the bits he knew, odd words filling the cab. "At least you picked something you can hear the words to." He turned, flashing a white smile again.

"That makes you sound old and you're not," she said, "but I know exactly what you mean."

As Aretha Franklin finished and Status Quo started, she found herself singing along with him, and as the miles passed by under the tyres of the lorry, they sang for the next couple of hours. It was the most fun that Susan, now Tabby, had had in a long time, and she felt at ease with her new lorry-driver friend. Whoever John was, like her, he wasn't giving much away about himself.

John had been right. It was lunchtime by the time they neared the city limits. Not wanting to disrupt his plans, they hadn't stopped along the way and now not only was she bursting for a pee, but her stomach was howling with hunger. In the last twenty-four hours she hadn't eaten or drunk anywhere near what she should have and she marvelled at how, even without fluids, her bladder still managed to complain.

"This is as far as I go," he offered by way of explanation as they pulled into a service station. "It's best you try for another lift here. You'll do better than at the depot where I'm going a couple of miles away."

Tabby looked around somewhat nervously. She'd struck lucky with John, had in fact actually enjoyed his company, and his singing, and was sorry their journey was at an end.

"If you're looking to get into the city centre, I suggest a smaller vehicle this time, a car or van maybe. Most of us heavy-goods vehicles go around the city rather than through it. Might be easier that's all."

Tabby looked at him trying to keep the disappointment from showing on her face. "It's been nice meeting you, John. And thanks for my safe carriage," she added, sounding like someone from a bygone era.

He smirked in response to her word choice. "I'm sure you'll fair well enough but keep safe, eh?"

Tabby waved as he pulled back out on to the road. The smell of food from café behind her caught her stomach and she made her way inside. She was famished.

CHAPTER 17

Marcus Smith was annoyed and his frustration at having to leave Hong Kong before he'd finished his business was beginning to show. Now he'd have to head home to sort out the mess that Susan had got herself into and then return, having rescheduled meetings for a later date. Now he had to deal with the fallout, both business and Susan, wherever she was.

Even for business-class passengers, airport passport control can take an age. He stood, foot tapping impatiently, waiting his turn. It seemed the woman ahead was having difficulties with the machine and simply stood waving her passport to gain attention from an officer. Marcus wanted to scream, "Move over!" and process his own. It was bad enough he was back at Heathrow so soon, and the time difference coupled with the thirteen-hour flight wasn't helping with his fatigue or temper. A uniformed official eventually appeared and stepped in to help. With the woman now finally out of his way, he slipped his own passport into the machine and wondered about Susan. He'd seen the full report on the news before he'd left, and since he'd been in the air, and therefore out of the loop for so long, hadn't had an update as to what was going on. All Julie had given him was the emergency number that went through to the command centre somewhere near the crash site. They'd been unable to tell her anything, but now he'd arrived, he'd finally get to the bottom of things. They'd talk to him.

Once Marcus had left the airport and was in his corporate taxi home, he dialled. After introducing himself he was put through to one of the coordinators on the disaster recovery team, a man called Dean Duffy, who was, in fact, a pathologist who had picked up the ringing phone in passing. Stating who he was and who he was looking for, Marcus hoped for some cooperation and answers. Was Susan alive or dead?

"Can you confirm that my wife was actually on the train first off? Susan Smith. Can you check your lists, please?"

"Yes, Mr Smith, I can confirm that your wife Susan was on the train, according to passport control. But as of yet we have not been able to locate or identify Susan at this time."

"What the hell does that mean?" asked Marcus, anxiety simmering with fatigue and tension, bubbling like a stew on the stove.

"It means that we have not identified her as deceased and we do not have her listed as taken for medical assistance. I'm sorry, sir, there is little I can tell you right at this moment. I know it must be incredibly hard for you."

Marcus ignored the remark and carried on, "A friend of ours sent down some items of her clothing for DNA comparison and I can tell you who her dentist is. How long will it take to find out for sure?"

"I know this is hard, but it will take several days. We do have a lot of casualties and we work our way through them as quickly as possible, but we have to do it with precision and accuracy as you can understand, sir. But having a DNA sample and her dental records will be a great help. As you can probably imagine there was luggage and belongings strewn over a wide area, and if your wife didn't actually have anything on her person at the time of the incident, it would have been very difficult to identify her."

"So, let me be clear," said Marcus, "you can't confirm if she is in a hospital, and you don't know if she is deceased or not?"

"That's correct, sir. I know it doesn't sound much help, but it's early days yet and the team are working as fast as they possibly can. You've done all you can so far, I can only ask that you bear with us while we search for your wife."

"That doesn't sound good," said Marcus resignedly. "The hospitals don't have her so that suggests to me that you have Susan. Is there anything else I can do to speed this process up?"

"There is one thing, sir," said Dean. "It would be helpful if we could send an officer to meet with you and get a clearer picture of who we are looking for. For instance, what she was wearing when you last saw her, a recent photo, preferably a smiling one so we can see her teeth. Anything you can tell us will be helpful in finding your wife."

"Yes, okay, if that's all I can do." He didn't hide his exasperation at all. "Send somebody around. You've got my address, you've got my number. I'll wait to hear from somebody."

"I'll get one of my colleagues to contact you. Thank you, Mr Smith."

But Marcus had already hung up; his side of the conversation was complete and he didn't feel the need for hollow pleasantries or condolences. Frustration boiled and he flung his phone across to the other side of the rear seat where it bounced off the side door and fell into the footwell. The chauffeur glanced in his rear-view mirror at Marcus but wisely decided against saying anything. No doubt he'd heard half of the conversation anyway. The possibility of a dead wife wouldn't be easy to comprehend.

"Damn you!" Marcus shouted as he travelled towards home.

CHAPTER 18

Julie was desperate to call Marcus. He'd told her what time he'd be landing at Heathrow, but she didn't want to intrude or, knowing what the man was like from the few times she'd met him, suffer his wrath. What Susan saw in him she would never know but each to their own. People said the same about her Richard, particularly Chrissy who suffered him for the family's sake. That's why she childishly pulled her tongue out to the man behind his back so often. And last night Julie had felt like doing the same thing, his article in the newspaper of more interest than her missing friend. It had annoyed her.

"Dammit," she said. She composed a short text requesting an update as soon as Marcus knew anything and hit send. She didn't expect a reply for some time, not even knowing if he'd managed to find out anything worth reporting back at this stage. But she had to try, she seemed to be the only person that cared. For something to do she called Chrissy, who answered in her normal sing-song voice.

"Hi sis," she said. "Any news?" Chrissy always sounded upbeat even when there was sour news, it was her way. Julie wished she could be more like her sister.

"Nothing as yet, no. But Marcus should have landed by now so I'm hoping he'll be on the phone. I've just texted him. I don't really want to intrude too much."

"He'll let you know as soon as he knows something, I'm sure. How are you feeling? Did you get a nap?"

"A short one, and you should see my bags now. I'm going to need some extra help from a facial this week."

On the other side of the phone Chrissy rolled her eyes at Julie's quest for perfection. It was understandable she'd have bags after the lack of sleep and worry from a missing friend, but the woman never cut herself any slack.

"Well, I heard on the news that it's slow going identifying the victims, so it may be some time before we know anything."

"My gut tells me that she is one of them. Otherwise why hasn't she called somebody? Even if she was lying in hospital in a coma, surely they would know who she was?"

"Not necessarily, Julie, how would they? Her handbag will have been thrown somewhere and unless she had ID actually on her, which she probably didn't, how would they know who they'd got in a coma?"

"True. Will you come over? Richard's at work and I'm all at a loss."

"Of course I will if you want me to, though I have a couple of errands to run first off, all right. So why don't I head over in, say, two hours? Will that work?"

"Yes," said Julie petulantly.

Chrissy picked up on her tone and felt immediately sorry for her – it can't be easy worrying about a close friend. "Look," said Chrissy. "Put your lippy on and nip out to that salad bar that you like and get yourself something nice to eat, and I'll be over soon all right? You'll feel better when you've eaten something."

"Okay," she said, sounding like a sullen teenager now.

What Chrissy really wanted her to eat was a big, fat, greasy Burger King, or a twelve-inch pizza, rather than the lettuce and carrots that the woman lived on. She certainly couldn't afford to lose any more weight with worry. Unlike Chrissy, there was no chance of her falling down a drain if she stepped on one. "I'll see you in a couple of hours," she said. "Keep your chin up, and I'll be there shortly."

Julie wandered back into her conservatory and sat down in a chair. At least it wasn't raining to add to the dreary mood. The sun was doing its best to brighten everything it touched, though it couldn't penetrate her heart or her head where the despair lay. Maybe Chrissy was right, she thought, maybe nipping out will give me something to do, and so she sauntered off upstairs to reapply her lipstick and five minutes later was heading out the door into town.

Her phone started to ring – Marcus.

"Hello Marcus, do you have news?" she asked almost desperately.

"They want to come over and talk to me, find out what she was wearing, get a photo. I'm finding this whole process deeply unsatisfactory; I don't have time for all this. But that's the way it is, and I have to follow. Someone will be around at 3 pm apparently. Are you able to help?"

At first Julie was confused. Why did Marcus need her at the interview? But she didn't question it, the man was not thinking clearly, obviously. Then it dawned on her – he wouldn't have the first clue about Susan's clothes or much of what she filled her time with when he was away abroad. For the last few years he'd known precious little about his wife.

"Of course, if it would help," she offered. "I'll see you at 3 pm at your place then."

Once again the phone call had been disconnected. She wondered if he'd even heard her reply. Julie's beloved Richard might be thought of as odd at times, dour even, but at least he wasn't the arrogant prick that Marcus Smith appeared to be. She was thankful for small mercies.

At 3 pm on the dot there was a knock at the front door. It was the police. As Marcus showed the uniformed officer into the sterile living room that Julie remembered from her visit previously, it seemed quite surreal what they were about to do. There were no pleasantries, no offer of refreshments from Marcus, though Julie wasn't surprised. Introductions were made. DS Alan Davies made his north-of-six-feet bulk comfortable on the sofa. While he was tall and broad, he wasn't overweight, though his size could be intimidating when he needed it to be. Julie noted his kind eyes. Brown curls flopped loosely on his head and Julie found them enchanting. Marcus's tone brought her back to the room. Anxious to get on with it, he barged in with his question first.

"Have you found Susan?" he demanded. It was not a question that the officer could answer, not yet anyway.

"Mr Smith," Alan started, trying to take control. "We have to follow procedure and that's why I'm here today. I will make notes and take some of Susan's belongings away with me to compare DNA to, if I may. But let me say this first off, I completely understand how you must feel that everything seems to be taking time. I feel for you, I really do. We have to do this the right way so please can you start off by telling me what Susan was wearing on the day that she boarded the train?"

Marcus looked at Julie. He had no clue, but neither did Julie. He turned back to the detective and said, "I've been away on business, I really have no idea what she would be wearing, but if she was going off shopping, she wouldn't be in her best finery, now, would she?"

Julie watched as Marcus tried to dominate the interview. Upset at the current circumstances or not, he was being rude.

Marcus piped up again, "And I believe you've already got some shoes and a mug for her DNA comparison. We sent those down by courier, or Julie did, I was still in Hong Kong." Julie nodded that yes that had in fact happened. Again, the detective nodded his approval. Trying to keep some control of the situation, DS Alan Davies changed the subject to the need for a photograph.

"Now, it would be really helpful if you had an up-to-date photograph of your wife, preferably one where she is smiling," he said, locking eyes with Marcus and holding them.

Marcus turned away with a deep sigh. When he was ready to speak, he asked, "Why do you need a smiling photo?"

Julie knew he was being awkward; everything seemed too hard for the man.

"For dental comparison. It makes the process that bit quicker. With facial-recognition software we can scan the photograph of her teeth and check it against any victims that could be a match. It just saves time if we don't have to get full dental records, but if you prefer, we could. Just let me know who we need to contact."

Marcus sat back in his chair, somewhat satisfied with the answer though he didn't reply.

The detective went back to his checklist. "Did Susan have any distinguishing marks at all? Maybe a tattoo, perhaps?" he questioned.

Marcus rolled his eyes and Julie caught the look. She wasn't aware of her friend having a tattoo, she'd seen her at the spa in her swimsuit often enough, and didn't think Marcus would allow her one. Unless there had been a tiny one hidden somewhere, only visible to her husband, which she doubted very much, she thought not.

Alan Davies was still waiting for a reply from Marcus who seemed to be finding more entertainment gazing out the window.

Julie said, "I don't think she does, but, Marcus, can you confirm?"

They both watched as Marcus shook his head – negative.

The detective ticked a box. "How about any fractures? Has she ever broken an arm, or a leg, or her wrist, perhaps? Again, something for comparison, just to speed up the process."

Marcus shook his head again.

Julie confirmed with the little knowledge that she had of her friend's private life.

"Why don't I just find that photograph," Julie said helpfully, standing. "Where will the photo album be Marcus?"

"In the cupboard in the dining room, second shelf down, you'll find them there," he said helpfully, though sounding disinterested.

Julie made her way out and pulled out a photo album, flipping through it as she walked back to the two men. She saw quite a few of Susan in various poses at various events before she finally found one that was relatively recent. It showed Susan's expensive dentistry off elegantly. Like Julie, Susan spent good money on her appearance and her mouth was no different.

"Here you go," she said, taking the image out and passing it to Alan.

He took a moment to look at the woman and then slipped it into his folder without saying a word.

The rest of the interview went by reasonably quickly with no more awkward questions. Just as the detective was about to leave, Julie asked if he needed anything else, beyond the shoes and mug she'd already sent, for DNA testing.

"Yes, I'll take another item of clothing. More shoes will be fine."

This time it was Marcus's turn to go up to the bedroom and rummage through the wardrobe, and Julie took the opportunity to have a quiet word without him in earshot.

"How long do you think this will take now?" she asked.

"I know it's hard," he said. "It may take some days. But at least now we have a photograph. That will make immediate comparison easier and then the rest should just follow through, but DNA does take a little while longer. As soon as we have some news, rest assured we'll be in contact with Mr Smith directly." His smile was gentle and encouraging, and Julie was thankful for his presence. Marcus was coming down the stairs, his feet thumping on each step. Alan took the shoes from him and slipped them into an evidence bag, and with everything complete made his way to his waiting vehicle out the front. Julie bid him goodbye from the door; Marcus didn't say another word. When the door was closed Julie followed him back into the living room, not quite sure if she should leave him be or sit with him for a while.

"We should hear something in a couple of days, Marcus. Now they have a photo hopefully it will speed things up a bit." She was trying to stay positive, just like Chrissy had told her to.

But as with their phone call, Julie felt like he'd already hung up.

"I'll see myself out."

CHAPTER 19

The makeshift mortuary was a series of refrigerated containers arranged in an empty hangar at a nearby airbase. As with any disaster, there simply wasn't room at local hospitals and funeral homes to look after so many victims all at once. And positive identification was each pathologist's main concern. Worried and expectant friends and relatives desperately sought confirmation as to whether or not their family member was either deceased, and while it might sound like a crude set-up, the makeshift mortuary worked surprisingly well. It was a basic template now used at disasters all over the world. The team that staffed the temporary centre were all part of the Disaster Victim Identification unit, or DVI, and attended the scene from all over the country. No one ever knew where or when the next disaster would strike, and so these temporary locations were earmarked and semi-prepared across the length and breadth of the country – just in case. If London itself ever had another large-scale disaster on its hands, the city had a designated area ready to go at a moment's notice. And that was all thanks to learnings from other disasters around the world, something that before the events of 9/11 most of us had never thought about.

Dean Duffy was a local, and only one of the many crew

members that worked around the clock trying to identify the deceased that were now safely stored and awaiting identification. Body parts, and thankfully there were few, awaited their return to their rightful owners. Travel safety improvements in recent years had prevented more fatalities, though had each seat in that train been fitted with a seatbelt, there would no doubt be fewer waiting patiently in the mortuary. At least tables and chairs were fixed to the floor in modern-day trains, and passengers being crushed or asphyxiated by their movement were not commonplace as before. Most of the injuries and deaths in this disaster had been caused by passengers being flung from their seats and hitting, with some force, a window or other part of the train. Maybe, one day, trains would be fitted with safety seatbelts too. It would cost a fortune. But then trains were never supposed to come off their tracks.

Nearly two full days after the crash, the team had identified almost a quarter of the now thirty-five victims, largely through visual identification, if appropriate, and fingerprints, though full DNA comparisons and post-mortems would be performed to confirm. The old days of simply checking for appendices or the gall bladder were long gone, cause of death and identification had to be accurate. If someone had indeed suffered and died from a heart attack unrelated to the crash, their death would be recorded as such. Males tended to have their ID on their person in the form of a wallet, making things easier, but with females this was not often the case.

"I think this could be Susan Smith," Dean said to his colleague Liz. Both were pathologists though Liz worked in the north of England and had responded to the call after the initial disaster struck. The photo he held in his hand certainly appeared like the deceased female, but death changed the way a person looked. As did a rail disaster. "Let's scan her teeth and compare first off, though I can see she's had extensive work to the incisors, maybe even the right canine," Dean said, examining her mouth gently. On first observation, they were a close visual match. The scan would tell them for sure. "And we'll do a DNA swab anyway though visually she fits. I'd say she looks a little older, but we'll see," he said, reaching for a testing kit to swab the inside of her mouth and wiping the long cotton bud around. Slipping it back inside its narrow tube, he labelled it and handed it over to his colleague. They moved on to the next victim they had a photograph of and surmised the same, an accurate visual fit. By the end of the morning, they had possible names for another ten victims, each awaiting either dental or DNA confirmation. It was a huge step forward. But it was easy enough to make a ruling when comparing victims to photographs the team had already gathered and were working with. Too tall, too short, too fat or too thin, some bodies simply didn't fit the description of who they were looking for. Among the bodies still awaiting identification, there were no other possible fits for Susan Smith and the two pathologists were comfortable with their conclusion so far.

It was a complete surprise then when the dental scan gave a negative result.

"Well, I didn't expect that one," Liz said, dumbfounded. "She looks so like the photo that I'd have put my own little finger on it." Dean and Liz stood open-mouthed at the result, not quite believing it.

"Let's get the dental records while we wait for DNA then, try and speed this up for her husband. I had the pleasure of speaking to him yesterday." He put air quotes around the word 'pleasure' as he spoke, his colleague understanding exactly what he meant. In times of absolute stress, it was easy for family members to forget their manners as they struggled with anxiety or grief. It went with the territory.

"Will do. But if they come back negative for our un-named here, there's nobody else that fits anywhere near her description awaiting identification. Do you think we may have an error somewhere?"

Dean scratched at his chin where salt-and-pepper, two-day stubble needed attending to. "I don't see how though, do you? This female is the only one that bears any resemblance whatsoever to this photo," he said, pointing at the picture of a woman with a bright, happy smile. Liz shrugged in response. It didn't seem possible, yet there had to be an explanation.

"Well, until we have a watertight positive ID, we can't release her name to her family. We've no choice."

"And if DNA is negative too, we're left with an anomaly, a mystery female. And since no one has contacted the helpline looking for her, who the hell could she be?" Liz voiced what Dean was already way past thinking.

"And where the hell could Susan Smith be?" he said, holding up the photograph again. "Because she got on that train in London."

"Let's take a look at that passenger list again. There's got to be a simple explanation."

CHAPTER 20

"I'm telling you, Chrissy, that man is weird." Julie sipped on an iced tea, though had she not been driving, her glass would have been topped up with gin and tonic. Her sports car parked outside Chrissy's house was saving her liver. They were sitting out on the small rear patio, the late-afternoon sun a delight to be out in.

"He's just upset, I'm sure. Grief and worry make you do things or act out of character, as he appears to be doing."

"I'm not so sure. I've only met the man a couple of times, and he's always been aloof, but now I just think he's actually bloody rude."

Chrissy smiled slightly at her sister's use of a curse word – she almost never swore, not ladylike she said. And while Chrissy swore it was only in private. To herself. And during road rage. But who didn't then?

"When will you get some concrete news? Did they give you any indication when it might be?"

"None, but I half expect Marcus to forget about letting me know when the news does come through. He's awfully distracted. As well as rude." She sounded like a sullen teenager again, something she easily fell back into. "She was my friend. I want to know what's going on." Realising that she'd used the past tense, Julie covered her mouth as if it would stop more past tense words from leaving.

Chrissy caught her horrified look. "I think you should face up to it, sis, it's been too long. She probably won't be coming home, not now."

"I know. I'm trying to get my head around it. But I keep hoping, as you would do too."

The front door slammed shut and two sets of footsteps could be heard heading through the house towards the kitchen and back patio. Harry and Thomas were home from school and would need feeding. Chrissy rose from her chair to greet her boys.

"Muuum," Harry protested as usual as he tried to brush her affectionate kiss off. Chrissy knew it bugged them both, it wasn't cool, but she would never give up being their loving mother. Julie watched on, amused. Her own children, two girls about the same age, were at boarding school, out of Julie's way for most of the time. She missed them, particularly when she was around Chrissy and her boys, but a decent education was what was required, and that was just what they were getting. Richard had been pretty clear on that when she'd fallen pregnant.

"What's for tea?" asked Harry, making his way across to the fridge and opening the door. Jam and margarine were taken out and Thomas grabbed the bread from the cupboard. On returning home, a jam sandwich was the staple for both boys before anything else was done. Chrissy shook her head in wonder and amazement at how much food the two of them consumed on a regular day, their slender athletic frames evidently needing the calories though they never wore them. They'd start to fill out soon enough. Age did that to you.

"Don't you have any contacts that could find out for me?" Julie asked.

"And why would I have contacts at the police or mortuary?

"Because of your job? I thought you were a bit of a private investigator nowadays?"

Chrissy felt the barbed comment, "a bit of a PI". She was a full-on PI, even had her licence now, though Julie clearly thought she was playing at it. But then Julie lived in a Nancy Drew kind of world where everything and everyone had a happy ending. Life wasn't like that. As she was discovering. The harsh reality of dealing with a train crash and identifying bodies in real life was a far cry from *Murder on the Orient Express* or *The Great St. Trinian's Train Robbery*. This was real life and could well have an ending that Julie didn't want to experience.

"That may be so, but the desk sergeant at my local constabulary is not going to hit the mark with this scenario, sis, this is big time serious stuff. The last report I heard asked if terrorism was involved. I wouldn't rule it out, not these days."

Julie acknowledged her sister's response with a petulant lower lip, returning to her thoughts as she sipped on her iced tea. A slice of cucumber floated on the remains of the golden liquid and Chrissy watched it bob and settle itself as Julie placed the tall glass back on the table in front of her. Julie stood to leave, straightening her pale pink blouse and bending down to retrieve her bag from the side of the chair she'd been sat in. In the kitchen the two boys were making their second sandwiches. A jam-pot lid clattered loudly to the floor, spinning before it settled.

"Marcus will keep you informed, I'm sure," Chrissy carried on and stood beside her. The two sisters walked out towards the front door where Julie's Mercedes was parked. The top was lowered. It was a smart-looking car, it suited her, and with the amount of hair lacquer Julie used, her hair wasn't in any danger of being blown out of style any time soon.

"Chin up, sis. Keep me posted, eh?"

A light nod from Julie as she slipped into the driver's seat and pulled away, leaving Chrissy wondering just how she could help. There must be someone she could contact to speed things along.

CHAPTER 21

Pathologists Dean Duffy and Liz Morgan pored over the passenger list one more time. Beside each name was a tick for those that had been identified. Some remained works in progress, still waiting on results and family members to be informed. Dean followed his finger down the list. Susan Smith was on it but the body that they had didn't match the photograph. Not from the dental scan at any rate. What was the explanation? It was confusing to say the least.

"I don't understand," Dean said, scratching his chin again. The bristles irritated him, a normally clean-shaven individual who was desperately in need of some rest. And a clean-up.

"The only thing I can think of is we have this woman here," Liz said, pointing to the name of Tabitha Child that still hadn't been ticked as identified. "We don't have any more bodies and there's nobody else in the mortuary that fits Susan's description, and yet we still have an unidentified female on the list. The bodies that are still awaiting ID are all male. We must've made a mistake some-where." She began to pace up and down, scratching her own head as if stimulating her scalp would bring an answer to the surface, like birds stamping the ground for worms. "We're going to have to look at them all again. There is no other way, we can't possibly have missed somebody, can we?" she enquired. Her eyes were filled with worry that they'd messed up somehow.

"I don't see how, but I don't see any other explanation either. And nobody has reported anybody else missing; we have everybody. I believe the police interviews with family are all done now." It was perplexing. "No, we have no option but to go through everybody again. But the first thing we should do is just do a total count because if we are one body short, that saves the whole process of ID again. There are thirty-five people on this list. Let's hope we've got thirty-five bodies."

It made sense and was the easiest way to look, but the news at the end of the exercise was even more perplexing. There were only thirty-four bodies in the mortuary. One body was missing.

"So let's assume that Tabitha Child is the body that is missing," Dean said. "First off, I've no idea where she could be unless she was walking wounded, and this is simply a clerical error. That would be the obvious answer so let's try that route first."

"Agreed," said Liz. In times of crisis errors could be made. "I'll get on and make some calls." Liz started towards the phone to ring the hospitals and find out if anybody had seen or admitted their mystery woman. But, as she reached for the handset, it dawned on her that the mystery woman was actually the one that was lying there in the mortuary there with them. It was *Susan Smith* that was missing. The dental results had come back negative so it seemed likely that the DNA test would also be the same.

The woman they were searching for was Susan Smith.

She voiced her thoughts to Dean who nodded his agreement. Once she got through to the hospital she enquired about Susan Smith, but no, nobody had been in and nobody had treated anyone named Susan Smith.

"It simply doesn't make any sense," she said to Dean again after the phone call. "That's just stupid. How can a woman simply vanish? She obviously got on the train because she went through passport control. Why wouldn't she actually then get on?"

"Maybe she changed her mind at the last minute. That would

explain the absence of her, but what it doesn't explain is who this body is here."

Liz mulled it over and came to the same conclusion about the same time as Dean. "Then this woman has to be the body of Tabitha Child surely? Susan Smith's the anomaly here, not that I would like to tell her husband our discovery."

"I agree. Let's work on the assumption, for the time being, that this victim is Tabitha Child. Yet no one has reported her missing and we've got no ID. So all we can do is go for dental and DNA and fingerprints and see if there is anything already in the system. And she's given birth more than once – so where are her children? And this tattoo looks like a custom job, rather intricate, wouldn't you say? Even for a small one, it's a work of genius," he said, pointing to the photograph of the woman's thigh. It looked like the centre of some kind of flower yet to fully unfurl as it bloomed. "We know nothing about her. And you know what, Liz? She could be Susan Smith's older sister when you look at her. Even in death there is an acute resemblance though just a bit older. Do you think they could be related?"

"Well, they could be of course. Just because she is called Child doesn't mean to say they don't have the same parents. Could be married. And DNA will tell us if there is a familial match since we have samples of Susan's DNA already. We will know if they are from the same family but, again, no one has reported her missing."

"Well, I'll get started on the tests. And I'll send this tattoo through to the detectives involved. They may have an idea, be able to trace it somehow. The sooner we can find out what's going on here the better because I don't fancy Susan Smith's husband coming down here shouting the odds. In all my years of being a pathologist, I've got to know the type that will kick up a fuss and he's that type. We don't need the headache or distraction."

"I'd better report in with the commander what we've discovered with our mystery woman. He should be able to help find out more about our victim, assuming of course Tabitha Child is her real name."

"What makes you say that?" Dean asked.

"Because I wouldn't be surprised if there's more to this discovery than we know currently. A disappearing woman who looks uncannily like our deceased? It's not your everyday bread-and-butter case is it?"

Dean didn't need to respond to that one. Indeed, it wasn't. But then no two disaster identification situations were ever the same.

CHAPTER 22

When Tabby had finished her meal, she'd spotted a small booth at the back of the diner. A sign above the glass door said 'l'Internet'. French was often easy to decipher even if you were a little rusty. She slipped inside, sat down at a terminal and fed coins into the slot. Then waited for the screen to come to life. The speed was more like the old dial-up, and it took a few moments to bring up the Google homepage. If she was going to be Tabby for a while longer, maybe an internet search could tell her more about the woman she'd now chosen to be. She entered 'Tabitha Child' into the search box and results filled her screen. All twenty-one million of them. The first results were from *Bewitched*, the TV series that ran back in the sixties, since the young actress played a character called Tabitha and she herself was a child.

"Useful. *Not*," Tabby said sarcastically under her breath. Scrolling down quickly through the next four pages, she didn't see anything else of interest. She clicked on the images tab at the top and waited for the page to load with photos of Tabitha Child, but it was more about the young actress, from all corners of the globe.

She tried 'Child, Tabitha'. Nothing. Zip. There were no images of any other Tabitha Child, not on Google anyway. She tried another search engine and this time the results were not quite so one-sided towards the young actress. But even scanning the few images that were posted, there was no one that looked like she did, or anywhere near.

"That's strange," she said, mumbling. "I can't be the only one, can I?" She was aware of the door opening and closing, someone entering and sitting at the adjacent terminal. She looked up from her screen. He looked like another lorry driver, probably getting his email. Or looking for a chat room.

"Facebook," she said, a tad louder than she'd intended, causing the man to glance up at her. She mouthed "Sorry," then remembered she wasn't in England any more, the soundless word not making sense in French. The search results were a little better, showing seven Tabitha Child profiles, all of which, going by their images, looked nothing like her or the real Tabitha. Everyone had some online presence but not, it seemed, Tabitha Child. It didn't ring true. Having no social media accounts she could understand, but, if you googled a name, generally there'd be something online, a local news story, perhaps, or a business profile of some kind. It appeared that either she was an extremely private individual and didn't want the world to know her, or... what exactly?

Maybe she wasn't really Tabitha Child.

"Really? You're a fake?"

The man glanced over his screen again. This time she didn't try and apologise, but took the hint, closed the terminal down and left the tiny room. Her brain chugged into gear slowly, sorting through what little she'd learned and quite how little existed of 'herself'. But the woman whose life she'd taken over had credit cards, a passport, a life somewhere and, she guessed, someone who looked out for her. Maybe that someone was Dominic, he'd said she was worrying him. He'd be due to call again soon. He'd want an update on her whereabouts and plans – like when she was heading back. Where did he fit in exactly? It was something to mull on as she travelled. It was time to get moving, find another lift. It didn't take her long. A woman travelling alone was not much of a threat to anyone.

An older man, a local, perhaps, who spoke perfect English had room in his van and Susan thanked him heartily. So far, travelling on her own had not been an issue. She hoped it stayed that way. Paris city centre was about an hour away and 'Albert' proved to be an enjoyable travelling companion. It was a shame their journey was only short.

"Well, if you're looking for a little peace as well as warmth, there's plenty of tiny villages dotted through the south of France. You could lose yourself quite easily if that's what you wish." He glanced across at her, a knowing smile on his mouth. She sensed he knew something. Susan turned to him, her eyes questioning. How could he possibly know anything about her? He pointed to her now yellowish-purple eye.

"Well, you've hardly any belongings with you either. A simple deduction. But that's none of my business. Personally? I'd head to somewhere like Albi first, then if that's too busy for you, head down to the mountains, the Pyrenees. At this time of year there'll be a café or two that might need your help. But Albi could be your best bet."

"Why Albi?"

"Medieval city. It's a tourist attraction. Lots of history but lots of summer work too." His smile filled his face and showed off his lack of good dentistry. He needed to have a chat to John about that. But Albert was right, she had to get a job soon, the little money she had left wouldn't keep her for long and life living on the actual street held no appeal whatsoever.

"How far is Albi?"

"About seven hours. But you got a lift just fine all this way and it's a fairly straight road down. You'll be there before dark. There'll be backpackers' places, plenty of cheap accommodation." He made it sound perfect, the best place to try for. Or should she spend some time in Paris? She was almost there after all. Her phone vibrated in her bag and she absentmindedly looked down at it, willing it to stop. Albert glanced again at her and she dipped her chin, not wanting to explain.

"It's none of my business," he said, his smile still in place. "But somebody's keen." The phone finally stopped, and Susan felt a message hit voicemail. Something else she still had to deal with. Ignoring it for now, she opted for silence and took in the sights as they entered the city centre. The architecture looked exquisite.

"I'll drop you here if I can," he said, turning to face her when he came to a stop. "It's been a real pleasure. Now, you look after yourself, won't you?" Bright blue eyes twinkled at her, the white-grey hairs covering his chin made him look older than he perhaps was. Whatever his age, his natural perception was finely tuned. Susan had enjoyed chatting with him and was sorry they'd have to go their separate ways. Once out of the little van, she bent her head in through the passenger window and said "Thanks again!" before he pulled away. A withered arm waved from the driver's side in the distance. Albert was gone from her life, a fleeting visitor.

She took out the phone and asked Siri to read her last message and voicemail.

"You'd better be on your way back after your reckless jaunt. Or have I to come and get you?"

Tabby's stomach curdled at the venom lacing his words as he spat each one from his mouth. Whoever Dominic was, she certainly didn't fancy meeting him in person. Glancing up into the distance again, she watched the last of Albert's van disappear around a corner. Dominic's words still rang in her ears and put a dampener on her own spirit – it didn't feel much like an adventure any longer.

She was completely on her own again.

CHAPTER 23

As the working day ended for pathologists Dean and Liz, they were both glad to be going home for rest and a meal. When a disaster such as the train crash happened it was all hands to the pump, every resource called in to help, and everyone simply got on with their task at hand. The first forty-eight hours were always the hardest – for both the team and the anxiously waiting relatives desperate for information about their loved ones. The longer they went without hearing anything, the more their minds told them to expect the worst. Upset was replaced by resignation, then anger, then upset invariably took over once again. It was a vicious emotional ride for anyone awaiting news that wouldn't come soon enough. But members of the DVI team couldn't survive or be of much use when sleep deprivation took over and the only answer was for them to rest. As Dean escorted Liz out to her waiting car, he rubbed his chin again absentmindedly.

"Maybe it will look clearer in the morning. There'll be some perfectly normal explanation, you'll see. We had it right all along, and Susan Smith is among our victims."

Her car beeped as the alarm deactivated and she stood with the driver's side open. "I hope you're right, Dean, but that still means we are a body short, remember? Tabitha Child's name is on that list and we only have thirty-four bodies accounted for."

"Body parts?" He was clutching at straws.

"Not enough."

"Then let's sleep on it. I'll be lucky to stay awake long enough to get through my front door."

"Are you okay to drive, Dean? Maybe get a taxi."

He slipped inside his own car and brushed the idea off with a flick of his hand. "Nah, I'm all good. See you in the morning." And, slowly, he pulled away, leaving Liz to stand watching until his rear lights disappeared in the distance. Slipping inside her own car, Liz made her way towards her hotel and, like her colleague Dean, hoped the next day would bring them some positive explanation. She didn't fancy giving the news they had a missing person to the senior identification manager, who would have more questions than answers. Maybe a good night's sleep would indeed bring some clarity to the unusual situation. She could only hope.

But the following day was to be a day much as the previous one. While both Dean and Liz worked tirelessly on identifying all but five of the remaining bodies, it was nearly 3 pm when they finally received a telephone call from the lab with DNA results for several of their remaining victims. Liz had taken the call and listened as result after result was read out. Dean stood by waiting, a mug of coffee in his hand.

"I see," she said, "and they are all a one hundred per cent positive match? Yes. Okay, yes please, email them over. You're sure about that last one? I know. Okay, thanks again."

Dean was just about able to follow the one-sided conversation and could only wait patiently until Liz filled him in properly. As she hung up, her face told him all was not well.

"And?" he said, a tone of enquiry on each letter stretching the word out.

"And it seems the plot thickens."

"Then I'm guessing nine of the ten are confirmation, but our mystery woman is still a mystery."

"Correct. There is nothing in the system, which is not unusual if she's never been arrested before. And we have no personal items to match DNA against so still no positive ID for our mystery woman. And she's definitely not related to Susan Smith, not a familial DNA match."

"Never a dull day, eh?"

"It would appear so." Liz put her mug down on her desk. "Let's try her driver's licence photo and compare that. We have her name, at least a partial visual would help us confirm or deny and go on from there. But who do we inform with that even?"

Dean shrugged. "I'll organise it."

"We've still got a lot of work to do here on our remaining bodies and I'd like to get them all ID'd before the weekend."

Dean nodded, something niggling the back of his mind. Dean strummed his fingers against his mug. He knew plenty of detectives involved in investigating the accident; he'd ask one of them about the unclaimed woman. Maybe the tattoo could lead them somewhere? And her driver's licence photo. And the fact she looked so alike their now missing Susan Smith, which there had to be an explanation for. His naturally inquisitive mind was working overtime on the possibilities but, catching the time on the wall clock, Liz's desire to complete IDs for the weekend dragged him back to the urgent job at hand.

She'd have to wait a while longer.

CHAPTER 24

Constable Jamie Miller, the Family Liaison Officer, or FLO for short, was the young woman tasked with informing Marcus that his wife, Susan, was confirmed not present at the mortuary. It was a delicate situation to handle but she would be joined by her colleague Detective Alan Davies, who would be the one to break the news. Alan had met Marcus the previous day. Her role after the official briefing was that of support. An appointment had been set up for both Constable Jamie Miller and DS Alan Davies to deliver the news, not a welcome task but a necessary one and all part of the job. The young Constable knocked on the front door. A moment later, Marcus's presence was felt before he'd even opened it. Jamie glanced at her colleague. Judging by the slight wince on his lips he'd felt it too. The door flew open and Marcus Smith stood glowering at the two of them. Alan was about to introduce the FLO but there was no interest from Marcus who was already disappearing back down the hallway, expecting them to follow. The man's body language spoke volumes. He headed into the kitchen and picked up his glass of wine. It was four o'clock and judging by the almost-empty bottle, he'd started early. Even dressed casually in his own home, the man screamed formality and order. The sharp crease in the front of his trousers couldn't have been any sharper, his double-cuff shirt any more starched. Alan doubted the man owned a sweatshirt.

"Can I get you something to drink?" he offered, almost toasting with his glass and probably knowing full well that the two wouldn't be drinking on duty. He did it as more of a tease, a 'look what I've got a you haven't' kind of mentality, and he seemed a little wobbly in his voice. Maybe it wasn't his first bottle of the day.

"No, thank you, not while we're both on duty, but a glass of water would be welcome," said Alan, asserting his male authority in what already appeared to be a hostile environment. Marcus looked into his own glass before taking a large mouthful and swallowing it down, half the contents now gone.

"Take a chair each," Marcus instructed, waving his hand at the two bar stools near where he'd been seated. There was no move from him to get their glasses of water. DS Alan Davies did introductions just to be sure that Marcus knew who they were and the roles they had to play in the investigation of Susan Smith. But it was Marcus that tried to run the show, as per usual, and was anxious to get on with it, not feeling particularly sociable.

"So I'm guessing you've got some news for me," said Marcus, almost defeated. He was expecting the worst. It had been forty-eight hours now.

"I'll get straight to the point," started Alan. "We haven't recovered a body matching the description of your wife, Susan Smith. There is currently no body in the mortuary that fits her description and there are no DNA matches."

Marcus looked up from his drink. It wasn't the news he was expecting and confusion creased his eyebrows. "You're telling me that my wife isn't dead? She wasn't on the train?"

"We're saying that we don't currently have your wife's body which would lead us to conclude that she is alive somewhere. But as yet we are unable to locate her. She wasn't admitted to the mortuary or any of the hospitals, but she was on that train. She did go through passport control. She is now officially missing."

"But that's impossible," said Marcus. "Why would she just disappear? And she's not called, she's not answering her phone."

"I can't answer that for you," Alan said. "But I can tell you this: we're doing everything we possibly can to locate your wife. But I will also tell you she is now listed as a missing person and because she is an adult in her own right, there is only so much we can do to find her."

Marcus erupted like a sleeping volcano. "What do you mean there is only so much you can do?" he bellowed, making the FLO jump visibly. "You need to get out there and find her!" His face was the colour of the red wine he was drinking, his voice raised to screaming pitch.

"I understand that, sir, but if she has decided to go missing, for whatever reason, of her own free will, then that's her prerogative. Obviously, under the circumstances, after the accident, we will be looking a little more closely but it's safe to say she is not in any of the mortuaries or the hospitals in the local area. We simply don't have Susan Smith." Alan stayed quiet for a moment, letting it sink into Marcus's head just what he was saying. There was a good chance that his wife was still alive somewhere, yet he didn't look happy or sad about that news.

Marcus remained quiet, his explosive temper simmering down.

"In the meantime," Alan carried on, "Constable Jamie Miller is here in the capacity of family liaison officer. She will act as the go-between between yourself and the team until we figure out what's happened to Mrs Smith. She's support and liaison and will stay here as long as you want her to. So if you have any questions, please put them through Constable Miller."

Jamie nodded and smiled slightly to Marcus who returned the gesture with a look of contempt. Alan was glad it wasn't his role to fill.

"I don't need anybody to babysit me, I'm a grown man. What I need is someone to find my wife. Today!" His skin was flushed crimson, blotches appearing on his neck.

Jamie was used to this reaction and had a standard line of reply.

"If I may, Mr Smith," she started. "You may feel differently when the news has sunk in and I'm here if you need me."

Marcus finished his glass of wine and topped it back up.

"So now I need to ask some questions," said DS Davies. Marcus looked up from his glass that he'd been holding with both hands as if it was in danger of running away without him. "You might think some of these questions are a little simple but they can give us an idea, while we're trying to build up a picture of Susan's life, where she might have gone. So let's start with the first one. Is there any reason that you can think of why your wife might have left?"

The volcano was back, spewing fire and ash. "Oh, for heaven's sake," screamed Marcus. "Is that the best you can do? No, I don't know where she might have gone or why she might have gone. This is as big a mystery to me as it is to you. I give her everything she wants, more, and she disappears, putting me through hell, letting me think she's dead. So no, I've no idea what's gone on, where she is or why. Maybe you'd be better asking some of her friends, I'm rarely in the country anyway." He caught his breath after yet another outburst. Alan hoped the man's heart was strong enough; he didn't fancy trying to revive him if he collapsed.

But sometimes, for a detective, it was what people didn't say more than what they did say that gave the clues, evidence or suggestions of what happened in a crime. The fact that Mr Smith was hardly ever in the country, leaving his wife in the unmistakable, almost sterile environment on her own? She was probably lonely and had had enough. But it wasn't his place to make assumptions. They had to find evidence. Though, as he'd already stated, she was a grown woman and entitled to disappear whether her husband liked that fact or not.

Watching Marcus Smith simmer with annoyance and drain his glass one more time, Alan hoped that if Susan Smith had run off, she had the stamina to keep on going.

CHAPTER 25

Unlike like Chrissy, Julie was a superb cook. It was the reason she'd got such an elaborate, well-designed, almost commercial kitchen. Yes, it was also there for show, like a lot of things in Julie's life, but when she had the time to spend creating, what she produced Raymond Blanc would be content eating. It was a shame she didn't cook more often. While Chrissy used a food service to deliver meals for her family if she hadn't the time to cook, Julie enjoyed going out to eat, to be seen in all the right places – something that drove Richard round the bend. He was a caring individual, and he loved his wife dearly, though he'd learned to tune out in those times when what she had to say really was of no importance to him at all. The general gossip or the petty things that went on in her life – the mundane, the banal – was of little interest. He really didn't care if the dry cleaner screwed up and her idea of a hellish day was the wrong colour varnish applied to her toes. Recently though, since Jooles, Jooles had opened, he had to admit to himself that conversation had changed somewhat. But Richard was sensitive to the fact that Julie's friend was presumed dead after the train crash and he'd decided to book somewhere more upmarket for a change, somewhere away from where they usually went out for dinner, to try and take her mind off it.

They'd spent their evening across town at a swanky place with starched linen tablecloths and silver cutlery, and Julie had shone as brightly as the diamonds embedded in her rings. For the first time in the last few days she'd seemed brighter, happier. Now they were on their way back home. Richard was at the wheel, choosing to stay sober and drive them himself rather than get a car. Ravel played lightly in the background on the sound system, *Boléro* about to reach a rather long, gradual crescendo with trombones, tubas and cymbals adding to the rest of the orchestra in heady full force. As they drove on through darkened streets, it couldn't have been any more dramatic had there been thunder and lightning. Julie's phone rang. Not connected to the Bluetooth it didn't interrupt the music and she bent to retrieve the phone from the bottom of her evening purse.

"Who could that be?" Richard asked. "It's gone eleven o'clock."

"It's Marcus," said Julie, surprised as she checked the caller ID. "I wonder if he's heard something?"

She swiped to open the phone and said, "Marcus, do you have some news?"

"I do, though I'm not quite sure what to make it. I suppose it's good news really."

Julie realised that Marcus sounded somewhat maudlin. He wasn't frantic, he wasn't being weird, he simply sounded awfully flat, but there was something else in his words. It was a kind of despair, almost wondering. And drowsy.

"Have they confirmed Susan's body, is that what you mean?"

"No," he said resignedly, "that's just it, they don't have her body. Everybody's been accounted for, everybody that could possibly be Susan that is. There *is* no Susan, she simply isn't at the mortuary and she's not been to any of the hospitals. I don't know what to make of it."

Julie took a moment for it to sink in what he was telling her. It wasn't the news that she'd been expecting either.

"So, they think Susan is still alive somewhere, is that what you're saying? Well, that's good news, isn't it?"

"And that's what I thought," said Marcus. "So where the hell is she and why hasn't she contacted me? She must know about the crash – she was on the train because she went through passport control."

"So she's somehow disappeared?"

"So it seems." Odd whimpering sounds made Julie wonder if Marcus had begun to cry quietly and she immediately felt for him. It was so unlike the man she otherwise knew so little about. He was always rampant, gunning for something, on edge, or just being a complete arse. But this was a different side to him she'd never seen before, a caring side, a concerned side that his wife was missing. The situation had turned into a whole different scenario. She also wondered if he'd taken something, his words sounded drowsy almost.

"Are you all right, Marcus?" she enquired. Perhaps he'd been drinking and taken a sleeping tablet.

"I'm fine. Sleepy." Maybe he had.

"So, what happens next?" Julie asked. She was conscious of Richard constantly turning his head, trying to understand what was going on on the phone, trying to catch odd words and make something of it.

"I've filed an official missing person report but, because she is an adult, they informed me that there is little they can do because she may have walked off of her own free will. They don't suspect foul play. There was an accident, yes, and a woman has since disappeared, gone. They'll take a cursory look, but then that's it."

"What can I do to help, Marcus?" Julie asked with a renewed gust of energy.

"I don't know. I just thought you'd like to know. I'm going to sleep on it and see what happens in the morning. I guess it's better than dead though, even with so many unanswered questions."

"Let's speak tomorrow. Get some rest."

As usual with Marcus, the phone line was already disconnected. Julie turned to Richard and relayed the conversation.

"What the hell is happening now, she's alive?" asked Richard. "But he thinks she's done a runner? Is that it?"

Julie put her head back on the headrest and closed her eyes for a moment. "It could be so. But if she has done a runner, where's she gone and why?"

"I guess she's got her reasons, if that's what's happened."

"I'm going to give Chrissy a call, maybe she can help."

"And what makes you think she can? She works in HR, doesn't she?"

"Keep up Richard," Julie said sarcastically, finding her sister's number and waiting for the call to connect. "She set herself up as a PI a few months back."

"A private investigator? I must have missed that piece of drama," he mused and turned his concentration back to the road as Julie relayed the facts to Chrissy. It wasn't hard to hear the loud "holy hell" from his sister-in-law. She wasn't known for being demure.

CHAPTER 26

Chrissy suggested she meet Julie in a café in Englefield Green and was sitting nursing a mug of milky coffee, waiting for her sister to arrive, and people-watching at the same time. She wondered about their lives, where they were headed, what they might be going back to later, and if they were happy. Each life different to the next. Blonde hair in the distance caught her eye and she instinctively knew who it belonged to. She smiled to herself as Julie approached, opened the café door and glanced around for her. Chrissy put her hand in the air to make it easier for her to spot and Julie wandered over, immaculately dressed as per usual. Chrissy couldn't help but notice the gazing eyes of both men and women giving her sister the once over. She was a stunning looking woman. She leaned in and air-kissed either side of Chrissy's head.

"Did you sleep?" Julie asked. "I didn't sleep at all."

There was no point in trying to answer before Julie finished with her own experience so Chrissy simply nodded her head.

"What exciting news, isn't it? At least Susan is alive. That much I do believe," Julie said happily.

"And you're obviously thinking I can somehow find her when the police can't. Is that why you wanted to meet?"

Julie readjusted her leather skirt before sitting down to join her sister, crossing legs that wouldn't look out of place at a hosiery photo shoot. "Of course, you are a PI, aren't you? I'm happy to pay."

"It's nothing to do with money, Julie," she said. "I'm just not sure what more I can do that the police can't. Why don't we wait and see what they come up with first?"

Julie looked petulant as she stared back at her sister. "But you're a private investigator now so you've surely got some other tools. They always seem to have on the television so I'm assuming you will be the same? You must have a geek friend somewhere that can track Susan via her phone or something?"

Chrissy gave an amused smile at the reference to television shows. Real life was rarely the same as a police show, a private investigator series or *Silent Witness*. The public had a misconception of what actually went on because in reality the true story would be somewhat less exciting. And a good deal slower.

"First off," said Chrissy. "You can only track someone's phone when it's turned on, unless you're the NSA, and since it's days after the crash there'd be no battery charge left. Or perhaps she dropped it and they found her phone at the crash site, one of many I should expect, but the battery would be dead. And the phone would be locked."

Julie looked crestfallen.

"And who would even be tracking her? Do you track Richard? I doubt that Marcus would be bothered, would he?"

"There must be other technology, there must be other ways to find her?"

"If she doesn't want to be found then no, not much. I'm betting her credit cards haven't been touched, she's not been on Facebook, obviously, and she's not bought anything on hire purchase understandably. And none of her friends you've tried have heard from her." Chrissy let the information settle before adding, "You might have to face the fact she doesn't want to be found and is living the life in Greece with a bronzed fisherman. That's what I'd do. Like Shirley Valentine did. Though it's better than dead."

"So, you're giving up before we've even started?" asked Julie.

"And what's with the 'we'?" Chrissy said, squinting slightly at her sister as she said the words. Was Julie thinking of tagging along? Surely not.

"Well," she said, "I just mean we'll be looking for her, but not me physically, obviously."

"What about Marcus? Does he know that you're speaking to me, looking to employ me to find his wife? Or has he got something organised himself?"

"I don't much care about Marcus because I don't think Marcus much cares about Susan. But I care, she was my friend— is my friend. She's still alive, remember?"

"Well, I think out of courtesy we should let him know that we're looking for her. He might be able to help."

"You know, maybe he *was* tracking her," Julie said thoughtfully. "She said he was a bit controlling. Maybe he was tracking her in some way and she didn't know about it? I wouldn't put it past him, it feels like something he'd do."

"I suspect if it was something he was privy to, he'd have checked it out already but, like I said, the phone will be dead, it would be useless. And the police will have checked that angle, I'm sure."

A young waitress came over and Julie ordered a green tea; Chrissy, a refill and a blueberry muffin. When the waitress had gone, Julie leaned into Chrissy and almost in a whisper said, "I think, looking back now, now that she has gone, maybe she has run away from him. She never said anything specific to me, that he abused her or anything, but I know she was dreadfully unhappy with the way he kept a mental grip on her. Maybe she just got sick of it. Maybe she was planning on running away all along when she went off to France for the day. Maybe she *is* hiding out in Greece somewhere."

Dramatic like a corny soap opera.

"You're forgetting the train crash, though, so I doubt very much she's actually in Greece. Or Paris. Still in England somewhere?"

"There are other ways of getting across the Channel once that train had crashed. Maybe she did get off, managed to get out unscathed. She could get to the airport."

Chrissy sat thoughtfully. "Those front carriages were almost completely destroyed, mangled completely from what I saw on news reports. And the Business Premier carriages are up front and where the main casualties were. I'm assuming that Susan, being one of your friends, was travelling in style, wouldn't you think?"

Julie wondered. "I would assume so, yes."

"Then we need to double-check that she bought a business ticket before we go off wandering around the country or further afield. Because if she was in the first carriages, the chances of this being some terrible error would be high. When that train derailed and the carriages were dragged sideways down the tracks... I don't need to spell it out any further."

"I'm sure I can persuade Marcus to have a look at the credit-card statement for transactions and I'll tell him that we're going to look into her disappearance at the same time." Chrissy caught the 'we' again but ignored it this time.

"I think that's wise. We need to at least keep him in the loop. He may be of help."

"How else can we trace her?" Julie asked, sipping at her green tea and watching Chrissy tuck into the blueberry muffin, crumbs sticking to her upper lip before she finally wiped them off. Chrissy stayed quiet while she chewed and thought. There was only so much she could do to find the missing woman, but there were questions she needed the answers to and that meant a conversation with Marcus Smith.

"Here's what I want you to do."

CHAPTER 27

Reluctantly, Julie had called Marcus and arranged for them both to go around and talk to him. There was certain information that he might know as her husband that could help Chrissy in her search, and it would also give them the opportunity to tell him what their plan was. Surely he wouldn't mind. Julie pulled up outside Marcus's place. He was still in the country, though he was due to leave the following day. Julie wondered if he actually would do in the midst of the chaos. It seemed odd that the man would hurry back to Hong Kong and his business interests, but that was his decision not hers, and since his wife wasn't dead, there was no funeral to hang around for or organise. Even so, it struck Julie as odd. She hoped Richard wouldn't act similarly if she were to run off. But then maybe Marcus was the reason Susan had run off.

The house seemed different somehow as Julie and Chrissy approached the gate. Marcus opened the door and let them in wordlessly, showed them both through to the kitchen at the back and offered them a bar stool each. "Can I get you two ladies a drink?" he enquired. "Tea? Coffee? Wine, perhaps?"

"Not for us, thanks," said Julie. It was a bit early, only just coming up to twelve o'clock and while she might partake in a glass of wine over lunch with the girls, she certainly didn't drink alcohol at lunch as a rule. But Marcus wasn't in his normal routine and quite possibly his body clock was still in another time zone. The two women watched as he poured himself a glass of red. They sat quietly, giving him space to speak first. After all, it was his kitchen, his house, his wife.

"So, what's this about?" he asked somewhat tiredly.

Julie spoke first, "Since we now know that Susan isn't lying in a mortuary, I thought I'd hire a private investigator to find her, with your blessing. Chrissy here," she said with an open hand as if displaying an auction exhibit, "is a private investigator. She also happens to be my sister."

Marcus turned to Chrissy and Julie watched as his eyes took her in, from her forehead down to her knees and back up again, and she wondered what he was thinking. His inspection wasn't suggestive in any way, not like he was looking somebody up and down in a nightclub, say, but he did appear to be checking her credentials by what she was wearing and the way in which she presented herself. Satisfied, he returned his gaze back to his drink, taking a long mouthful before speaking.

"I thought about that idea myself," he said, "but I've got to get back to Hong Kong so I haven't done anything about it. I thought I'd leave the initial investigation up to the police. They've got to be in the best position, surely?"

It was Chrissy's turn to take that one. "That may be your impression, Mr Smith, but since she's obviously gone off on her own the police simply don't have the resources to look for her as an adult. They barely have enough to look for missing at risk children. Literally hundreds of thousands of people go missing in the UK every year. So please don't set your hopes on what the police will do for you right off the bat. But there are things that a private investigator such as I can do. But let me also say don't feel that it has to be me if you prefer to use somebody else."

"That's very good of you to give me the option," said Marcus sarcastically. Chrissy bristled visibly and Julie started to speak.

"Marcus, whichever way you choose to go, there are some basic questions we need to ask you." Chrissy caught the 'we' again and made a mental note to talk to Julie about it later. There would be no 'we' during this investigation – not after today anyway. If Marcus gave his permission, and even if he didn't, Julie was her client, sister or not. So whatever Marcus wanted didn't really matter, but they certainly needed his help. His approval would be nice too.

"So we've got a couple of questions to ask."

"Fire away," said Marcus, without raising his head. He couldn't have looked any less interested if he'd tried.

"Lots of families have tracking devices for members of their families even if it's only *Find My iPhone*. Did you and Susan share anything like that? Did you monitor each other's movements, maybe, just to make sure each of you was safe?" Chrissy thought she'd wrapped the question up rather nicely, didn't make it sound like he was snooping but that they were watching out for each other. She did notice the slight smirk appear on Marcus's face, his lips creasing at the edges even if it wasn't intentional. The answer to that particular question was a definite 'yes' but he still hadn't spoken. After a long moment, Chrissy gave him a nudge. "Which one did you use, Mr Smith? Just so we know what we're dealing with."

"What makes you think that we used one?"

"Come on, Mr Smith, I wasn't born yesterday."

Marcus let out a deep sigh but still didn't speak. He wasn't making it easy.

Chrissy ploughed on, "The most common one is *Mspy*. I suspect if it wasn't *Find My iPhone* it was something like that, am I correct?"

There was no mistaking the glare directed at Chrissy. Finally, he spoke.

"Yes, okay, yes. I liked to know what she was up to, that she was safe. No harm in that, is there?"

"So you have the control pad on your own phone then?"

"Yes. I guess your next question is what was on her texts and emails?"

"Well, I was coming to that, but since you mention it, what did they contain?"

"Nothing out of the ordinary. She wasn't seeing anybody, if that's what you're thinking, but since the time of the crash there have been no more texts or emails or phone calls or anything. I've checked: her phone is not responding, offline. I can't even find the location of it, and the battery is almost certainly dead."

He took another long mouthful of his wine and Julie remembered how he sounded the previous night. Perhaps he hadn't been sleepy but maudlin drunk instead. He was headed that way now.

"Well, that's helpful to know there's been no activity on her phone. I could do with checking your credit-card statement. We need to know if she was actually in a Business Premier carriage or further back. Given the state of those front carriages, this is important. So we just need to know what ticket she bought."

"I'll get it for you."

"Actually," said Chrissy, "it won't show on the paper printout yet. They'll be on your online banking on your phone. You could check for us now."

Both women watched as Marcus took his phone out, entered his passcode and hit the banking app. He scrolled through. There hadn't been much activity since he'd been back, he hadn't been anywhere himself, really not in the mood for shopping, so there were only a handful of transactions over the last few days. They were all Susan's. And they stopped on the day of the crash.

"This one here," he said, pointing. "That's the train company and that's a business ticket judging by the amount."

"So we know that she went through passport control," Chrissy said, "but we don't know what happened after the crash and that's where our investigation should start."

"Do you think you both can find her?" It was the first time Marcus had seemed genuinely interested.

"We'll do our best," said Chrissy and smiled inwardly for saying 'our' best not 'my' best.

It looked like she had a tag-along apprentice after all.

CHAPTER 28

"I really don't understand that man," said Chrissy. They were back at the car and were both well out of earshot of Marcus, who was no doubt finishing off the rest of the wine at the kitchen counter. "He seems so disinterested. I mean, he even said he was going back to Hong Kong for heaven's sake. He really doesn't have his priorities in the right order. Unless Susan never was a priority of course. I've never met anybody so arrogant and dislikeable in all my life." Chrissy thought about Julie's Richard: at least he wasn't arrogant, but he wasn't the most likeable soul either. Still, you couldn't pick your in-laws; they were acquired for you.

"What now?" said Julie.

"Well, we need to find out if she is still in the country. She went through passport control at this end, but it would be good to know if her passport was pinged somewhere else. Because if she decided to get herself somehow to an airport or a ferry port, she'd need a passport to get out of the country. And I also need to know if they've found her handbag. Is she carrying ID with her and in what form? If her passport is still in her bag, and it's stored somewhere with the rest of the luggage and belongings from the accident scene, she has to be still in the UK somewhere."

"And how are you going to do that?" enquired Julie. "You're not exactly a policeman. I mean woman."

"I know that. I might need to use one of my contacts. Not entirely legal but then that's the joy of being a private investigator – I don't have to play by the same rules the police do." She started the engine, pulled away from the kerb, and headed back towards home. "Maybe Marcus needs the distraction of going back to work, and as long as we can get hold of him and ask questions, it's not a biggie really."

"So, do you have a contact, someone that can find out if her belongings have been found?" Julie asked.

"Not on the local police side, not yet, but that's not to say I can't get one."

"What can I do?"

Chrissy glanced across at her sideways, and slyly asked, "What you mean is what do I *want* you to do?"

"Well, I'm obviously going to be helping," Julie said indignantly. "She is my friend and I'm going to help find her."

"And how do you propose you do that? Follow me around like a lost puppy?"

"Noooooo." She drew the word out like a child, making it painfully longer. "There must be something I can do, flutter my lashes somewhere, perhaps."

She had to concede that one. "You might come in handy on that score." Chrissy's idea of expensive face cream was when Nivea was full price and not on offer. "We should head back home then, and write out all the things that we would do if we were running away ourselves. How would we do it? How would we survive moneywise? How would we travel? All those things. Because even if she did this on a whim – because, let's face it, no one would have expected the train to crash – she's surviving somehow and somewhere."

"It'll be fun," said Julie. "Like kind of making it up as you go along."

"Well, if she did do it on a whim, that's exactly what she will have done. What we don't know is if she is still in this country or if she's rattling around Europe somewhere."

"What do you think to Marcus tracking her for heaven's sake? Why on earth would he do that to her? Because I can tell you it wasn't to keep her safe, he's not like that. And I bet she didn't know about it either. Talk about breach of her privacy."

"All part of him being an arse, I think. Maybe their relationship was somewhat more controlling than you first thought. He doesn't need to leave a mark on her skin to be abusive. I wouldn't like to cross him."

"And that house," Julie said with a shudder.

"Not my cup of tea," said Chrissy. "I like my sofas to be comfortable, not like something you'd find in a royal palace. I can't imagine swinging my legs up and spending a Sunday afternoon reading on any of that furniture."

"Maybe that's why she had a room down the bottom of the garden," said Julie. "Surprising, isn't it? You think you know somebody until something like this happens and you don't know them at all."

"I guess we're going to find out an awful lot more about Susan Smith if we're going to find her. Are you ready for that?"

"Damn right I am," said Julie, smiling.

CHAPTER 29

Detective Alan Davies wanted to see Susan Smith's belongings, what she was travelling with that day. Maybe there was something in her purse, her handbag, maybe, something to tell them where she'd been headed and what she might now be doing. While it was easy enough to see her credit cards hadn't been used, cash was the only way to go if she was going to disappear properly. Unless of course the whole escapade was a planned one. Maybe not from the crash, but she could have had an alternative ID set up and ready to go, along with the funds to look after herself. It wouldn't be the first time he'd come across a person with separate identities. He remembered an individual, a bigamist with two wives and two sets of children, living two very separate lives. It must've been a complex set-up every day, but he'd pulled it off. For more than fifteen years he'd led both families astray with his tales and excuses, neither any the wiser to the other's existence. It had all come out at the man's funeral. He hoped Susan Smith wasn't going to turn up at her own funeral. But having spent a few minutes in the presence of her husband he could fully understand why a woman might want to leave and not tell him where she was going.

The crash had happened days ago and the tracks were now

clear, trains moving freely again, with all the debris taken to a hangar, though luggage and personal belongings would be elsewhere. He needed to track them down and liaise with the disaster commander no doubt. It was his first major disaster in his career as a detective and protocols changed when something like this happened. Since the local constabularies hadn't got the resources to look after the incident on their own, the DVI units were set up to run at a moment's notice. He made the call back to his DI and asked who was looking after the belongings and where there were currently being stored. As soon as he had the answer, he headed straight over. They too were in a hangar at a nearby airbase, which was also the site of the makeshift mortuary. There wasn't much of a rush to get the belongings back to individuals, it wasn't a priority, and for many of the items it would be hard to know who they belonged to anyway. Unless ID was on each bag or each laptop, they would have no way of knowing whose was whose. In the end everything would be disposed of, forgotten.

Upon arrival he made himself known to the attending officer and explained what he was looking for: a lady's handbag and maybe an overnight case from the business carriage. The man, somewhere in his early sixties, looked doubtful. Resignedly, he said, "Best of luck, mate, it's carnage in there. I hope you've got some help?"

"I'm on my own, I'm afraid, so let's see how far I get before it goes dark."

"I'll bring you a coffee in an hour then, shall I?" the grey-haired man chuckled as he went back to his position at his makeshift desk.

Alan Davies stood in the doorway looking at the vast collection of belongings. There was no order to it. They had literally been dropped into the room to be sifted through at a later date – if ever.

"Let's get going then," he said as he walked further in, scanning as he went, looking for smaller bags, looking for an overnight case, looking for a lady's handbag. He pulled on latex gloves and opened the first bag that he came to. And then the second, and then the third, and then the fourth. By the time he'd found handbag number fifteen, he felt like giving up. But instead he thought of the detectives that had searched for the Yorkshire Ripper all those years ago, those that had undertaken the manual task of searching through reams and reams of paper records trying to locate a single vehicle among many thousands, and how they finally discovered it in the last few pages that were left. That's where they got their result.

"Bingo," he said into the darkening room. He hadn't realised how long he'd been searching until he'd glanced up at the fading light. In his hand he held Susan Smith's handbag, complete with phone, passport, wallet and other items that she'd carried that day. It was all in there. But would it reveal further clues as to where she'd gone? Maybe, just maybe, she'd still made it to Paris, though by somewhat different means than she'd originally intended.

CHAPTER 30

He knew he should have gone back home for some much-needed rest before he had to be back in the following morning, but pathologist Dean had a hunch grumbling in his stomach, though what about he wasn't sure. But it was there and it was causing him a degree of inner unrest. He couldn't place what it was but, like an intense thirst, it needed quenching. He'd arranged to meet DS Alan Davies at a pub nearby, and was sitting with a pint of lager in front of him when he spotted the man's unruly mop of hair bobbing its way through the crowded bar. Friday-night drinks after work were in full swing as the big man approached the tiny stool at the table. It had been a while since he'd seen him and he hadn't changed a bit. Dean stood to greet him and shake his hand.

"Good to see you again, Alan. You keeping well?"

"Not bad, thanks. And you?" Alan always had a pleasant way about him that made him popular with most. He was like a giant teddy bear, his curls disarming people somehow.

"Always. I see too much death in my job to let myself or my mind slip," he said, patting his hard stomach. A weekend warrior, he enjoyed his off-road running and competed locally when events didn't coincide with his heavy schedule. Death, unfortunately, had its own timetable. "What can I get you to drink?"

"Lager, thanks."

Dean stood to place the order. "Back in a minute," he said, gently easing through the crowd towards the bar. A moment later he was back and conversation resumed.

"Thanks for coming out here," Dean said as the detective wiped creamy froth from his upper lip, almost half the pint glass gone in one long swig.

"You sounded like something was on your mind and, in my line of work, when something gives you cause for thought, it's worth looking at. Gut feeling doesn't win juries over, but if your gut is talking, it's always best to listen." He took another giant swig, leaving only the bottom two inches of amber fluid. Maybe he was taking a taxi home.

"And that's just it. Something tells me there's more to a woman we have in the mortuary than we can find. Firstly, she looks a lot like another woman from the train, one now missing and off our list. And secondly, no one has come forward to claim or report her missing. No one. And most people have someone that would miss them. Yet she doesn't appear to, even though she has signs of giving birth – several times in fact." Dean paused and sipped on his own lager, taking in somewhat smaller amounts than Alan.

"Have you got photos with you?"

"Yes, here," he said, opening a folder that had been on another stool beside him. He handed it over and watched as his colleague studied them. Alan flipped back to the woman's facial shot,: she looked badly banged up and bruised. There was also one of the thigh tattoo.

"That's a beauty, an artist for sure," he said, studying it closely. "And you think she looks a lot like the missing woman, Susan Smith?"

"She certainly does. But she's not Susan Smith. DNA says so. And the only other woman on the list is Tabitha Child, though we can't confirm it's her at all. I'm hoping the tattoo and dental records will help, but since we've no idea if she's even from England, it could be a while."

"I see the resemblance now. And you want me to run this tattoo, see if that matches somewhere, and whatever else I can dig up on Tabitha Child, is that it?"

"Yes. We're stumped for now."

Alan picked up the tattoo picture again and held it close. He appeared to be interested in the dead centre of the flower.

"We've got a guy back at our station who should take a look at this image. A bit of an expert on tats. I can take this with me, I presume?"

"Of course. What are you thinking?"

"I'd rather not say as yet. Let him take a look first." He tipped the remainder of his lager down his throat. Dean wondered if he even tasted it, it went down so fast. Dean tossed a bucket of water down the drain slower than this man drank his brew. An empty glass smacked the table.

"Another?"

"Better not," he said. "But back to your mystery woman. If the tattoo doesn't tell us anything, and no one comes forward looking for her, she'll stay put in the fridge for a while?"

"No other choice. Afraid so."

"Then let's see if we can't find out her name, then. I was out at the hangar looking for our missing Mrs Smith's handbag, but I didn't look for your mystery woman's. Maybe her stuff is still in there? I stopped when I found what I was looking for. Perhaps I'll drive out there again in the morning, take another look." He stood to leave, Manila folder of photographs in his hand. "I'll let you know what I find out," he called back, leaving Dean to finish his barely touched pint. The gentle throb of voices lubricated with alcohol filled his ears and he sat back, resting his weary head against the wood-panelled wall. It had been a tough few days, and there was still a ton of work ahead of him.

And a nameless woman occupying a refrigerated container.

CHAPTER 31

Now it was Alan's turn to have something gnawing away at his stomach. Back in his vehicle, he let his brain run its built-in scanner over the mystery woman and, in particular, the tattoo on her thigh. While it was only small, a part of it had sparked something deep in his psyche, something from the recent past he was sure of it. But could he be mistaken? He was tempted to drop in at the home of his tattoo specialist colleague – just to see his reaction. Or if there even was one. The clock on his dash said it was coming up to 8pm. It wasn't that late; it wasn't like it was midnight. Justifying it to himself, he changed course from driving towards home and made his way back across town to see if his gut was correct. He decided it best to call ahead first, in case the man was out enjoying the evening somewhere else. His car filled with a ringing tone that stopped almost immediately.

"Evening, Alan." Caller ID made anonymous calls almost impossible these days.

"Evening, Carl. I wonder if you're home? I have something I could do with you taking a quick look at."

"Well, if it won't wait until Monday, I'm betting it's urgent so come on round."

"Thanks, I'll be there in ten."

"I'll put the kettle on," he said, before disconnecting the call.

Alan pulled up outside the large terraced house and by the time he reached the front door, Carl was opening it for him and he headed inside. Alan's stomach rumbled at the smell of Chinese takeaway that still lingered. He detected sweet-and-sour something, the vinegary tang playing with his nostrils. It must have registered on his face since Carl said, "There's leftovers if you want them?"

"Please, if they're going spare," he said as they made their way through to the back room. A TV was playing close by, and Alan assumed the rest of the family were ensconced watching a show. Had he pulled Carl away from something?

"I don't want to intrude..." he started, but Carl waved his hand at him that things were fine. Alan watched as the microwave turntable started its slow rotation, his meal beginning to steam almost instantly. The two men waited for the hum of the machine to finish before Alan stated his business as Carl placed a plate of hot sweet-and-sour chicken and fried rice in front of him. He'd been correct about what his nostrils had picked up. A few prawn crackers sat on a side plate nearby and Carl slid them over.

"May as well finish them off too," he said, refilling his wine glass. "You want a drink?"

"I'd better not, thanks. I've just had a pint." Alan tucked in with gusto. He hadn't realised quite how hungry he was, lunch had been way too long ago. When he'd shovelled in a couple of large forkfuls and allowed the food down to his awaiting stomach, he paused for a moment then slid the photo of the tattoo across to Carl. Between chews he asked, "What do you make of that?"

Carl picked it up and studied it carefully. There was obviously a reason why his colleague had driven over, something concerned him about the inking. He reached for his reading glasses, scanned it again, and then moved to open a drawer on the far side of the kitchen. He pulled out a magnifying glass and waved it at Alan's questioning look that read, 'You've got a magnifying glass – at home?'

"Age catches us all, my friend," he said as he once again bent his shoulders and concentrated on the image of a half-opened rose. Alan let him peruse and think while he worked on demolishing his plate of food. By the time he had picked up the last of the prawn crackers, Carl was looking at him intently.

"You think this has been done to conceal an original tattoo, a tattoo that points to all kinds of crap?"

Alan wiped his mouth on the corner of a tea towel that was nearby and said, "I do. And since you've spotted it too, I know I'm not imagining it."

"Where in holy hell did you come across this?"

"She's a mystery woman in the mortuary at this point. A victim from that train crash."

"Holy flaming hell. But you said 'mystery woman'?"

"It seems no one has come forward saying she's missing so she's lying in her own fridge awaiting an ID. The only name on the list unaccounted for is Tabitha Child. Mean anything to you?"

"No, but I see what you're getting at. You want me to check for an alternative identity."

"Yes. Because this is serious. She's not simply a woman with no fixed abode or family. She's important. Or should I now say *was* important. She'll not be a fat lot of use now she's in the mortuary."

"Do you think they know that she's dead?"

"I don't see how they can do. But look, I don't know for sure it's her, hence why we need to cross-check and find out her real name. Because if it's not her, then we have another victim on our hands."

"Sounds like she's already a victim, being dead and all."

"Can you look her up and let me know?"

Carl looked at the image again. There, in the centre of the half-opened rose, was a tiny but distinctive tattoo that had since been covered by the more appealing pale-pink petals of the flower. The original tattoo now formed the centre. He wondered why the woman had gone to so much trouble when she could have had the original removed. Maybe it had simply been a case of it being easier and quicker to do so, or maybe she wanted to keep the memento as a reminder, though Carl couldn't think why. There was only one reason she had a stigma tattoo, the inference obvious when you looked for it.

Just like a rose's reproductive organs, this woman had had her uses at some stage.

But she hadn't lived long enough to tell.

CHAPTER 32

Dominic watched the tracker icon flash on his screen and sighed heavily, contorting his mouth with dissatisfaction. Tabitha Child was in the centre of Paris on a spur-of-the-moment and somewhat stupid jaunt. What was she thinking? Was she trying to get herself killed? Her being out in the open with no backup close by was tantamount to suicide, but since he couldn't keep her locked up, a prisoner, there was little he could do. Except get her back somehow. She was under no legal requirement to stay put, but it was in the interests of her own safety to do so.

People like Tabitha, that found themselves in witness protection, sometimes through no fault of their own, found it tough, he knew. Being witness to a crime, a murder on the street corner below your flat, for instance, a murder you witnessed from your own window, could land you with unwanted attention from gangs or other people that weren't keen to have you stand up in court and tell the jury exactly what you had indeed observed. Intimidation, then, was scary stuff, particularly when threats involved your children or other family members. Protection, therefore, was the only alternative. Or let the bad guys get away with it.

He knew it was tough. Many people he'd handled in protection fell apart at some point, though it was usually the men, not the women. Men tended to miss their girlfriends, sneaking out and risking the wrong people learning their whereabouts, desperate for a quick lay. Some missed their mothers, and it was these natural situations that caused the protective team the most headaches. Women tended to be less hassle, particularly if their spouse and children were in the programme with them, but, again, the men still loved to be with their mothers. When things did fall apart and a protected person had to be moved, it generally happened in a bit of a rush. That meant midnight flits to yet another nondescript house in yet another town some distance from the last one. Setting up again in a small and often undesirable town at the opposite end of the country to their previous life, along with another set of IDs, was a nuisance for all concerned, and it was expensive. The notion you'd be given a flash house, car and a job were not the reality. The pull of their old life could be strong at times and it was hard not to give in and call it a day. But to what end? Tabitha had, up until this point, been a model protected individual, but he'd noticed her rest-lessness of recent. He should have seen something like her running off looming in the distance, but he'd missed the signs.

At least with the phone tracker Dominic could monitor Tabitha's movements from a distance. He thought back to the messages he'd left her – perhaps he'd gone overboard with the threat of 'collecting' her, maybe in hindsight he'd actually scared her into staying away even longer, left her in no rush to get back to the confines of the house. He knew he'd go stir-crazy himself if he had to go through it but such was life – you couldn't control everything that happened.

He watched the screen intently. The dot had been stationary for a while so she was most likely having a bite to eat.

"Time for a visit I think, Tabitha. Don't go wandering off too far while I get myself there."

He had to at least try and persuade her back, she'd been gone too long and if it came out she wasn't where she was supposed to be, he'd be in the shit. And that would mean deviating from his own plans and he wasn't going to let her ruin those. Dominic checked flights, chose one that he could get to in time then closed his laptop and slipped it into his bag before heading out. If he was going to Paris, he needed a change of clothes and his passport. So a quick pitstop home and then on to the airport. Her being in the city centre somewhere was handy as it was quick and easy enough to get to. Persuading her to go back with him? That would be the hard part. He'd figure something out along the way. There was no way he was going to let her screw things up, not at this late stage.

"I'll be on my phone if you need me," he said casually over his shoulder to no one in particular as he left the room. He didn't need to check in with anyone, not yet, but he'd casually mentioned his departure in passing for anyone paying attention. He doubted they had been: their heads down, concentration in their shoulders, eyes focused on the screen in front of them. He had a job to do – get Tabitha Child back home where she belonged.

And without any hassle.

CHAPTER 33

Tabitha Child wasn't the only woman being tracked. As soon as Detective Alan Davies plugged in Susan's iPhone to charge, her whereabouts, or rather the phone's whereabouts, pinged up on Marcus's screen as a notification where he was sitting in the departure lounge at Heathrow. He too was about to board a plane, heading back to Hong Kong while the police and the two oddball women, as he'd termed them, searched for his missing wife. He doubted either party would return having had any real success, though the massive detective with the messy hair had notified him they'd picked her handbag up from the hangar. Wherever she was, she hadn't kept her identity with her. If Susan was still alive, and it was a big 'if', she obviously didn't want him to know the fact, or indeed where she was hiding out or why.

Their marriage had been over for some time, though he had never got around to telling her. It would at least save on a rather expensive divorce, and the embarrassment and time wasted on such. This way, with his wife simply disappeared, possibly dead, he could save face. He didn't need her. Or the insurance money. He could now focus back on the job in hand before he lost the deal all together. Buying ailing companies and selling off the valuable parts didn't earn him many close connections, but Marcus coped by enjoying his own and rather special kind of outlet. His mouth smirked, curling slightly at the memory of the lithe young woman that had slithered from his bed only a few days ago. Perhaps he'd call her back for a repeat performance, she could massage his soul from the inside.

Or he, hers.

It was only a twelve-hour flight back to a life spicier than the stone-cold presence he shared with Susan in Surrey. If she did return, and he doubted she would, maybe he'd buy himself a bolt-hole of his own, somewhere more pleasing for when he was in the UK. Or he could stay away more often. Either was preferable to the current situation. But since he doubted her return, indeed hoped for her continued absence, he could do what he liked from this point on. He'd never particularly liked their home together, but she'd seemed to like its vastness, to begin with anyway. Something to show off to her friends. But when they'd lost interest, so had she. The obvious thing to do was sell up.

The phone he'd been staring at in the business lounge vibrated – his plane was boarding. He dismissed the notification and flicked back to the tracker screen where the live dot pulsed its location at a local police station somewhere in Kent. For all his bravado, Marcus Smith found himself once again pondering the disappearance of his wife. He'd loved her once. She'd been loyal all along; he should know, he'd been watching her for long enough. But that was what men did, wasn't it? Looked out for their spouses? Watched over her? A sign he cared? And when she'd had the nerve to disobey him, he'd shown her quite how to respect him and he'd never had to remind her again. Certainly, she'd needed a verbal reminder, but that was all it took. Like with a petulant child, it was important to nip bad attitude in the bud before it festered into something else.

Marcus gathered his briefcase and overnight trolley bag and sauntered to the lounge exit, taking his time. The departure gate was a little way off, but Marcus Smith was in no rush. The plane wouldn't leave without him.

CHAPTER 34

Chrissy hung the call up and settled back in her office chair. It wasn't the news she was hoping for. Valance Douglas, the tech wizard she'd contacted, couldn't help her with what she needed, not legally anyway. And she wasn't about to break the law, or rather he wasn't prepared to break the law for something like a missing adult woman that had most likely simply deserted her husband. A missing child presumed abducted? He'd have been in immediately, but he'd drawn the line on his involvement with Susan's case. Now, without confirmation of whether Susan's passport had been used to gain entry into France and possibly beyond, Chrissy was still in the batting box, waiting to swing at a ball that wasn't going to come anytime soon.

She slammed her fist on her desk. "Damn it!" she shouted, making Julie jump. Julie had driven over and had been sat nibbling on half a biscuit while Chrissy made a couple of calls. Now Chrissy was unsure how she could possibly find out the passport status without a contact and without bribing an official.

"So, what else did they teach you at PI school?"

Chrissy sat thoughtful for a moment, her fingers rubbing both temples simultaneously in an attempt to stimulate a thought.

Preferably one they could use. "With no digital footprint, no other friends to contact, and no leads whatsoever to follow, we're somewhat limited. And she clearly wants to stay hidden or else she'd have called someone by now." She continued to mull things over before adding, "There is a simple explanation to all this, you know, though I've no clue as to what that is. But what if we can't look via passport control. There must be another way."

"What other way?" Julie had finished her nibbling and was playing with the few remaining crumbs of biscuit on the small plate, her long pale-pink fingernail moving around in slow circles as her finger teased the tiny edible rubble underneath it.

"I'm wondering if her luggage and handbag have been located. If her bag still has her wallet and passport in it, at least we'll know she's still in the UK. Or she's stowed away somehow, most likely on a boat rather than a plane. People do it all the time coming into the UK, surely one woman can do it going the other way?"

"We haven't considered the ferry, have we?" Julie said slowly. "It might be easier to board. I'm thinking about *Home Alone 2*, you know, when a large group went through ticketing in a hurry, and Kevin McCallister got left behind and ended up getting on the wrong flight."

"That was a movie, Julie. It wouldn't really happen." Chrissy was tempted to roll her eyes but it gave her a thought. "But, you know, maybe that's not such a crazy idea," she said, sitting bolt upright and running a scenario through in her head. "If you were intent on getting through, you'd find a way, wouldn't you, and that might be to tag along with a large group."

"Or perhaps you could use the passport of someone that was a similar build and look to you?"

"Possibly, yes. But not on a plane. Too hard. And the trains weren't running so that leaves a car ferry or a foot passenger on a ferry. It has to be one of the two and I'm going for foot passenger. Or she's still in the UK."

Julie shook her head, no. "She was going away anyway and now she's run off. So something's bothering her. If that's the case, she wouldn't stay here, she'd keep going south. That's what I'd do too. Maybe she *has* gone to Greece."

"Have you been on a ferry recently?"

Julie wrinkled her perfectly powdered nose up in disgust.

Chrissy received the answer loud and clear. "No, I guess you're more of a plane kind of girl. So, I'm saying, unless she had another passport of some kind – and we have no way of knowing, but assuming she hasn't – she couldn't get on a flight, but there's a slim possibility she got on a boat or ferry. Shall we test it out?"

"You mean, get on a ferry and cross the Channel?" By the look of horror on Julie's face, you'd think she'd been asked to swim in a muddy bog.

"You wanted to tag along, sis. If Susan hadn't planned to leave and has for some reason chosen to on a whim, she has few options to choose from, so let's get creative and try and think how it could have worked for her. We have nothing else to work with, nothing. Now, I'm going to grab a bag of clothes, and if you're dead set on coming, you'd better do the same."

Julie looked a little unsure. Could she leave Richard on his own for a day or two? The shop could manage, no problem there. She oversaw things rather than being scheduled on the staff rota anyway and everything was running smoothly in that respect. Could she be tempted?

"What's it to be, coming or not?" Chrissy stood with hands on her hips while she waited for Julie's response. Instinctively she knew the answer, but she wanted to hear her sister say it. Would she be game? Slumming it on a stinky diesel ferry could be an amusement in itself. When Julie stood, she knew she had her. "And one other thing before we get going," said Chrissy. "We play by my rules, okay? No nipping off shopping or getting a chipped nail fixed. Neither of us know where this little jaunt will take us and the more I think about it, the more I'm inclined to take a couple of days' worth of clothes. I suggest you do the same – but travel lightly. You'll have to carry or lug around what you pack so bear that in mind. You won't need your stilettos, but you will need your comfy walking shoes." Chrissy watched Julie's face drop. "What is it?"

"I don't possess any walking shoes."

"Really? And you a shoe-shop owner?"

"Yes, really." There was a moment's silence between the two women. "But I can get some quick enough," she said, her face brightening.

"Great. Now, why don't you nip home, pack, and drive back over. I'll pack while you're gone and organise things here for the boys. I'm sure you've got stuff of your own to sort out. Oh, and don't forget your passport."

"Yes, ma'am. Anything else?" Julie said in mock salute.

"I don't think so. I'll look up the ferry timetable while you're gone." Chrissy checked her watch. "By the time you're back, it will be lunchtime, so we'll leave straight away. It's got to be quicker by car so we'll press on without the train. You just concentrate on yourself, and get back here as soon as you can, all right?" Chrissy was watching Julie intently, looking for signs of nerves or excitement, neither of which showed.

Then, "Right, I'll get off and get back."

The two women headed back downstairs in silence, each thinking about the journey ahead, their search to find a missing woman, one who it appeared didn't want to be found.

Once Julie had waved goodbye from her Mercedes, Chrissy stood for a moment to enjoy the morning air. The temperature had risen a handful of degrees since her sister's arrival and the sun warmed her bare arms.

"The continent should be nice at this time of the year," she said to herself, closing the front door behind her and heading back upstairs to pack. "So, Susan Smith, where did you head to if you did go by ferry?"

It was a question she didn't have the answer to – yet.

CHAPTER 35

Chrissy was standing on the doorstep and looking on in amusement at the size of the bag Julie was pulling from the boot of her car. Her earlier instruction on travelling light had gone in one ear and out the other.

Julie glanced at Chrissy's bag and pointed, "Is that it? How can you pack so little?"

"I could ask you the opposite," Chrissy quipped as she gathered her own up. "Let's get going, because we have a couple of stops to make on the way. And some calls. So you can be PA while I drive, okay?"

"PA? I can do that," she said, brightening. Julie watched as Chrissy easily lifted the bigger bag into her own car and tossed her own much smaller bag on top, closing the lid with a satisfying clunk.

They were both ready to go. Chrissy asked, "What did Richard say? What did you tell him?"

"I left him a message; he was in a meeting. He'll be fine," said Julie, waving a dismissive hand. Chrissy glanced at her sister. The news wouldn't go down too well with Mr Dour when he found it. Adventure was not a word the man understood.

"Are you sure about that?" she asked as they pulled out of the drive and the gates closed behind them. "What will he do for food?" Chrissy couldn't help the light-hearted dig at the man. There would be no way he could survive on a desert island, though he'd be all right making money if there was internet access. Perhaps he could order a takeaway.

"Already taken care of," Julie said smugly. "Ordered to deliver later today. He'll never know I've gone." She looked as smug as a child with a bar of chocolate, mischief shining in her eyes. "Anyway, you mentioned a stop on the way. What's the plan?"

"Glad you asked," Chrissy said as they picked up speed, heading out towards the M25 and the south. "My thinking is this: when that train crashed with Susan on board, and we can assume she was on board, for some reason she got off it. That journey from Ashford is straight through to France so, unless she jumped from a highspeed train, she got off at the crash site a way south of the town. Agreed?"

"That makes sense, yes."

"So she mustn't have been badly hurt. There are no hospital records for Susan Smith attending for treatment so, unless she's still lying dead in a ditch, she managed to get away unscathed and hide out. Agreed?"

"Yes. I'm hoping so."

"So, if you were her, what would you do to get away unseen?" Chrissy gave Julie a moment to come to the same conclusion she'd reached earlier while packing her clothes.

"You'd keep away from CCTV," Julie said. "So that means off public transport, though it would have been bedlam that day in the town. So, if I had the funds, I'd grab a taxi out of there pronto because car hire would leave a trace..." Chrissy didn't fill the silence but let Julie think. "But taxis have cameras too. I'd flag a lift, which would be better still. But there's no way of finding a member of the public that might have been her good Samaritan, is there?"

"My thoughts exactly! Not without a nationwide hunt, no."

Julie beamed at Chrissy, pleased she'd had the same thought as her sister. "So we're headed to the taxi rank in Ashford? And you've got a photo of Susan to ask around with?"

"Private investigator 101. There can only be one place she got off and keeping a low profile means one witness. The taxi driver, I'm hoping. We need to find out where they dropped her."

"It sounds simple enough. But what if it was a member of the public, not a taxi?"

"We have to try the taxis first, then cross the next bridge when we come to it."

"Okay. So, what can I do while you drive?"

"You can find the detectives that went to see Marcus then confirm where Susan's bag and luggage are being stored. My guess is she hasn't got them with her because they'd have been flung all over. And a bag would slow her journey down. And we know she hasn't used her credit cards or phone. And, while you're at it, ask him to see if her passport has pinged anywhere yet."

Julie thought for a moment about where to start, who to call first. Marcus would know the detective's name but she didn't fancy calling him. She decided to start with the casualty bureau that had been set up. She hoped the call centre operators would be less likely to follow police procedure when it came to giving info out. Hopefully the telephones would be staffed by civilians and not officers. She dialled and prepared her best tearful voice.

The trembling she mustered was an Oscar-winning performance and Chrissy drove open-mouthed as she listened to the sob story that Julie relayed about her missing 'sister'. By the time she'd finished and hung up, she had the name of the detective working the misper case and the location of where all belongings had been sent after the accident, though she wouldn't be able to retrieve them herself. Julie turned triumphantly to her real sister, Chrissy.

"You can close your mouth now, you're not a goldfish in a bowl. I told you I'd be of use."

Chrissy had to concede the point and, steering with one hand, pulled on her drink-bottle nozzle with her teeth before taking a long pull – more for something to do with her mouth than a need to quench her thirst. Perhaps Julie had other hidden talents she could make use of during the investigation.

CHAPTER 36

After a slow journey around the notorious M25 then the M20, Ashford loomed in the distance nearly two hours after leaving Chrissy's place. By the time they'd parked up in the town centre, Julie's bladder was almost bursting.

"There'll be a loo in McDonald's," Chrissy said helpfully, but judging by the look on Julie's face, it wasn't a place she frequented. Not now and not ever. "Suit yourself," Chrissy added with a shrug. It wasn't her bladder.

"I'll head to M&S. Then we can perhaps get a cup of tea and a sandwich?" Julie was already craning her neck to figure out which way the shop would be. Though she had no clue, she set off anyway, heading in the direction that most people appeared to be walking in. Chrissy locked the car and fell into step with Julie, who teetered in wedge heels and a rather restricting skirt hem. Neither were a match for Chrissy's shorts and sandals, but she hung back to walk alongside her sister. Trying to be helpful, she searched for the store on her phone to check directions.

"Well, the bad news is M&S closed down a month or so ago."

Julie groaned to a standstill. "But the good news is there's a public toilet not far," said Chrissy helpfully, reading the PeePlace

web page, and steering a now near desperate Julie around the corner
in the right direction. "I'll wait here, it's on your left." Chrissy
watched her scurry off as fast as her hemline would let her and took
the opportunity to find out where the taxi ranks were located from
her phone. If Susan had indeed jumped in one from the crash site,
there were five to choose from. The one directly outside of the
station probably wasn't going to be it since the accident happened
downline several miles. With no trains entering the station, there
would be little point in a taxi driver sitting there waiting. She
picked the most likely based on position alone and figured out the
best way to get to it. It wasn't far but, for Julie, it could be a
mission. A moment later, the blonde hair of Julie could be seen
approaching slowly.

"You can't hobble around like that for the rest of the day.
What's in your bag that's more appropriate?"

"More of the same, I'm afraid," she said, somewhat
embarrassed.

"Then I'm taking over," Chrissy said matter-of-factly. She
spotted Debenhams – there'd be something more suitable in there –
and the two headed over. Thirty minutes later, Julie was wearing
shorts and flat sandals similar to Chrissy, though with her lacquered
hair she didn't look quite as casual. Still, she'd be able to walk a hell
of a lot easier. Julie had refused a T-shirt and opted for a pretty,
floral, short-sleeved shirt instead. Heads would still turn. Chrissy
grabbed the same shirt in a different colour for a spare and paid.

"Let's drop your clothes back at the car, then we'll tackle the
taxi ranks. Here's a picture of Susan," she said, passing her a copy. "I
suggest we take a rank each and see what we can find out. Let's
hope the drivers today were working at the time of the crash." It
was a long shot, but what else did they have to work with? In most
missing-person cases, those searching for them knew little to
nothing of their movements but had to start somewhere. For them,
that somewhere was the town nearby the scene of the accident.
With a little more speed, Chrissy and Julie each headed off to separate ranks, each hopeful of finding the driver that could have taken

Susan on somewhere. They had two ranks each and agreed to check in when they'd done both. That left one more to approach for whoever finished first or they'd go together.

It was an easy story to recite because it was true. A friend of theirs had been missing since the crash, had they seen her that day? She could be wounded and needing help, overlooked and frightened. Maybe they'd taken her, disorientated, to a clinic or chemist, perhaps? Which of their driver mates were on that day, could they ask them? There was no need to sugar-coat the story or extend the truth. They were looking for their friend and since the police's resources were stretched, they were looking for the woman themselves.

"Are you the police?" asked a driver with a strong accent that could have come from somewhere in Africa. The man's skin was the colour of liquorice, his teeth bright like Polo mints.

"No, I'm not, no need to worry. I'm only interested in finding my friend from that day. Were you working?" Chrissy asked, as she pressed the photo back under the man's nose. "She's got shaggy blonde hair, nice-looking, do you recognise her?"

"Sorry, lady. I was here, but I didn't pick her up. She sure is pretty though. Good luck in finding her." It was a story she was getting used to hearing and when she'd finished with the handful of drivers waiting at the rank, she asked the last man about their control centre. He was halfway through what looked like a steak pie, a blob of gravy on his ample chin. Chrissy motioned with her finger on her own chin and he wiped it off with his handkerchief.

"Thanks."

"Would your controller have a record of who was working around that time? There's got to be a way of finding the driver."

"I expect they do. I'll radio in, hang on." Chrissy waited patiently as he placed his pie in his lap and relayed the information back to base. And when they asked, no, she wasn't the police. The radio was loud and clear and Chrissy heard every word so she wasn't surprised when the answer came back that they weren't giving her that info. The dark man shrugged an 'I tried' look and Chrissy thanked him for his time. "If you hear anything, call me," she said, scribbling her mobile number on the back of a taxi business card she'd grabbed from the man's top shirt pocket. "I'm extremely worried about her. She could be hurt," she added and handed it him. It was all she could do before leaving and heading off to the next rank. She wished she'd brought more of her own cards to hand out, but she had already used the ones in her bag.

She hoped Julie was faring better than she was. She didn't need to wait long before she found out.

CHAPTER 37

By the time Chrissy had joined back up with Julie at the rank she was investigating, she was almost out of breath from jogging over. She could see her sister in the distance, chatting to a man, seemingly deep in a serious conversation. Chrissy approached the driver's door, which was open. The man's long legs stretched out in front of him, resting on the tarmac, casually crossed at the ankle as the two chatted. Julie spotted her and excitedly introduced the man.

"This is Joe, and he thinks he had Susan in his car that day," she said, beaming as if she'd won the prize, which maybe she had. "She's definitely still alive, Chrissy!"

Joe turned to Chrissy and locked her with his intensely dark eyes, though they were tuned in friendly. Like a chocolate Labrador's only darker.

"Can you tell me what you know, please?"

"I will, missy. Like I just told your sister, it was about lunchtime and I was working up at the hospital. We rotate, you know? Anyway, I took your friend to the bank, the HSBC on the high street, then on to the ferry at Dover later that afternoon. She paid me by credit card and looked really tired. Said she'd had a nosebleed, and I told her of my daughter and her nose bleeds, though my daughter didn't get a black eye at the same time like your friend had. A real shiner that'll be. I dropped her off at the ferry terminal and came back home. That's about it." He beamed at them both, glad to help.

"Did she talk about much while you were driving? Perhaps say where she was going?" Chrissy needed more.

"She slept a lot of it, but she was trying to get to France because we debated driving across to Gatwick. She settled on the ferry and Dover. And she got locked out of her iPhone so I showed her a trick to get back in for some basic tasks, until she could get it unlocked properly." His eyes smiled as he recited how he'd helped the missing woman. "But when we arrived at the terminal, she paid and left so there's nothing else to tell. I wish I could help you more. I know what it's like when someone you love goes missing." Joe's chin dropped and a silence encased the three of them. Neither woman wanted to intrude on his thoughts so Chrissy thanked him for his time and wished him a good day. The two women slowly pulled away, heading back towards the shopping area. When they were out of earshot, Chrissy broke the silence, "So she's definitely alive! That is good news. At least it's confirmed. But we now also know she headed to France somehow. And she has a credit card and phone."

"But he picked her up from the hospital, a hospital that has no record of Susan Smith needing medical attention."

"For that I have no explanation," Chrissy said. "Other than she left before they got to her? A & E would have been in uproar."

"Maybe."

"Are you thinking this was a planned run then? Because how else would she have a credit card that Marcus doesn't know about? You saw for yourself there had been no activity on the account. Same goes for the phone. A burner phone, perhaps?"

"Burner phones don't normally come in the shape of an iPhone, too expensive. And how did she manage to get locked out of it? It's not hard to remember your passcode is it? An extra credit card on a different account I can understand, though I wonder now if it's under another name, her maiden name, perhaps. Same for a passport?"

"Hmm. I hear you. What next, boss?" asked Julie.

"Let's go to the bank, though I doubt they'll give us anything. We might get a reaction if we flash that picture, even though we already know she went in there. I wonder why she didn't use the ATM instead?"

Julie shrugged. They knew so little and it was frustrating.

"Not helpful, sis," Chrissy said in warning tone. "We need to find her other phone number somehow. GPS will tell us where she is if she still has it with her. But how can we do that?"

"Can't we tell the police what we know already? Maybe they have powers?"

"They might have powers, but they can't conjure up her location without knowing the phone number at least." They were now walking down the high street, approaching the bank. "Did that detective that found her bag definitely have her passport?"

"He said so, and purse and phone. So she must have duplicates, but what are the chances of that accident happening on a day when she had her alternative ID at hand? You don't think she caused the accident somehow, do you?"

Chrissy pulled up short. Always the drama queen, Julie had let her thoughts go off the rails with that one. "And how in hell's name could she do that?"

"Just putting it out there," Julie added petulantly.

"A long way off base, sis. Even James Bond would have struggled to achieve such an accident single-handedly." Chrissy held the bank's door open and they both slipped inside and joined the short queue. Chrissy still had the photo in her hand. "We get one shot each so watch for any reaction, any at all when you show it, okay?"

Chrissy went first, introduced herself as Chrissy Livingstone, PI, but it was obvious the young male teller didn't recognise the woman in the photo. He also confirmed he wouldn't be able to help anyway, privacy and all. A dead end.

And the same went for Julie, the teller she spoke to merely shook her head. Even if they could, there was little point trying to get CCTV footage because it would only show what they already knew – Susan Smith had been in the bank. And then left.

It had been a long shot, but it needed trying. If someone had seen Susan that day, Julie or Chrissy could have asked what she'd been in for, what she'd wanted and that might have given them another lead to follow. As it turned out, privacy won over and they were no further forward.

When they were both back out on the pavement, Chrissy said, "Let's grab a drink and figure out our next move. And I'll ring that Detective Davies myself and fill him in. He might have an idea now we know a bit more."

Feeling a little flat, Julie had to agree. Maybe if they pooled what little knowledge they had, they'd have a location to head to, because right now the two sisters couldn't cover the whole of Europe on foot – not on their own.

Susan Smith was officially alive and on the run. But where to?

CHAPTER 38

The police tech team were constantly overwhelmed by their work-load. Cybercrime was a rapidly growing business for scumbags of all types and their crimes spanned a vast array of topics: from child-pornography rings to malware on little old ladies' computers and everything else in between. Their work was important, sometimes desperately so, and a never-ending stream of high-priority cases kept them busy. So faced with a simple task like a cracking open a missing person's phone, it was easiest all round if the detective on the case did it themselves – provided they had the skills – and then figured out afterwards how any evidence could be used in a court case if need be.

Detective Alan Davies didn't possess those skills, but he knew a woman that did. Bridget was the team's go-to girl when they needed something tech-related doing on the side. A petit blonde that fancied herself as a bit of a Lara Croft, geeking out was her passion. When she wasn't a detective by day, Alan knew she felt quite comfortable roaming the streets after dark and her role didn't dictate her waking hours. Bridget Knox had a personality that it was risky trying to get to know in any depth; the aura she emitted sent a message that was impossible to misread: keep out.

Like an old mineshaft.

And he knew he wasn't on his own with those thoughts. So it was with some trepidation that he approached the cluttered desk of his colleague. He tried not to pay attention to the disarray in which the woman worked, but she was surrounded by day-old coffee mugs and empty nut packets. She sensed him before he had chance to open his mouth in greeting.

"What do you need?" Her face stayed firmly glued to her screen as she spoke. "Speak to me. What is it you need this time?" There was no malice, simply concentration. Still, Alan almost flinched at her direct manner.

"I could do with this phone unlocking, please. It's charged now, but locked. Can you get inside it for me?"

"Of course I can," she said, taking the iPhone from him. "What are you looking for when I get in?"

"Anything that might tell me why its owner, Susan Smith, is now a misper. She was on that train that crashed and appears to have done a runner."

"Oh, how exciting."

There was no hiding her thoughts, but Alan gave her a questioning glance. "I'm sure her husband and family don't think so."

"I mean, running off after the accident. Taking the chance to flee. You don't naturally run off for no reason when the opportunity presents itself. Not normally. Any clue as to why?"

"That's what I'm hoping to find out from her phone, why and where she's gone."

"Right. I'll take a look, see what I can find. Though if she's done a runner and left this behind, I doubt we'll find much. She'll have another phone by now, probably had a second all along."

"Let's see before you cast your aspersions. Maybe she left a breadcrumb or two."

Bridget raised her blonde eyebrows at his terminology as he turned and left her desk. Alan's version of breadcrumbs came from his cheese-and-onion sandwich and not from a digital trail, she mused. Still, he made her smile. Not many men did. Bridget watched him head towards the back of the room and, not for the first time, wondered what he'd be like in bed. Two distinctly different-sized bodies could be a challenge, but her imagination would figure it out. She'd always liked Alan, he fascinated her. Still, there was time. Turning back to the phone in her hand, she plugged it into a cable already set up on her personal laptop and did the necessary. It took a few seconds to gain full access and change the passcode to something easier to remember. She settled back to read emails and texts, and snoop around the various apps and settings that were Susan Smith's life. Apart from work emails, a few texts and voice messages from concerned friends, there was nothing of obvious interest. Susan Smith's life as a consultant appeared relatively stress free.

Until she noticed the tracking app. It had been installed to be hidden from the user and Bridget worked quickly to trace it back to its installer: one Marcus Smith. Making a note to tell Alan, she took her talented snooping skills up another level. If a man was tracking his wife in secret, he had a reason. Either Susan was having an affair and her husband suspected so, or he spied on her for pleasure. It wasn't hard to find him and dig a little more.

"Now, what are you up to in your own private time, Mr Smith?" she chided as she tapped her keyboard rapidly. What floated up on the screen she was glued to would be gibberish to any onlooker. If any of her colleagues looked over her shoulder, there would be no way in hell that they could decipher what scrolled past. Unless they had Bridget's skills. Which they didn't. When she was satisfied with where she was at, she rested back in her chair to read. Alan Davies wasn't the only person to have breadcrumb issues. There, laid out in front of her, were Marcus Smith's activities in all their digitally traced glory.

"Told you, you were the one with issues, Mr Smith. You like to spy because you like to manipulate. You're a bully. A good-looking one but a bully all the same." Bridget's fingers danced across her keyboard and her fine mouth creased into a curve at the edges as she set about copying the information she needed. Bullies only spoke one language and that was control. If he'd been eavesdropping and tracking his wife, who clearly had been going about her own business, a good proportion of it sat at home from the geo data she could see, Bridget wanted to know what the man himself was up to. Maybe he'd had a hand in the woman's disappearance? Was that why he was back in Hong Kong while the police searched for Mrs Smith? Whatever he was or had been up to, Bridget Knox wanted to find out more.

"Let's see how you like being spied on," she said with satisfaction. With one last keystroke, the life and times of Marcus Smith was filtering live on to a separate screen. Satisfied, she made her way to Alan and gave him the news of the tracking-app find.

CHAPTER 39

Alan Davies was still reeling from Bridget's news: Susan's husband was monitoring her movements and eavesdropping on her communications. Why? He was pondering the question over coffee and a Crunchie bar when his mobile rang. He didn't recognise the number, another mobile, but accepted the call anyway. Dealing with so many various individuals each day, he couldn't store them all in his phone and have prior knowledge of who they all were.

"DS Alan Davies," he said, licking chocolate off his forefinger then wiping it on his trouser leg. It was still sticky.

"Hello." A female voice soothed his ears. It was almost like a cat's purr. "This is Julie Stokes. We spoke earlier today about Susan Smith. I'm her friend?"

"Yes, how could I forget," he said, smiling. Her voice was like gentle harp music to his stressed shoulders and he closed his eyes while he listened. He was also conscious he was enjoying the sound. "What can I help you with?"

"I've been doing my own investigation," she cooed. "And I thought we could pool our knowledge, see if three heads would be better than one. We're all after the same result, are we not?"

"Three heads?"

"Oh sorry, yes. My sister, Chrissy Livingstone, is a PI. I'm her PA."

Alan rolled his eyes at the mention of a private investigator. They often got in the way of police business. And they did things a little more out of the box than the rule sticklers. He'd not come across Chrissy Livingstone professionally. He skipped forward. "So, what information do you have?"

"I was hoping to get a question answered from you before that, if I may."

"And what's your question?"

"Well, it's about her passport. It's still in her bag along with her purse and phone, I believe. Is there a way for you to see how she might have used a passport to gain entry to France? Maybe in her maiden name?"

"So you think she's gone to France."

Julie groaned at her mistake. She'd given the game away. She took a deep breath and sighed heavily. Alan carried on, "I'm not a detective for nothing. Why don't you tell me what you know, then I can see how best to help?"

And so Julie did. About Joe the taxi driver, the hospital pickup, Susan's phone, the ferry, and of course her trip to the bank. He added the information to his own newly acquired intel, courtesy of Bridget. Perhaps Susan Smith was a person at risk and warranted further resources after all. If her husband was, or had been, controlling her in some way, that was most likely the reason she'd fled. Or she simply wanted to run away – more adults than children did.

"What ferry do you believe she crossed on?"

"It would have been mid-afternoon when the taxi dropped her, around 4 pm, so I'd check a couple in case she missed the first one."

Alan smiled at Julie's idea and was tempted to add "No shit," but restrained himself, allowing the thought to drift off. "I'll see what I can do. Anything else?"

"Chrissy and I are heading to the ferry now and will make some enquiries at Dover. Will you let us know what you find out, please?"

Even though DS Alan Davies was under no pressure to inform someone outside the official enquiry of anything, he found himself nodding to the phone. "Let's see what comes up, eh?" Non-committal for now. But the woman's voice was mesmerising in his head. "But before you go," he wanted to add a caution. "It's great she really is alive and well enough to travel, but have you thought that she might not want to be found? From a police point of view, now we know she is alive and on the move, strictly speaking that's the end of our enquiry." The other end of the line went quiet. Julie had gone silent.

"Oh, I see. But that doesn't seem fair or right, Susan is on the run from something or someone." It was time to tell him about Marcus and the tracking app. "Her husband was tracking her every move. Did you know that? He's an odd person, rather controlling, and I fear for her safety. Isn't that enough?"

So the PI team had been doing their own investigation. How could they possibly have found out about the app? Alan chose his words carefully. "I can't promise anything, but let me see what my DI wants to do. If there is a problem with her husband and she is in danger, he may let me carry on. That's all I can say."

"But can you at least find out about the passport? It would help us greatly, even if you can't do anything more."

Alan sighed. She had a point but handing over that kind of intel could land him in the shit. "No promises."

"I'll await your call. You have my number." And then the soft purr of Julie Stokes vanished, much like Susan Smith. Alan sat looking at his phone.

"What the hell happened there? Are you nuts?" he said louder than he meant to.

Bridget glanced across questioningly, her eyes bulging, chin dipped. "What have you done?"

"Hopefully nothing." Changing the subject, he said, "I need to find out what passport was used on an afternoon ferry on the day of the train crash. Dover to Calais, around 4 pm. Can you get a list of passengers for me, please?"

Bridget swivelled her chair back round to face her screen. "I'm on it."

The rest of the afternoon flew by, mainly with paperwork. There were reams of it, everything in triplicate, everyone's arses covered, 'I's dotted, and 'T's crossed. A defence team would have a field day in court if it wasn't so, though the tiresome task was another drag on resources. Then, at five o'clock, Alan ventured over to Bridget's desk for an update. An almost-empty bag of roasted almonds was sat by her mouse and he leaned in to grab a couple. Quick as a fox, she slammed her hand down on his to prevent him swiping any and he called out in surprise.

"Damn it, ask first," she said calmly as she removed her hand from his. "Ask, and you will receive. Take, and you're in trouble." There was something in her clear-blue eyes that told him he'd been warned. It took him a moment to rebalance himself and state what he'd ambled over for in the first place.

"How did the passport list go, have you got anything?"

"Just got it actually. I'll print it off," and he watched as she collected the pages from the nearby printer. There looked to be three or four of them. She handed them over and he glanced down the first page. Nothing immediately stuck out. He scanned the other three pages and was almost at the end of the total list when he gasped out loud.

"Something interesting you?"

"I'd say so." He stared at the name, Tabitha Child. How could a dead woman be travelling to France on a ferry?

CHAPTER 40

Tabby had half-heartedly explored Paris for a couple of days before finally deciding it wasn't the place she wanted to be. It was expensive, far too busy and, at the same time, desperately lonely. She felt isolated, disorientated, and her chest was constricted with an anxiety level she'd not experienced before. The trip to Paris she'd originally planned would have been the polar opposite to the one she was experiencing right now. It was to have been harmless fun, to fulfil a role she'd contemplated many times but never played. Then, when the opportunity to truly become someone else presented itself, she'd snatched it. And then things had spiralled out of control and she was left wondering what to do next.

So, where *did* she want to be? While the answer wasn't yet obvious to her, Paris most certainly no longer felt right, if it ever had. Too many people bustled and jostled; backpack-laden tourists headed for famous landmarks, locals zipped and zoomed, busy, intent on their own business. Everyone around her appeared to know their plan for the rest of the day: where they were driving to, where they were sleeping, where they might be in the evening. But Susan knew none of those things and it bothered her. She still had some cash, she'd been frugal, but the ferry, backpackers and food so far had meant a chunk had already gone and there was no way of getting any more. But what could Paris offer her now? Busy meant a summer job wouldn't be too hard. Busy meant a youth hostel or similar on a budget. And busy meant she could disappear easily. Yet she felt Paris wasn't it. She checked the phone for the time. Maybe it was time to let go of it. It wasn't like she could use it much, only listen to messages and read texts to keep up the pretence of being Tabitha Child. But to what end? Who knew Tabitha was 'missing'? And no one would suspect Susan Smith had a dead woman's phone, why would they? But the GPS aspect had been gnawing at her of recent: what if someone had put two and two together? It was coming up to 3 pm.

There was, however, a tiny feeling of comfort that she was still somehow connected to her old life, though it was absurd. It was like finding comfort in someone else's soft blanket. Marcus would be worried no doubt and she contemplated that for a moment, a smile creeping across her mouth. She'd loved him once. They'd ambled on doing their own thing, trying to carry on the farce and be the model affluent couple. If he could see her now, sat on a bench in Paris, dressed as a scruffy hitchhiker, he'd have something to say and it wouldn't be pretty. The smile vanished at the notion. Dull years had taken their toll on their relationship and their feelings for each other. Her own contract work had not been met with his approval and had been the subject of so many rows, but he'd conceded to her keeping it part-time. While he didn't know much of what she did, it had allowed her to bring in her own contribution to the household. He just never saw any of it. Had the day to go it alone always been on her own agenda? Is that why she'd built up a reserve? Tabby was tempted to draw on some of that money and check into a hotel. A hot shower and a decent meal were a strong pull, but she also knew that Marcus spied on her. Did he also know about her other accounts? She wasn't going to give him the satisfaction of tracing her. She'd manage as she had been up to know.

Abruptly she stood up, the decision of what to do next as clear as spring water running down the French Alps. Move on south. To

Albi. It sounded like a wonderful place to get lost in with its medieval buildings and cobbled streets, and a tourist trade to help her find work. While her French wasn't up to much, she'd force herself to become fluent as quickly as possible. Being immersed in it daily would be the best way of learning. A job waitressing wouldn't be hard to find, she felt sure. But she needed to get there first. She set off walking towards the main road where Albert had dropped her off a couple of days ago, all her worldly belongings in her backpack. All she knew was it was about seven hours south, depending on the route she found herself taking. It wasn't the hitchhiker that made that decision but the driver of the vehicle you happened to be travelling in. And a zig-zag journey was to be expected. But Albi sounded like the place she'd feel a little more at home in. Not the bright lights of a bustling capital city. Not any more anyway. Once upon a time in her life, it would have been; a handful of days ago, it would have been; but that was all behind her now. Going forward, Tabby Child, as she was now known, would be looking for work and a place to call home for the foreseeable future. When she reached the busy road, she stuck her thumb out and hoped for a safe travelling companion. A moment later, a woman's voice caught her attention as it called out close by behind her.

"Where you headed?" It was English accent and she turned to see who was enquiring. "Thought you might be English," the woman said. Tabby gave her a look that said 'how?' to which the woman, somewhere in her early thirties, caught on. "Your pale skin. Only us Brits have skin that colour," she said, laughing, and her eyes appeared to dance without the cover of sunglasses that rested between her fingers. "So where are you heading?"

"South. To Albi, eventually. Are you going that way?"

"Certainly are. Well, Toulouse actually, but Albi isn't far from there. Get in." The woman pointed with her thumb at the seat behind her own and Tabby opened the door. Putting her head inside first, she quickly took stock before committing her whole being to the back of yet another stranger's car. Along with the woman were two men, both about the same age as her, one of whom was driving. He turned to greet her, and Tabby found herself looking straight into his eyes. They seemed friendly enough.

"Welcome aboard," he encouraged as she shuffled herself and her bag on to the back seat and smiled at the other occupant, sitting alongside her, who held his hand out in greeting.

"I'm Will," he said and nodded to the other two up front. "And that's Kirsty and Jez." She introduced herself as Tabby, which now seemed like the truth, fastened her seatbelt and the car pulled away from the kerbside. Remembering she still had the phone, she pulled it from her bag and let it slip out the open window. It landed on the tarmac behind them. Peering out and behind, she could only just make out the slim, dark shape as it lay where it had landed. Her 'lifeline' had gone, as had any GPS.

"Didn't you want that any more?' Will asked, a bemused smile filling his mouth.

"No, not where I'm going, no."

If she had felt all alone earlier on, she felt totally alone now.

There was no more Dominic either.

CHAPTER 41

He breezed through passport control and headed out towards the exit and the taxi rank.

Dominic hadn't bothered to take much more than a clean shirt and underwear on his trip to Paris. He knew he wouldn't be long. He certainly wasn't intending to stay long. Pick up Tabitha Child and get her the hell home, back to the safety of her secure location. Or to another if need be. What had she even been thinking about going off on a silly jaunt without mentioning it to him? It was a great way of getting herself killed.

Charles de Gaulle Airport was vast but well equipped to deal with the number of visitors that passed through daily. The centre of Paris was only about fifty minutes away by taxi and he joined the queue, which thankfully moved forward quickly. The taxi coordinator at the front allocated rides, doing a wonderful job, arms directing waiting passengers in two directions. Dominic only had to wait three or four minutes before he was able to slip inside his own car and head away from organised mayhem.

"Paris centre, *s'il vous plaît*," he directed and he pulled out his phone. The driver nodded and they moved off in silence. Dominic had plenty of time to give him the exact location closer to their arrival. On his phone, the dot flashed its location, which he noted hadn't moved much at all while he'd been on the flight. She'd only travelled a few streets over from the last position he'd recorded. That was a good thing, he mused, and he hoped she stayed put until he got there himself. He also hoped she was going to accompany him without a making scene, because if she started being stroppy, he wasn't sure how he was going to get her back to the airport and home without attracting the interest of the local police. There was also the small matter of explaining how he'd come to locate her in the first place, because there was only one feasible way he could have known. That alone would generate anger. Nobody liked to feel spied on. But Dominic didn't want the formality of letting the French police know of his plans. If he kept under everybody's radar and managed to get the woman back quickly and quietly that would be ideal.

Dominic laid his head back on the cracked leather headrest and closed his tired eyes for a few minutes. They felt gritty from the plane and the change of dirty air blowing around the airport. These were never the cleanest of places, and certainly not easy on the environment. The faint odour of aviation fuel seemed to have accompanied him into the small space of the taxi. Forty minutes later, he was aware of a voice nearby – he'd fallen asleep. When he finally opened his eyes, he was looking straight at the driver, who had pulled over and was trying to raise an actual address out of him in broken English. Dominic sat up and lifted a finger in instruction to wait a moment and the driver screwed his face up in a frown. Dominic checked the icon on the phone. Tabitha Child had moved. He studied the road, recited the address and, without any further communication, the driver pulled away aggressively, a horn blaring from somewhere behind them. Dominic was jostled in his seat as the driver took his annoyance out on the steering wheel, throwing the vehicle around bends roughly. All the time, Dominic watched the flashing marker as they gained on it and when he was close enough, he instructed the driver to pull over.

"*Arrête, s'il vous plaît.*" Although probably not entirely grammatically correct, it would have to do. At least he'd tried to speak the language. The taxi pulled over and Dominic handed over his credit card. There'd been no time to exchange a few notes to euros and he made a note to find an ATM. He grabbed his small bag and slammed the door shut. The driver was apparently still indignant as he peeled away back in the direction of the airport.

But Dominic had more pressing things to think about than a stroppy driver and he headed off in the direction the tracker was showing him. According to the location, she was only a hundred metres or so in front of him. He took a deep breath in and held it a moment before releasing the air with a whoosh. He only had one crack at this and he had to get it just right. His eyes searched the heads bobbing up and down as their bodies carried them forward, looking for the shaggy blonde he'd come to know so well. At least it wasn't raining, he thought, umbrellas would have made things tricky and spotting her would have been virtually impossible. He picked up speed, pushing through the dense foot traffic of rush hour in Paris. With one eye on the tracker he could see he was close, only a few feet away. But still he couldn't see her head. Had she dyed her hair? he wondered. But as he scanned the women ahead of him, he saw that, unless she was wearing a long-haired wig, nobody fitted the bill.

"Damn," he said quietly to himself with annoyance. "Where the hell are you?" He increased his speed to get further ahead of the crowd and when he looked back at the tracker, he could see it was now behind him. "What the..." He pulled into a doorway and scanned each face heading toward him, but he knew she wasn't one of them. Another glance at the blue blob that flashed at him, and he knew instantly what had happened.

Somebody else had Tabitha Child's phone. And they were stood three feet away.

CHAPTER 42

At ponderous times such as these, Detective Alan Davies found the best thing to do was find something to nibble on. He was a giant after all, and giants needed regular fuelling. The mere motion of his jaws working through a bag of peanuts jostled his grey matter into a productive combustion engine. At least peanuts were a tad healthier than a bag of Maltesers, though the fat content and the size of bag he was currently troughing through wouldn't be kind on the calorie front. Bridget's almond idea had a lot to answer for. Still, he needed the fuel for his brain and it gave his fingertips something to do other than push a mouse around a mat. He was searching the police database for Tabitha Child again. An unidentified body lay in a fridge back at the mortuary and the only name left on the pathologists' list was hers. And now her name had shown up on a passenger list for an afternoon ferry to Calais on the day of the train crash. And since nobody had reported the woman missing, which was odd in itself, Alan was beginning to wonder if something much more complicated was going on. He had the woman's passport picture on the screen in front of him and he'd emailed a copy across to the pathologist. If the woman staring back at him was the woman with the tattoo, then how on earth had she also made it through passport control? He dialled his colleague Carl, the man that had so graciously let him clear up the sweet-and-sour leftovers on Friday night. And the one who'd recognised the drawn-over tattoo.

"What can I do you for?" he answered brightly. Alan could hear waves in the background.

"Are you at the beach?" he enquired, jealousy sounding in his own ears. An ice cream and a walk along a promenade would be nice right about now.

"I am indeed. Come on over and join us. I believe the water is cold as all hell," he said, laughing. "You're only an hour or so away, you can be here for fish and chips later."

"I'll pass, thanks. But listen, I've had a bit of luck on a case I'm working on and it might be linked to another. Did you manage to find out anything on that tattoo I showed you?" A seagull squawked overhead, filling the otherwise empty phoneline from Carl.

"I was about to call you. Are you ready for this, my friend?"

"What have you found out?"

"Well, here's the problem: the file is locked and that means one thing under the circumstances." Alan knew what that meant. It also explained why the pathologists had no prints or DNA to work with.

"Protected witness," he said. It added up to what he knew already. It made complete sense. "So that tattoo *has* been covered up. We didn't imagine things."

"It seems not. Look, keep me in the loop, would you? Out of interest?"

"Of course. I thought that was all put to bed a couple of years ago, the ringleaders behind bars?"

"But now a woman with the same tattoo turns up dead."

"From a train crash, remember? Nothing sinister there but I hear you. Thanks for that, Carl. I'll speak to you later."

Alan sat back in his office chair, swivelling it slightly from side to side as he popped another couple of nuts and chewed. The office was almost empty now, colleagues gone home for the night, a couple of night-shift staff making a start. He noticed Bridget was still at her own desk. He moseyed over.

"Can you get into a locked file on the database?" he enquired nonchalantly.

"Only if I want the sack," she said, swivelling round to look him in the eyes. "And no, I don't want the sack, so don't bother asking. There's no way to not leave a trail, even if I could get in." That wasn't what he wanted to hear, but he'd no intention of pressing the issue.

"You'll need someone with a higher pay grade than me." She turned her chair back to her own screen and carried on typing furiously. Discouraged, and obviously dismissed, he went back to his own desk to think about what to do next. He called back over to Bridget.

"Did you, by chance, ask for the CCTV footage from those afternoon ferries?" Her head shook side to side, no. He double-checked his list of names and the ferry time and made the call himself. Security agreed to put the file on a USB for him to collect. Alan checked the clock – full-blown rush hour. The motorway would be like a car park for the next two hours. He wondered about the two women, the PI and her PA, Chrissy and Julie. They said they were heading down to the ferry. Would it be out of place for them to pick an envelope up for him?

"Of course it would, you moron. Plus, they'd be able to feel it was a USB stick easy enough." But it was tempting and would save him a great deal of time. If they were heading back this way anyway... and he did want to confirm who was using Tabitha Child's passport. Because as he glanced back at the woman still staring out at him from his screen, he had an inkling just who that might be.

The missing Susan Smith. But he needed proof.

CHAPTER 43

It made sense to ask the PI duo to pick up an envelope. Surely they wouldn't consider snooping at police evidence? That would buy the pair a whole heap of trouble. They were passing through anyway, it was no different than using a courier service for one lousy tiny package.

"Except this one contains evidence, I hope," Alan mumbled as he found Julie Stokes' telephone number and dialled. Her familiar purr made his pulse spike like an arrhythmic attack, though he did his best to ignore it. Never having met the woman, he wondered what she looked like – perhaps she'd be a blonde.

"Alan," she purred. "How nice to hear from you again. I'm putting you on loudspeaker... How can Chrissy and I help you?"

The spike stabbed him harder in the chest. He cleared his throat before attempting to speak. "And hello to you, Chrissy," he said, out of courtesy. A moment later a different voice filled his ears, one without the soft purr. This one was gritty, and more assertive, like a tradeswoman – Chrissy Livingstone.

"Hello to you, DS Davies. What can we do for you? Do you have news?"

"Nothing else to report, no. But are you, by chance, still passing through the Dover ferry terminal at all?"

"We are, yes. Almost at Dover in actual fact. Why?"

"Could I trouble you to bring a small package back this way? It's at the information desk in the ferry terminal. Only, it would save me a trip and if you're already there... Makes sense. But only if you don't mind, I don't want to put you to any trouble." He winced at the saccharine coating he'd added to his words, as if he were talking to a young child or an elderly lady.

"It sounds exciting. What's the package? Don't tell me it's drugs?"

Julie laughed at her suggestion. Of course it wouldn't be drugs.

"I can tell you for certain it's not drugs, but it is important." He could hear mumbled words in the background as if they were having a private conversation.

"Hold on a moment, please," Julie said, and Alan struggled to hear the conversation between the two women. He caught the words "couple of days" and wondered what they were discussing. Chrissy spoke next.

"What Julie failed to mention is we're planning on going across to France for a day or two so we won't be heading straight back. Is that too long for you to wait?"

There was no way he wanted to wait for the camera evidence. He'd have to find another way. "Okay then, not to worry, I'll get it picked up somehow. It was only on the off chance, since you said you'd be there." It seemed he had a slow evening ahead of him, starting now. "Where are you headed then?" he found himself asking. Perhaps they had a lead on their friend. He wasn't going to get their hopes up with his own suspicions so kept quiet about the contents of the envelope.

"Calais, then not entirely sure. We'll figure it out. Any news your end?"

"Nothing to report, no." He kept it non-committal. "Anyway, I'd best get off so have a good trip," he said and hung up before either party could say another word. He sat for a moment, hands steepled in front of him, chin resting on his fingertips. He felt someone hovering near his shoulder.

"There's always an easier way, you know," Bridget announced. "They could put the file in a cloud folder, and you could download it this end. It'll take a while, but not as long as a trip to the coast and back." Alan turned and watched as the blonde slipped her arms into her bright-red raincoat. The contrast between her pale hair and the vivid colour was startling – he was reminded of Marilyn Monroe. Her idea made sense.

"Bridget," he said loudly, "you're a genius. Why didn't I think of that?" He picked his phone up and hoped the person he'd not long ago spoken to was still there and able to upload it for him.

"Because *I'm* the brains here," she said and gave an exaggerated wink as she turned briskly and headed for the door. "Ciao," she called, red mackintosh flapping as she walked.

Indeed, the file could be uploaded to the cloud and a link sent to him. They'd just dropped the USB at the information desk, but it was no bother. Alan thanked the man heartily and figured he'd grab a burger from next door while he was waiting. It could take some time to sift through and find what he needed so he may as well refuel while he had the chance.

Chrissy was parking up at the ferry terminal. She had a nose like a truffle pig rummaging around an oak tree and knew instantly that whatever it was in that envelope, it was important. And the detective sergeant wasn't sharing, which was beginning to aggravate her. Weren't they both on the same side, weren't they looking for the same woman?

"Stay here, I'll only be a moment," Chrissy instructed as Julie prepared to get out of the car. There was no sense in them both going to the desk. This way she could pretend she was a colleague of the detective without actually saying as much. Impersonating a police officer was not a bright thing to do, not to mention a criminal offence. Chrissy hoped whoever was manning the desk at this time of day would be bored stiff, uninterested and would hand it over without comment.

Once inside the terminal building, she spotted the desk and headed over. A young male in his late twenties was assisting an elderly man and Chrissy waited patiently while he explained what the café on board stocked by way of snacks. Chrissy wondered if the old man was debating whether he should stock up before boarding or not and willed him to decide and move on. With a faint roll of her eyes, Chrissy smiled as she approached the counter and prepared to empathise with the younger man.

"Age comes to us all eventually," she quipped, "though you're a way off yet." It came out flirtier than she'd have liked, judging by the tiny pink blotch that appeared on his cheeks. "There should be an envelope to be picked up. For Detective Sergeant Davies." No lies thus far. She watched as he turned and retrieved it from a tray on the top of his workspace. He double-checked the name on the front before handing it over.

"Here you go."

Chrissy smiled her thanks and headed straight back towards the door without another word. When you'd got what you came for, why risk saying anything else that might arouse suspicion? As soon as the envelope had entered her hands, she knew what it contained. The obvious outline of a USB drive shifted inside, resting with a light thud in one corner, and she ran her finger over it.

"Let's see what's so interesting on this little beauty," she said as she opened her car door and slipped back inside.

"Pass my laptop over, would you, Julie?"

CHAPTER 44

When an unauthorised person attempts to access a police file above their pay grade, an alert is sent to those that might be interested in such activity. Detective Chief Superintendent Morton reached for his phone and immediately called the detective whose login details had registered. Why would he be snooping around and trying to access the file of a protected witness? After introducing himself and asking that same question of the man, he was told it was yet another detective that was interested.

"And what's your colleague's interest, may I ask?"

"You'd have to double-check with him, sir," Carl said as he struggled to keep his two-year-old from clinging on to his lower leg as he walked. Her delirious giggling was distracting him from paying full attention. "Hang on a moment and I'll get his number for you." The only way to stop her laughter temporarily was to stop moving. It gave him the opportunity to find what he was looking for and pass it on.

"Thanks, I appreciate it," Morton said and then he was gone, leaving Carl to the clutches of his young daughter.

It didn't take long for Morton to get Alan Davies on the phone. The detective was waiting patiently for his burger order not far from the station. Not recognising the number that flashed up when his phone rang, he was tempted to let it go to voicemail, particularly as it was nearing the end of his shift, but something told him to accept it.

"DS Alan Davies," he said and waited.

"Detective Chief Superintendent Morton here. DS Carl Bradley passed your number on to me."

"What can I do for you, sir?"

"I'm interested in your interest in a locked file actually. Can I ask what it is?" When a chief super calls and asks why you're interested in something, you tell them. But this simple misper case, which was fast turning into something a whole lot more intricate, had Alan's internal antennae vibrating. He should choose his words with care.

"Simple really, sir. A woman's name popped up after the train crash, but we can't find much about her to confirm an ID. It was a simple file search, nothing more. Is there a problem?"

"You know as well I as do, sergeant, that a simple file search wouldn't ping my attention. Would you care to tell me more?"

"There's nothing more to tell. I'm trying to confirm her ID and find any next of kin."

There was a silence on the other end of the line that Alan felt was calling him a liar. Maybe that was his paranoia talking, but the antennae in his gut was still telling him to be cautious.

"And the name you have to work with is Tabitha Child?"

"Yes, sir." There was empty silence again while Alan waited for the chief super to respond with more. When he didn't, he filled the void with a question of his own. "I'm guessing there's something special with this file? Are you able to tell *me* more?"

"No, I am not. Where is she now?"

"In the temporary mortuary at the airbase still." Alan didn't want to give any more away until he had some answers of his own. "Can I ask why you can't help confirm her ID?"

"Leave this with me."

And he was gone.

Alan stared at his phone. He became aware someone was calling his name and dragged himself back to the here and now to claim his meal, somewhat perplexed by the strange conversation he'd just had. Why would someone, and particularly a senior officer, not want to help confirm the ID of a woman that was lying in a chiller nearby? He wracked his brains about what he knew of protected persons and the way things ran. Individuals had false identities to protect them from something, usually life-threatening, but she was already dead. And then there was the tattoo that both he and Carl knew was bad news. And there was the small matter that her passport had been used to board a ferry to Calais – after the crash. Something didn't smell right and now a higher pay grade knew the woman was dead. And the chief superintendent wasn't for helping him out with confirming her ID either, which in itself was strange. Or was it all his own paranoia, having seen her tattoo and linked it back to the past? If the woman, who was now deceased, had had some involvement in a crime from at least fifteen years ago, did it even matter? The ringleaders were safely tucked away in prison. And, back then, they'd had no reason to suspect more victims being involved. If his mystery woman had been a victim, there could well be more out there that would rather forget what had had happened to them. Like she had tried to do with the overlaid tattoo.

He needed to get back to his desk and scroll through footage of passport control and the surrounding buildings. Tabitha Child had been caught up in the tangled silk web strands and had somehow broken free. After all she'd likely endured, a freak rail accident seemed an unjust way to leave this earth. Nobody was watching over her any longer.

Susan Smith was somehow caught up in it all and could now be in grave danger.

CHAPTER 45

Dominic felt like a grade-one idiot. Tabitha had given him the slip. The last message he'd left on her voicemail ricocheted through his mind. Had he scared her off for good now? Had he gone too far? He had to make certain she was safe; there was too much riding on her staying alive. That was what safe houses were for, that was what the protected-persons programme was all about, keeping them safe. The startled youth, who Dominic had forced down a side street with his arm tucked painfully behind his back, had told the truth. He'd picked the phone up off the street less than an hour ago and had been taking it to a mate's place to try and unlock it. It was of no use to him as it was. Through the mix of pidgin English and French, Dominic had understood and believed the boy. Eventually the youth had straightened his jacket back into place and left the deserted side street, rubbing his sore arm as he went. A tirade of likely curse words floated on the air like the grey vape from an e-cigarette. Dominic had been left standing there, wondering where it had all gone wrong.

It was about to get worse. His phone vibrated in his pocket and he groaned outwardly as he saw who was calling.

"Where are you?" Chief Superintendent Morton asked.

"Paris actually, sir. Why?"

"Do you know Detective Sergeant Carl Bradley, or Alan Davies?"

"Can't say that I do. Why?"

"Because they've been looking at a file. Tabitha Child's to be precise. And apparently she's dead." The air between their two lines spiked with an electric current though no one said a word. The static was silent.

"That's not possible. She's here, in Paris."

"You'd better explain to me how, then, because she's on a deceased list from the train crash." The chief super's words had an edge to them as sharp as a jagged wine glass, a shard slicing into nearby flesh. Dominic, or DS Dominic Berger as the chief super knew him professionally, flinched as if he was the one being cut. Morton carried on, "She's in a fridge awaiting her formal ID."

"Sir, she can't be, she texted me only yesterday. We've been in contact."

"Then what the hell do you think she's doing in Paris?" the man screamed. "It's called a safe house for a reason! How the hell did you let this happen? Because I can't think she got permission for a fun day out!" The man's voice bellowed into Dominic's ears and he was glad he wasn't stood in front of him to experience his wrath at such close proximity. The man's stale breath was legendary. It was time to come clean and tell the chief super what he knew.

"Look," he said, taking a steadying breath of his own. "The first I knew was when I got a text saying she was taking a short trip. Obviously, I was as mad as hell and told her to get back home, but she hasn't. So I've come to Paris to take her home."

"And have you? Got her back to take home?"

"Not as yet, no." The silence at the other end of the line was like a sonic boom in Dominic's ears. He knew he was going to have to tell his boss that he messed up, that she'd given him the slip. "She ditched her phone earlier today. I've no idea where she is now." He sounded like a young Dominic, in deep trouble and resignedly expecting a dressing-down from his father.

"Tell me, have you have spoken to her since the train crash, actually verbally spoken to her, heard her voice?"

"No."

"I thought not. So, can you tell me this, how has a now dead woman pinged at passport control, travelling on the Dover to Calais ferry?"

"So she *is* alive then." Dominic sounded hopeful. After all, he'd been communicating with her only yesterday. Or had he? If she'd been killed in that crash as his superintendent had just said, he couldn't have been.

"You tell me!" the chief super screamed. "Because she can't be in two places, she can't be alive and dead, you incompetent prat! Find out what the hell is going on or you'll be directing traffic, if you're lucky enough to still have a job when this is all over. Now get back here, pronto!" The line went dead, his superintendent had hung up. Dominic closed his eyes and rested his head against the glass window of the shop behind him. It felt cool to his skull that was still ablaze from his boss's angry words. Something was clearly not right. She had to be in France, he couldn't have received a message from her if she was dead. And yet her passport had pinged at the ferry. Apparently. He glanced down at the phone he'd retrieved from the youth, the one Dominic had foolishly tracked. The kid said he'd found it on the kerbside not an hour ago, but it was locked so it hadn't been of any use to him. Dominic had wanted to hit the lad about the head with it. But the fact that it was locked proved that no one else could have sent those messages – not unless they knew the passcode. It wasn't that easy to break into a phone. Taking a long deep breath and releasing it, he pondered his next move. Tabitha Child was somewhere up ahead of him, though he had no clue of the direction she was going in. Or she was actually lying in a cold fridge back home. There weren't two of them. And if his chief super said she was in the mortuary, she would be. He was never wrong.

The only possible way to explain the events was that someone else was travelling as Tabitha Child. Someone had sent texts from a locked phone and had deceived passport control by pretending to be Tabitha. Or had she somehow set this grand scheme in motion to give him the slip? Was the woman in the fridge a decoy? Something had gone wrong with her plan though, if that was the case, because if Tabitha Child had attempted to fake her own death, she wouldn't be using her *own* passport and phone. No, the real Tabitha had vanished and was likely unaware of the train crash killing her decoy. That was the only explanation he could think of that fitted.

Tabitha Child was on the run.

And Dominic was going to bring her home.

There was no way he was going to let this fall apart now. His own future was riding on it.

CHAPTER 46

Since Chrissy had picked up the USB from the ferry terminal, she had assumed it was going to be camera footage from CCTV and of course she was correct. It was a grainy image when it came: video footage of people milling around, dragging luggage behind them and generally passing the time until their departure. Chrissy glanced at the timestamp: it was mid-afternoon on the day of the train crash. The taxi driver had thought it to have been about four o'clock that he'd dropped Susan off. The fare had stood out because she'd paid by credit card and the amount was larger than the local ones he'd taken that day. But Chrissy wanted to see more footage. If Susan had got on a later ferry, she would have hung around the terminal a while longer, and Chrissy needed to find out as much as she could about her sister's friend. As the taxi driver had said, it was about 4.10 pm when Susan Smith entered the building. It was Julie that noticed her first, pointing to the screen with an audible gasp. They watched as she made her way to Burger King and then on to passport control. Chrissy made a note of the timestamp because Susan Smith had to be travelling under a different identity since her real passport was back at the police station, with Alan Davies. They needed to know what that name was – it would make their search going forward a whole lot easier because she'd likely have credit cards in the same.

Julie sat back in her seat and put her hands over her eyes. Chrissy gave her sister a moment before speaking. "That confirms it then, Susan has taken off for some reason, and she doesn't want anyone to know where. Otherwise, she'd have been in touch, she'd have answered her phone."

Julie for once was speechless. Maybe seeing her friend preparing to run had disappointed her.

"Do you think that she's running away from Marcus?" Chrissy asked.

Julie removed her hands from her face and rolled her eyes to the ceiling while she thought through recent events. "I really have no clue," she said tiredly. "I didn't realise things were so bad between them, but if he is the reason, she quite clearly doesn't want him to know that she is alive and kicking. She's got everyone worrying and she hasn't contacted me so she is obviously intent on starting a new life somewhere for some reason. I'm her friend. Or so I thought. And I hadn't a clue!"

Chrissy ignored her sister's dramatics. "The thing that strikes me," said Chrissy, "is that she's got no luggage, she's got nothing with her, so this wasn't planned in that respect. She's just literally got on a ferry and gone to France; she's doing this on the hoof. I doubt she's got a secret hideaway somewhere with all her new belongings ready for a new life, but of course I could be wrong." She thought for a moment before adding, "The good thing about the spontaneous hoof is she'll make mistakes. Let's hope that works in our favour."

"So we know she's gone to Calais at least. What do you suggest we do now, then?" Julie's words sounded weary, adrenaline had surged and left her body, leaving her tired.

"First off, I need to make a copy of this," she said, pointing to the USB drive and beginning to do so while she was talking. "And then we need to get it back to the information desk because DS

Davies will probably be sending someone down to collect it, and then I think we get on a ferry ourselves."

Julie glanced at Chrissy and asked, "She's gone to Calais, but how on earth can we find out where she went from there? She is an anonymous person travelling at the moment." She sounded like she was ready to give up.

"Look, as you've seen she's travelling without any luggage, only a handbag, so she's got to get some belongings somehow and she's going to need a bed for the night, because by the time she gets over to Calais it's early evening. She'd be looking for somewhere local to rest. That's what I'd do anyway. She's been in a train crash, remember."

"Okay, so if I was on the run and I'd got no money – and we have to assume she doesn't have much – and no baggage, I'm not going to be staying in the environment I'm accustomed to. She won't be checking into a nice hotel, now, will she?"

"Definitely not. No, she is more likely to be doing this on the cheap and that means backpackers' accommodation, wouldn't you agree?"

"Totally," said Julie. "So let's go over there and we'll google backpackers' places on the way."

"Sounds like a plan," said Chrissy. "There can't be that many in the town, and we've got a photograph of her so we do the old-fashioned thing and show it around, see if she's been there. And if she has been and since gone, we need to figure out where, because if she is headed to Paris, we'll never find her in that jungle."

"Let's hope it doesn't come to that," said Julie. "Let's hope that someone does recognise her and can at least give us a name."

CHAPTER 47

By the time the two women had bought their ferry tickets it was around the same time of day that Susan herself had passed through the ferry terminal. All Julie and Chrissy could do was recreate her journey, go through her steps and follow that way. This wasn't a James Bond movie where things slotted neatly into place. 007 wasn't going to conveniently find a waiting boat, with the motor running, that was powerful enough to chase after the bad guys. In reality, it was hard and laborious work using plain, old-fashioned shoe leather to solve the case of a missing person. Particularly if they didn't want to be found. There was no digital footprint to be followed, and the tracker that Marcus had installed was of no use if Susan's phone wasn't with her and switched on.

With two tickets purchased and the envelope back at the information desk – Chrissy had feigned surprise that there wasn't *another* small package awaiting collection – they made their way through the documentation process and on to the ferry. It seemed Kevin McCallister couldn't have squeezed himself *Home Alone* style through passport control. Things had tightened up somewhat since his escapade. The women took their seats and Julie pulled out a glossy magazine, her perfect nose instantly buried among the pages.

Chrissy took a moment to check her own emails; Susan Smith wasn't her only case. There was one from the college she'd been working with. They'd had another incident and were asking if she could call.

"Damn it," she cursed to herself, wondering how she was going to manage the added workload, particularly since she was leaving the country.

"I'm peckish. Do you want something to eat or drink?" Chrissy asked the top of a blonde head.

"Water, please."

Chrissy headed towards the café, leaving Julie to her fantasy world for a while. Having Julie tag along on the trip had not been what she'd envisaged but, since Susan was her friend, how could she have said no? Still, she'd been useful so far and she could well be further on. A young man smiled brightly as she approached the counter and ordered coffee, a muffin and a bottle of water.

"Sure thing. Coming up," he said, pressing ground coffee down with a tamper and clipping the full arm into the machine. The aroma filled her nostrils and she watched him work as he forced steam into a jug of milk. Whatever happened to instant coffee? she wondered. Did they even make it any more? She dipped inside her bag and pulled out the photo of Susan.

"I know you probably see hundreds of people every day," she started, "but do you remember seeing this woman recently? Three days ago, perhaps?" Chrissy held it up for him and watched his reaction as he looked. Nothing appeared to register, though she let his eyes linger. Maybe there was something circulating in the back of his head.

"I couldn't be sure," he said, the words creeping slowly out of his mouth. "She sort of looks familiar."

"Oh? How so?"

"Well, I can't be a hundred per cent, but I did notice a woman a bit like her sat over there, on her own," he said, pointing to a quiet spot away from the majority of travellers. She caught my attention because I noticed quite a bruise here," he said, pointing to his brow and eye. And there was a stain on her shirt. I assumed maybe blood, like she'd had a nosebleed. Or been in a fight. Then she seemed to sleep a while so I kind of kept an eye on her but didn't speak to her. She looked a lot like the lady in your photo though."

Chrissy's pulse spiked. Another clue. "Did anyone speak to her that you know of? Only, she's missing. And my sister and I," Chrissy said pointing to Julie across the way, "are looking for her." The young man smiled in the direction of Julie. He had the perfect vantage point from where he worked to notice a great deal, Chrissy thought.

"No, she didn't speak to anyone that I'm aware of. Thinking back, she seemed sad maybe. You know, you can just feel a vibe from someone sometimes. I like to think I'm in tune like that."

"How about luggage, did she have a bag with her?"

"Not that I saw, no. But day trippers often don't." He clipped a lid on her coffee cup and smiled, her order complete.

"You've been helpful, thanks," she said and handed over her card to pay. She gathered her order and balanced the three items as best she could while walking back to Julie, who was still engrossed in her magazine. A perfectly moisturised and manicured hand slipped out to receive the bottle of water and Chrissy rolled her eyes at her sister.

"Hey," she said, somewhat excitedly. "The guy at the coffee shop over there reckons he saw Susan," she said, pointing. Julie looked across at the still-smiling man and obliged him with a smile in return. He was likely smiling at Julie. She ploughed on, "And get this, he said she had a bruise above her eye and had maybe had a nosebleed, which would fit with the crash. Oh, and he said he sensed she was sad."

"Interesting. And on her own, I assume?"

"Yes. A bit banged up but on her own. And no luggage."

"Great, that description should jog memories when we get to Calais."

Chrissy sat down next to her and pulled out her phone. "I've got some work to do for my other client. Can you look up the back-packers' places for when we get there?"

"Hmm?" Her head was submerged in glossy pages.

"Julie, I have other clients. Can you do the search, please?"

With an exaggerated sigh, Julie laid the magazine down and did as she was told. As Chrissy watched her obvious displeasure at being given an order, she remembered why she'd been reticent at letting Julie tag along. With more important things on her mind, she dialled the college.

There'd been another incident. It was not the perfect time to be heading to France.

CHAPTER 48

There were around eight different places that Susan Smith could have headed that fitted the bill: backpacker or cheap hotel. Chrissy looked at each one individually, figuring which one she would have gone to if it was her on foot. Particularly if she was feeling a little banged up after the accident. She wouldn't want to be walking far or wasting money on anything other than a bus into the town. On arrival, the two women headed straight over to the bus station and the courtesy bus that took tourists into Calais itself. From there they'd simply start with the first possible location on the list. Julie's bag soon became a problem, its wheels not enjoying the cracks in the pavement, and Chrissy was getting tired of her moaning at the exertion of keeping her it under control.

"We probably should have left that at the terminal in left luggage," Chrissy said, though not helpfully.

Julie, not one for criticising, was tempted to say something snarky but refrained; it wasn't in her demeanour. "Where can we leave it now, then?" she questioned, somewhat whiney.

"The only thing we can do is check into somewhere we'll stay ourselves and leave it there, because we won't be headed back home tonight."

Julie nodded.

"Let's just check in at this next one," Chrissy said, pointing in the distance. "Then we can leave the bag and have a quick look around to see what's what before having dinner."

"Okay," Julie agreed, sounding relieved her struggle was almost over.

Chrissy could see a small family-run hotel or motel not far ahead. "There is as good a place," she said. "It might not be up to your usual standards, Julie, I warn you now. But at least it will have a shower and a bed and we can get something to eat. And leave the bag, more importantly." Looking at Julie's face, Chrissy took pity on her and took the bag handle herself. She dropped her own sports bag on the top of it and used the main bag to transport her own. "Let me take over then," Chrissy said, and Julie smiled her appreciation.

"Thank you," she conceded in the demurest way she could. Chrissy was tempted to roll her eyes. She often marvelled at how different the two of them were and had joked at times that she was the milkman's daughter. But when you placed Julie next to their mother it was most likely that Chrissy was the odd one out.

Five minutes later they found themselves in the reception area of a cheap hotel. It smelled of fake pine air freshener, and judging by the deep-green, swirling-patterned carpet that was laid, it hadn't seen a decorator in at least twenty years. Chrissy hoped the bath would be clean and there'd be no stray hairs in the beds, pubic or otherwise. If *she* was thinking those things, she knew damn well that Julie would be. Once checked in, Chrissy carried the bag up two flights of stairs, opened the door and watched as Julie flopped down on one of the beds – a single. The room was as tired as the reception had been and as tired as they both felt. Pulling the bedclothes back for a closer inspection she could see the sheets were in fact clean and devoid of any hairs. After a quick scan of the bathroom, she was satisfied that, even for a tired place such as this, the cleanliness standards were up to scratch.

"Why don't you go and have a shower?" Chrissy encouraged. "You might feel livelier when you're cleaned-up and changed."

"I think I will, if you don't mind," she said and prised herself back up off the bed and moved towards her bag.

"Here," Chrissy said. "Let me lift it for you," and she put it on top of the old luggage rack, opening it so that Julie could find her toiletries and whatever else she needed. A moment or two later Chrissy could hear the shower running and she called through the door that she was popping back downstairs. Armed with a photograph, she figured she may as well make a start in the hotel where they were staying. The stairs creaked as she went down the two flights and at the reception she pinged the old brass bell and waited. The middle-aged woman smiled at her return and in almost perfect English she asked, "Is everything okay?"

"Great, thanks," said Chrissy, "but I wonder if you might help me?"

"I will if I can," she said. "What do you need?"

Chrissy showed her the photo of Susan Smith. "We're looking for a friend. We know she came through Calais a couple of days ago. I wonder, have you seen her at all? Maybe she stayed here?"

The woman looked but it wasn't the result Chrissy had hoped for. "Sorry no," she said, shaking her head rather too quickly for Chrissy's liking.

"Please, take another look, she may be in danger," she urged, and the woman took another look.

"I would have remembered her, she is a good-looking lady, but no, we've only had families and couples this week. I don't think we've had any single people to stay at all this month, and I don't recognise her, I'm sorry. I do hope you find her though."

Chrissy said her thanks and wandered off back upstairs for a shower of her own. One hotel down, a few more to go. Maybe later on or tomorrow they'd have better luck. If they didn't, Chrissy really was at a loss of what to do next without a name.

CHAPTER 49

By the time DS Alan Davies had finished his burger and was viewing the relevant time frames of passport-control CCTV, he reasoned he was only going to see what his gut already knew: the woman on the footage was Susan Smith and she was using Tabitha Child's passport. The burning question was why. The next question was, did the two women know one another, had they planned it all along, whatever it was? He sat back in his chair and looked at the freeze-frame on his screen. There was no mistaking Susan Smith. The younger-looking Tabitha Child replica was headed to France and maybe beyond, but at least now he had a name to work with. But unless the woman used credit cards or anything else in Tabitha's name she would still leave no trail for him to follow. He bet that was the idea.

The other, real Tabitha Child was lying in a cold fridge, while Susan had taken over her identity. With the involvement of a chief superintendent to add to the discovery of the tattoo on the real Tabitha Child, Alan really did have concerns for Susan's safety. He wondered if Susan knew what she had got herself into.

Wiping his mouth on a napkin, he debated his next move. Maybe he needed to go back and search through the luggage and find Susan Smith's overnight bag as well as look for Tabitha Child's handbag and her own overnight bag. Maybe either of those could give him some clues, though he wouldn't be surprised if he found them both empty, a ruse all part of some elaborate plan. He checked his watch; it was almost 7 pm. There was no way anybody would still be back at the hangar. Or would they? He picked up his phone and dialled the contact that he'd spoken to before, but there was no reply. It looked like he was going to have to wait until the morning.

He wondered about Chrissy and her sister on their way to France and how they were doing. He doubted they would catch up with their friend Susan, but if they did, he'd be interested in talking to her himself. He also wondered if they knew her now-assumed name that she was travelling under. He'd agreed that if he found anything out, he'd let the two women know, but so far, he hadn't done. Should he tell them? It would save them a wild-goose chase, knowing that their friend had in fact passed through Calais travelling as Tabitha Child. But where to, nobody knew.

"Oh, sod it," he said and picked his phone, calling the number he had.

"Hello," Julie purred.

Alan smiled at his internal overreaction again. Not many women had an effect on him, but this one seemed to. "Detective Alan Davies here," he said, trying to be formal and put some authority into his voice.

"I know," said Julie. "I recognise your number. Do you have some news?"

"I do actually."

"Then I'll put you on speaker for Chrissy."

"Hello again DS Davies," Chrissy chimed in. "What do you have?"

"Hi Chrissy. Well, it seems your friend Susan did go through passport control at Dover, though she is not travelling on her own passport. Now, I can't tell you what name she is travelling under because it possibly links to another case, but I can tell you that your friend is alive and well, and is travelling alone or appears to be travelling alone. I just thought you should know."

"Oh, that is good news," said Julie, trying to put on some level of surprise. Having already seen the CCTV footage herself, she was doing her best. "So what happens now?" she asked.

"Well, nothing really, I'm afraid, from a police point of view. If your friend wants to run off, she is quite entitled to do so and there's not much else I can do."

"Oh, that doesn't seem fair," purred Julie again. "There must be something? Can you please tell us the name she is travelling under? Maybe we can trace her that way."

"Not at this point, I'm afraid, but at least you know your friend is alive."

"Well, thanks for calling," Chrissy finished, somewhat abruptly, and hung up.

Alan slumped back in his chair wondering if he'd done the right thing. Maybe he should have said what name she was travelling under; it would have made their job a bit easier and maybe his own in turn. But with links to another case, his decision not to tell them would have to stand. If Susan Smith travelling as Tabitha Child was about to run into trouble, he didn't want anyone else ending up in a similar situation. No, tomorrow he'd go and check the contents of their luggage, though knowing that Susan was now travelling as Tabitha Child, he wasn't expecting to find that particular handbag or its personal contents. Susan Smith already had those. But their overnight bags could tell a different story.

He'd better ring Marcus Smith and let him know of his discovery, that he could confirm she was alive, there was no doubt of it now. At least he'd be pleased – Alan assumed.

CHAPTER 50

Marcus Smith was bleary-eyed having been woken around 1 am. While he was often up late, his jet-lagged body clock had sent him to bed earlier than usual in an attempt to get back on an even kilter. The deep-sleep disturbance had perturbed the man and he answered his ringing phone with all the finesse of a dragon with a sore tooth.

"Who the hell can't wait until a reasonable hour?" he screamed by way of greeting the caller.

A beat passed before Alan spoke. He was glad he was so far away and didn't have to deal with the man in person. He pitied Susan once again. "It's Detective Alan Davies, sir. I have an update for you."

"Yes? Right. What is it?" Alan could imagine Marcus rubbing sleep from his eyes and trying to focus himself.

"I have some good news for you, sir. It appears your wife Susan is definitely alive. We haven't managed to fully locate her at present, though we do know she's travelled to France. She is alive though, as I said. I thought you'd like to know."

"Alive? That is good news. Thank you. But in France, you say? When will she be home? I'll fly straight back." Alan could hear movement. Maybe Marcus was getting out of bed. It was an image he didn't want to contemplate for too long.

"Sir, we haven't actually located her. Not her exact location that is, and since she's an adult..."

"Yeah, you said already, she can do what she pleases." Alan didn't need to say much else. Although he was tempted to throw in that Mr Smith didn't sound too thrilled about his wife being alive and on the move, it was best to keep his thoughts to himself.

"I wanted to inform you of the development. Maybe she'll be in touch with you soon." He doubted it. He was reaching for something else to add to the awkward conversation. Right now, Alan was rooting for Susan to carry on running. "I'll let you get back to sleep, sir. Perhaps we will talk again tomorrow."

"Right."

Marcus hung up, leaving Alan staring at his silent phone. "What a complete arse."

CHAPTER 51

Chrissy and Julie had written a list of the various backpacking motels and cheap hotels around the town. There was no point looking much further than them until they'd canvassed the immediate vicinity, because a woman on foot, with presumably limited funds, wasn't going to get very far. That was their reasoning and, that's what they themselves would have done. They'd split the list between them, but by mid-morning, gathered at the café where they'd agreed to meet, both looked and felt deflated. It was obvious neither had had any luck. Chrissy ordered coffee for herself and green tea for Julie. There was no point asking if her sister wanted a muffin, but Chrissy was happy to share her own so bought the bigger size of the ones that were on offer. Just in case. With all the walking they were doing Chrissy wasn't too concerned about the calories.

Julie slumped down in the chair opposite, resting her chin in her hands, elbows on the table. "My feet are sore," she whined, and Chrissy couldn't help but grin. It was a good job they'd bought the cheap sandals in Ashford, otherwise she probably wouldn't have any skin left on her feet.

"I figured you wouldn't want a muffin, but you can share mine, or I can easily get you one?"

"I'd love a muffin, actually."

Chrissy raised her eyebrows and said, "Did I hear you right? You want a muffin?"

"Stop being sarcastic. Yes, I would like a muffin, please."

Chrissy watched as Julie rubbed her temples; she must've been feeling rough. Sliding her own muffin across the table, she headed back to buy a replacement for herself. "You'll feel better when you've eaten that, sugar does that to you. It's called comfort eating."

"This is exhausting," Julie said, breaking a small piece off the top with an elegant finger. Chrissy didn't think she'd ever seen such beautiful fingernails on anybody else. Certainly not on her own hands. "The real life of a private investigator isn't glamorous at all, it's quite the opposite. It's nothing like Magnum."

Chrissy bit into her own muffin and watched Julie picking at her own. "Who's Magnum?" she enquired.

"A sort of old cop show, but without the cops." Julie raised an eyebrow in question. "I should've realised you wouldn't have watched it; it was a long time ago. Eat your muffin and cheer up."

The two women sat in silence for a while, coffee and sugar supplying sustenance for the next stage of the day. They'd still got more on the list to visit and Chrissy was hopeful that somebody in Calais had put Susan up for the night. It was just a matter of finding out where that place was. And Chrissy's college client was adding to her concerns. Aware she may not be giving it the time she should, she made peace with herself by deciding that she'd find a couple of hours later to work on it. Family connection or not, the Susan Smith case was draining her mental resources.

It was close to two o'clock when they had their first spark of luck. Chrissy was in the reception area of a backpackers' place, the last on her list, and the woman behind the desk glanced at the photograph and said yes, she remembered her, she had been in. Chrissy asked her to repeat herself because she'd spent the morning hearing no after no after no. Had she heard the woman correctly?

Susan had in fact been in and stayed there? Finally, another break-through. Things were looking up.

"Yes, she stayed just one night and then set off early the following morning. Had breakfast and was gone."

"Was she travelling alone?"

"Yes. There was something about her that stuck in my mind. I see so many people through here every day, but I noticed her." The woman seemed to be thinking as she spoke, her words getting fainter in memory as if Susan were dead. "But she seemed so quiet, and had a nasty bruise above her eye. I felt a bit sorry for her." The woman drifted off again, remembering.

"What time did she leave the next day?" Chrissy asked.

"Not long after breakfast. So 7 am, maybe? I saw her head up to the main road, no doubt to catch a lift like many of the others that stay here do. Obviously, she is long gone by now."

"Did she give you a name when she checked in? Because I'm guessing she didn't use her real name." The woman looked suspicious at the question and Chrissy wondered if she'd pushed it too far. Time for a sob story. "It's her husband that she's running from, that's all. It's nothing more sinister. But I'm worried about her so any information you can give me, please, I'd appreciate it." That would explain the bruise. The woman looked thoughtful again, maybe thinking back to the past, maybe her own friend in trouble, or herself. Finally, she took a deep sigh before taking a look at that bookings for that day. Chrissy could only see the top of her salt-and-pepper head as she searched. Chrissy waited until the woman had found what she was looking for without saying another word, not wanting to fill the empty space with idle chit-chat.

"Here it is. She checked in at about six o'clock and gave the name 'Tabby Child'."

Chrissy filed the information inside her head. It didn't mean anything to her – yet. "Thank you so much, you've been extremely helpful," she said, beaming. It was excellent news, and now they had a name. It would make things easier going forward.

Chrissy left and, once outside on the pavement, called Julie to save her wasting any more time. They agreed to meet back at the café. Once they were both together, Chrissy recited the story that Susan Smith had been in but was travelling under a different name.

"Tabby Child?" asked Julie. "Why on earth Tabby Child? What a weird name. I wonder why she chose that —what's the relevance?"

"I have no idea," said Chrissy. "But we're getting closer to finding out."

CHAPTER 52

Chrissy and Julie were buoyed by the news. Susan Smith had stayed locally and had changed her name to Tabby Child, though neither woman understood why that particular name or if it mattered even. Maybe it was a reference to a favourite toy she'd had when she was younger, or maybe it had been a bunny rabbit. Tabby sounded like a cat either way.

It wasn't far to where the receptionist at the backpackers thought Susan would have caught a lift from, where most hitch-hikers seemed to start out from once they'd left the accommodation. Many headed on for the bright lights of Paris after leaving Calais and Chrissy hoped that Susan hadn't done the same. It had been hard enough trying to find a missing woman up to this point, never mind in the midst of the hustle and bustle of a capital city. And with only a name to go on. And when someone didn't want to be found... As they set off together it was Julie that said, "You know, Chrissy, we haven't told Marcus yet that she is alive, never mind that she has changed her name. We should tell him."

"I know, you're right," Chrissy said, "but something is telling me not to say anything, not yet. I don't quite know why, but Susan is running away from something and maybe Marcus *is* that something."

"I know what you're saying, and I've felt the same thing. Who knows what goes on behind closed doors? And while she is my friend, she is not likely to tell me everything. For instance, I didn't realise that things were as bad at home as they must have been, because she didn't mention this," Julie waved her arms to encompass her surroundings in an exaggerated action, "at all to me."

"I guess some things are best left unsaid. But you know that room down the bottom of her garden? Well, that's the kind of place that I see her living in more than the mausoleum of her home. And I think she spent most of her time down there, save for sleeping. She had pretty much everything set up, like a studio flat-cum-reading room-cum-office. So, what *was* going on behind her closed doors, do you think?"

"I knew she was unhappy and lonely, but I thought they just lived separate lives. Fallen out of love somewhere. But if it had been as simple as that, why would he track her? That just seems extreme, particularly if you're not that bothered about the woman that you live with any more. I suspect while he is away in Hong Kong, he's doing his own thing, if you understand my meaning. And why stay together now anyway, either of them?"

"Well, we should tell him at the very least, I suppose. It's not our place not to and we don't have to give too much detail, only that she is alive and well and is headed to France. CCTV confirms it. We don't need to say any more just yet," Chrissy finished. Then, "I'll call him towards the end of the day."

"I agree." Julie looked relieved it wouldn't be her breaking the news.

They weren't far from the service station up ahead where a small gathering of people milled about. It appeared to be a popular place catch a lift. Since they now had Susan's assumed name and a photograph, and they had basic details of her minor injuries, somebody might remember seeing her.

"I guess we should split up again," Julie suggested. "It worked last time and we can cover more ground. I'll start at the left and you start at the right, and we'll see what we find."

Chrissy smiled to herself. She suspected Julie was enjoying herself being out in the fresh air. She had not mentioned Richard once since they'd been away and Chrissy wondered about that too. He was a bit of a bore, but she assumed her sister loved him dearly. Otherwise why were they together? Some people stayed together because there was nothing for them to separate for.

But then she could say the same about Susan and Marcus.

Chrissy watched Julie saunter off in the sunshine and hoped that she'd put some sunscreen on, because with her English-rose skin exposed to the French sun, she would likely burn. Chrissy approached the first vehicle, a transit van, and went around to the driver side, pulling out the photo of Susan Smith.

"Hi," she said, surprising the driver a little. "I'm looking for my friend. I wonder if you might have seen her. She passed through here a couple of days ago, looking for a lift."

The man gave the photograph a quick glance and said, "I've just arrived, love, so no, I haven't seen anybody yet," and wound his window back up.

Chrissy moved on to the next vehicle, a family car with children in the back and luggage visible through the rear window. She doubted they'd have seen Susan either; they too looked like they'd just arrived. She tried anyway.

"Just arrived, I'm afraid," said the woman at the wheel. "Sorry."

There seemed little point asking car drivers. It was the regular travellers up and down from France to the UK that she needed to speak to, and that meant lorry drivers and maybe transit-van drivers. She scratched their agreed plan and wandered over to where a handful of lorries were parked. It looked like Julie had had the same idea so Chrissy started at the opposite end of the row and crossed her fingers. Looking up at the first cab, she found it was empty, but she spotted a man wandering towards her and figured he was probably its driver. He was a typical trucker stereotype: work boots, baggy jeans, T-shirt, beer belly. As he got closer, she called out to him and he raised his eyes away from the newspaper he'd been scanning while he walked. She explained who she was looking for and why, and asked him to look at the picture, but immediately she knew it was a waste of time.

"Not seen her, I'm afraid. I'm up and down this road a fair bit, but this is the first time this week for me." Chrissy's heart dropped again. There must be an easier way.

"Is there any way of making this easier?" she asked him. "Only I can't stand here for the next two weeks asking lorry drivers if they've seen my friend. Is there some way of contacting your trucking buddies, I don't know, like maybe an app? Perhaps you have such a thing for truckers, your own social app?"

"Well, I can get on the radio and ask about, that would be the quickest thing. There may be an app, but I don't know about it." At least he was trying to help her out and Chrissy was grateful.

"As in CB radio?" Chrissy asked, not trying to hide the incredulousness from her words. "Do you still use that? I remember my grandad having a CB radio."

"Cheeky. But yes, we certainly do. Truckers, cabbies and a few others still use CB because it's free and no need for a licence any more. It's quieter these days, but there's still a fair few of us lot on it."

"Would you mind asking then, please, because it's really important that we find her."

"I'll give it a go, hang on."

She watched his bulk climb up into the cab and pull himself into his driver's seat with the door still open. He picked up the radio handset and said that he was looking for a blonde lady who had been picked up from this location. He asked if anyone had seen her in the last couple of days, if anyone had given her a lift.

Chrissy shouted up to him while they waited for a response, "She's got a bruise around her eye, maybe had a nosebleed, and travelling most likely on her own. The bruise, it could be important. Does anyone remember picking up a blonde lady with a bruised face?" Chrissy asked eagerly, then listened while the trucker relayed the message. They waited, listening to empty airwaves. It seemed nobody was going to respond. Chrissy felt even more deflated. She let her shoulders hang loose and was ready to walk away.

"Let me give you my mobile," she said, "just in case someone does come back to you later when we've gone. That way you can give me a call." She pulled out a slip of paper with her number on it, which would do in the absence of her card. She handed it up to him and was just about to say goodbye when the radio crackled.

A friendly-sounding male had picked up someone fitting that description, a young woman, a couple of days ago, and had dropped her just outside Paris, at another service station where she was going to get another lift. Sorry he couldn't be any more help, that was as far as he took her.

Excited now, Chrissy shouted up urgently, "Did she give a name? Can you ask, did she give her name at all?" The driver pressed the button to speak and again relayed the message over the airwaves. Both waited patiently for the man to respond. "Yes, Tabby," they heard him say. He remembered so because his daughter's cat was called Tabby.

CHAPTER 53

The following morning, bright and early, Alan was ready and waiting at the hangar, flask of decent coffee in his hand. He was greeted by the same grey-haired, older gentleman that had showed him in last time. Chuckling lightly, the man pointed to Alan's flask and said, "Come prepared for a longer stay, have you?" Alan's own brew would be a good deal better than the instant, chemical-created stuff the older man had generously provided.

"Something like that," Alan chided.

"Then I'll leave you to it," he added, opening the padlock for the detective, before shuffling off back to his post.

Once again, Alan was faced with the mountain of belongings, many bags intact and others badly damaged, items of clothing spilling out haphazardly. He wondered if they'd ever find their way back to their rightful owners, and if those owners even cared. The walking wounded would claim on their insurance and receive money for their replacement; the dead, not so bothered. He placed his flask down on an upturned box and, looking back at the haphazard pile, wondered if he should have perhaps brought sandwiches too. It was going to take some time. He got straight to work sorting through the handbags, looking for Tabitha Child's. He wasn't expecting to find it, not if Susan was already using the woman's passport, and since he'd already gone through most of them when he'd been looking for Susan's handbag, it didn't take him long to figure out it was as he expected: missing.

But both their overnight cases? That was a different story.

It was almost two hours later when he came across Tabitha's case. He was a little surprised that a woman travelling Business Premier hadn't carried a designer case, but here it was, a generic trolley bag that looked much like any other. Not surprisingly, the combination entry was locked and he didn't have the code. He pulled out his multipurpose tool and, finding the small knife, slit the cloth edge of the zip all the way around. Prising both sides of the bag open, he laid the case and its contents flat to take a closer look. There were two changes of clothes, a black cocktail-style dress, a pair of black stilettos, toiletries and a small mesh bag fastened with a drawstring. He slipped the toggle on the thin cord open and peered inside. It looked hairy.

"Huh?" he said to himself as he put his hand in and pulled out a wig. Holding it up with one hand, he straightened it slightly to look at the style more closely. A short, dark bob with a fringe at the front that reminded him of one of the dolls his sister had had when she'd been much younger. The doll had been called Lulu and was supposedly French, though that had all been part of the child's mind, not the manufacturer's intention. Alan smiled at the memory of the doll at the dinner table and wondered why a woman would be carrying a wig for a short trip away. There was little else in the case and so he put it to one side while he carried on searching for Susan Smith's bag. When he came across the case, he was surprised to find it was identical to Tabitha Child's.

Alan pulled it closer and slit the zip fabric to gain entry. It contained almost identical belongings: a couple of changes of clothing, a black dress, a pair of black stilettos and toiletries. There wasn't a wig in Susan's bag. The similarity between the contents of the two cases made Alan sit back on his heels and stop for a moment. There were too many things adding up in a way that was as murky as the small pond at the bottom of his grandmother's garden. So much so that the thought sparked something in the back of his mind: had they been travelling in the same carriage on purpose? A coincidence, maybe? He reached for his phone and called Bridget.

"Yep?"

"Bridget, I need a quick favour. Can you double-check if two passengers were travelling in the same carriage for me? Susan Smith and Tabitha Child?"

"Hold on, won't be a mo." Alan held his phone with one hand and tried to unscrew his flask with the other, holding it between his thighs. By the time Bridget had the news, he was sipping from his mug and enjoying the taste of his own brew. He needed a biscuit.

"They were. Susan Smith was a handful of rows behind Child. Why?"

"Don't you think it odd that the two women who look fairly similar are in the same carriage? With identical cases containing almost identical items? And one is missing, one dead? And one of those has a locked file?"

"Wow. They were up to something!"

"I'd say so, yes. Can you do me another favour and put an alert on Tabitha Child's credit cards and passport? I want to know if either get used again."

"Already done."

Alan rang off and went back to Susan's bag. He felt around the edges of the case, feeling the lining, running his fingertips over the cloth, his suspicions on high alert that there was something else to find. He needed to look closer. There was more to this than what was obvious on the surface. He slipped his fingers inside a small fabric pocket and they froze on contact. The unmistakable feel of an envelope, firm, rigid, level-edged. He pulled it out. It was sealed. There was nothing on the front. Alan held it up to the light, but the hangar was not a bright space, there was no need for it to be. Since he was looking for a missing woman, there was no harm in opening it to see what was inside. His inner antennae were sparking like firecrackers bouncing down an alleyway.

Carefully, he prised it open, rolling the sticky edge of the flap back and pulling out a fine, film-like item. It wasn't greaseproof paper, but it was similar in its flimsiness.

There was no mistaking what it was.

It was a tattoo transfer. And it was identical to the one on Tabitha Child's thigh.

"Holy hell."

CHAPTER 54

Detective Alan Davies didn't hear the grey-haired, older man enter the hangar with his own coffee mug and a plastic tub of assorted biscuits in hand. The discovery of what the envelope contained had knocked him off balance a little, and he was pacing up and down the area he'd cleared of luggage. Walking helped him to think.

"You'll wear a hole in the concrete if you keep that up," the man said, smiling. But it broke through Alan's trance-like state.

He lifted his head, eyes refocusing like a telescopic lens. "Sorry, I was miles away."

The man offered the tub of biscuits Alan's way and the detective took a couple at random.

"Time for a break. I thought you might like the sugar, only I didn't see you bring anything other than your flask," he said and sat down on a large upturned case and sipped on his own coffee.

While he didn't need the distraction, Alan appreciated the gesture, his stomach grateful for the fuel. He could spare five minutes to talk to the man and ease his boredom of guarding a largely unoccupied building.

"Have you found what you were looking for?" the man enquired, dunking a shortbread into his hot coffee and letting it soak for a brief moment.

"I've found the relevant luggage now. Though I doubt I've found any answers, only more questions." Alan sat on an adjacent bag, poured coffee from his flask, then stuffed the first biscuit into his mouth, allowing crumbs to fall into his lap. Brushing them away, he added, "Just when you think you're getting somewhere, the proverbial fly drops in the ointment." He bit into the remaining biscuit.

"Life's like that sometimes, my friend. If you're at the base of the wrong tree, you should stop barking."

Alan puzzled at his philosophy and watched him finish his shortbread. "That's a bit deep isn't it?"

"Depends on your perspective. I'm full of great advice; it's a shame I never take any of my own," he said, grinning. "My favourite is this: 'woman with skirt up can run faster than man with trousers down'. I find it covers most eventualities in life, and if you're worrying about something unnecessarily, it's a great distraction for the mind. You can't help but visualise it."

Alan couldn't help grinning at the man's logic. "Well, it seems I've got a woman with her skirt held high above her waistline, and I appear to be the man with trousers around his ankles. She's off and running, and I'm sipping coffee here in a draughty hangar, pondering her next move."

"So what's puzzling you? What isn't making sense?"

"I was barking at the wrong tree until just before you came in. So at least I can stop barking at that one now. The problem now is, I need a new tree."

"And you need to pull your trousers back up and get going, am I right?"

"Something like that. Do you always talk in riddles, indirectly?"

"I find it stimulates my mind, keeps me sharp. A bit like doing puzzles, but I add them to conversation. More fun too."

The two sat in silence while they sipped their coffee and pondered. Alan felt like the Karate Kid, recipient of Mr Miyagi's uniquely bestowed wisdom, and waited for the older man to say something else. Instead, he stood, drained his mug and picked up the plastic biscuit tub.

"I'll let you get back to it then," he said and headed back out from where he'd come, leaving Alan to wonder what the answer would be. Like in the story of the Karate Kid, the solution wouldn't appear overnight, it would take time and effort. He just needed to know where to spend his efforts.

He needed a new tree.

And he needed to make a phone call. He dialled, ready to ask the pathologist a question.

"Dean, it's Alan Davies here, have you got a minute?"

"Of course, have you some news on our mystery woman back here keeping cool?"

"Maybe. But first I need you to double-check something."

"I'm about to get on with another autopsy, but I can check for you in a couple of hours or so. What do you need?"

Damn, Alan was hoping for an answer while he waited.

The pathologist picked up on the delay. "Sorry, mate, best I can do."

"No, I understand. Listen, can you double-check the tattoo on our mystery woman is real, see if it smudges? I'm guessing you will need more than water to do the job."

"Not been asked that one before. Everything all right?"

"Not sure yet, but I'm looking at a different tree to bark at."

"I'm sure that makes sense to you. I'll call you back when I've done it, okay?"

"Thanks, Dean, I appreciate it." Alan was about to hang up when Dean added something he wasn't expecting.

"She seems to be generating a bit of interest, our mystery woman."

"Oh? How so?"

"Can you believe I had Detective Chief Superintendent Morton stinking the place out with his cigar odour last night? And he wanted to see her specifically. Unusual, don't you think?" Alan could hear a woman calling Dean somewhere in the background, back in the lab he assumed. "Look, I've got to go, but I'll call you later."

Alan was left with an empty line again. Slipping his phone back into a pocket, he wondered about the interest the woman was attracting. After his conversation with the chief superintendent the previous night, and the locked file they couldn't get access to, he was starting to feel uneasy about the whole thing. And with his latest discovery rattling around his skull, he had to be careful who he let into his circle of trust. Dean, the pathologist, was on his side, as was Bridget. But Carl had asked to be kept informed, why? As had the chief super, why? And was anyone else watching from a distance?

Perhaps he needed to look at things differently, because since he'd found the contents of Susan Smith's suitcase, there could only be one explanation.

The two women not only knew one another, they had something planned.

He had to find out what.

CHAPTER 55

It was both exciting and frustrating news, all at the same time. The service station where Tabby had been dropped was an hour outside Paris and a common meeting place for those that used the roads up and down to the ferry.

"We need a vehicle," Julie said, stating the obvious but excited at the news.

"And when we get to Paris? What then? Because even if we show her picture at the service station, we already know she's gone to Paris. Before we set off, is there any point to this? Are we really going to knock on every Parisian door and ask if Tabby Child has been by?" Chrissy was trying to figure out their next move, a move that would preferably propel them forward instead of maintaining their current pace of creeping. It wasn't happening fast enough for her. They desperately needed something else.

They were walking slowly back to their hotel. It wasn't even lunchtime, but the sunshine was bright and hot in the sky. Chrissy turned to Julie. "So put yourself in her shoes again. You've woken after a night's sleep and a meal, and grabbed a lift to just outside Paris. Where are you heading and why? And, remember, you've likely not much money or belongings, and you've a shiner of a bruise on your face. What's your plan?"

Julie looked up at the blue sky, feeling the heat on her shoulders. "And it's summer and I'm free, on the run from a bore of a husband that I may or may not know tracked me. Oh, and I've been lonely for some time, and if I had a phone, I've not called anyone."

Chrissy added Julie's extra information to her own thinking and the two women stayed silent, quietly focusing as they walked back.

"You know, *Shirley Valentine* came up earlier. Maybe she really has gone off on holiday to Greece and is thinking of staying," Julie said, remembering.

"What, you think Susan is like her? A bored, suburban, middle-aged woman with a mundane and routine life. Chips and egg on a Tuesday teatime, or whatever night it was?"

Julie took the bait, "And she met a gorgeous man that turned out to be a bit of a fake, and only after one thing. But she fell in love with the place anyway and worked in a café for a while before her husband went to find her and try and take her home." Julie looked as if she was daydreaming as she recited the bones of the plot. Chrissy couldn't help but smile. Julie's husband, Richard, was a bore, but she couldn't see her sister running off to a fishing village in the sun, not without her heels and nail varnish.

"What are you smiling at?" she enquired.

"I was thinking about you actually. I couldn't see you running off; strappy sandals are of no use on a Greek beach."

"Ha, ha, very funny."

They were back outside the hotel now, and it looked as gloomy as it had the previous day when they'd arrived. They really needed to modernise the place, plant something cheery in the flower beds at least, give the front some street appeal.

"Let's carry on walking," Chrissy said. "I fancy an ice cream, and we've still some thinking to do."

"Oh, not for me, but I'll sit with you."

"Come on, sis, a single chocolate scoop won't hurt. Let your hair down."

Instinctively, Julie touched her stiff head of hair. She relented. "I'll have one scoop then. In a cup, not a cone."

Life was full of concessions. Chrissy wanted to slap her sister on the back, in a congratulatory gesture, but was conscious she'd think she was taking the micky. There were tiny cracks, however, of Julie relaxing and being less formal the more time they spent together. Their trip was doing her sister good.

Sitting on a stone wall, looking out at the beach in the distance, both women slipped ice cream into their mouths from tiny wooden spoons and savoured the taste. The summer season would be in full swing in a few more weeks, the sun too hot to bear for some, but the temperature right at that moment was perfect, and Chrissy pushed her legs out in front of her to allow the sun to work its magic.

"You know, if it was me in Susan's place, I wouldn't be headed for a city, not at this time of year."

"Oh?"

"No. Would you? Think about it, Julie. You've been lonely and cooped up in a big tasteless house with a husband you deep down know doesn't love you any more. After she's got over the shock of the accident, she'll want to explore a little. Though not here, it's too close to home." She took another spoonful and teased it off in several sweeps with her mouth, deep in thought. "So she's on the move, and I'm betting, as each hour passes, enjoying her newfound freedom and gaining a little more confidence as she goes."

"You think she's happy about this then?"

"I think she'll be learning to be, yes. *And I'm also betting that the more time passes, the more likely it is that she'll slip up and make a mistake.* It's clear Marcus isn't going to chase her, and the police aren't too bothered, she's simply another adult gone AWOL. In another week, nobody will be looking for her with any vigour."

"That's sad, don't you think?"

"That's life is what I think. And that brings us back to: where has she gone? And where will she be in a week?" Chrissy scraped the last of the chocolate from the tub, disappointed she'd only had two small scoops and not three. Getting up off the wall and tossing her tub into a nearby bin, she added, "I'd head down south for the summer. Not to the coast or Greece – too busy and I wouldn't want to risk being seen. But I'd find a happy middle place to hide in for a while. But Paris? Not a chance."

"And if she hasn't got a suitcase as big as mine with her," Julie said, smiling at her own dig, "then I'd agree with you. There is no draw to Paris itself. Cities can be lonely places, and that's one of the things she's perhaps running from. She wants some time to readjust, reinvent and revitalise. Like a butterfly," she said, adding enthusiasm with her arms raised in the air.

Chrissy rolled her eyes at the drama of it all. She smiled at her sister and said, "Come on. Let's find a large map and see what the best options would be to do just that."

CHAPTER 56

Dominic had the same problem as the two women did. Just how do you find a person that doesn't want to be found? If they are not using credit cards or anything else that transmits a digital footprint, it's virtually impossible. But Dominic had put so much work into this – he didn't want it to fall apart now – and the phone call from his boss, Morton, had rattled him somewhat. He pondered his next move. In reality there was nothing much he could do from where he was right now: he had no resources handy and no obvious direction to go in. Paris was a big place. If she was, indeed, still in Paris. Had she ever been? It didn't make any sense. He had to believe that Tabitha Child was alive and well, and was up ahead, though he had no idea how close or how far away.

He could have kicked himself. His chief super had been right to ask if he'd actually spoken with, or set eyeballs on, the woman, because no, he hadn't, not for a few days if not longer. And that had been before, back in Kent, at the house. He should have seen this coming and he was left feeling like a complete fool.

His phone vibrated in his hand. It was Morton again. Dominic didn't fancy picking it up and getting another dressing-down, so he let it go to voicemail. He needed the space; he didn't need somebody clambering around the inside of his head kicking rocks around. If Tabitha Child was dead, somebody was impersonating her. If Tabitha Child was alive, he was going to find her. He wasn't going home empty-handed. When Morton rung off and the voice message had been received, Dominic dialled in to listen to what the man had to say. What he heard turned his blood stone cold. It wasn't the news he wanted or expected. Morton had been to the mortuary and had seen for himself the woman lying in the fridge, complete with the tattoo that confirmed exactly who she was. The pathologist was anxious to give the woman her identity back after the train crash, but Morton hadn't confirmed her name. He had merely said it wasn't the woman he was looking for and left it at that. No one was any the wiser.

Dominic couldn't believe it. There was little point going on now. Tabitha Child was dead and that meant the case was over. As was his own reward. Whoever was using Tabitha Child's identity, sending texts, didn't matter any longer because it wasn't the woman they'd been protecting all along, the woman now unable to supply the vital evidence. Dominic turned to head back, feeling totally defeated and somewhat angry at his own stupidity, that he could have been taken in in such a way. He hailed a taxi back to the airport. A flight home earlier than scheduled and an expensive taxi ride were going be the least of his worries when Morton got hold of his collar. It would probably be the end of his career.

Dominic was sitting in the departure lounge when he had a thought. Maybe there was another way around this. Tabitha Child was lying in the mortuary, yet somebody had successfully gone through passport control impersonating her. Morton had told him her passport had pinged. He needed to find out who had used it. It didn't take him long to come around to a conclusion. If somebody had Child's passport, and, probably, her other belongings, it would likely be somebody that had been travelling on that train with her or near her. In the same carriage, maybe. But who?

An opportunist.

And the opportunist would have to look a lot like Tabitha

Child. How else would she be able to use the woman's passport successfully? Would it be possible for them to use the opportunist in place of Child? He mulled it over while nursing a bottle of beer before his flight. Maybe it was time to dial Morton and run the idea past him. It wasn't crazy once he'd tossed it around his mind a couple of times. If they could find the woman that had impersonated Child, maybe she could be of use in the trial somehow after all. Since all the forensics and medical examinations had already been completed, they only needed her coached testimony. It was simple and, more importantly, it could work. He waited for the call to connect and when Morton answered in his usual gruff manner, Dominic garbled the idea in a hurry.

"It's not over," Dominic explained. "The similar looking woman could take over from now, once we find her. Our plan is not necessarily lost, we can use this still, we've just got to figure out who the woman impersonating Child is and locate her." Dominic gave his boss the details of how the rough swap might work.

Morton stayed silent on the other end while he thought the swap through. "It's worth further investigation. Find out who she is then. However you manage to do that God only knows," he said, "but I'd start with the CCTV at passport control, that is the obvious place. But bring her back alive. We don't want any more dead bodies." He exhaled loudly into Dominic's ear. As Morton hung up, Dominic imagined the man's cigar-tinged halitosis from his exasperation and grimaced at the thought, thankful for the distance.

Dominic made the call back to the office to request CCTV footage of both Dover and Calais passport control. It had been a tiresome case and he was exhausted. Looking after a protected person was not the easiest job at times, particularly when they did stupid things like running off or getting themselves killed so close to when they were needed to give evidence. They made his head hurt and he wondered why he'd ever left his last role. Working in vice had had its ups and downs, but it was a good deal more interesting than babysitting headstrong adults. And it paid better too.

His phone buzzed and a glance at the screen told him it was a colleague, another detective back at the office. "That was quick," he said.

"The footage was already handy apparently. I've sent you a link to it. I thought you'd like to know that you're not the first person to order it, for Dover anyway," said a male voice.

"Oh, who else?"

"A DS Alan Davies. Do you know him?"

"I've heard the name before. So he's got the footage too?"

"Appears so. Anyway, just thought you should know. Your case is proving popular."

And then he was gone.

Was this case ever going to be straight forward? Dominic doubted it and another detective being interested in it wasn't good news. He might already be one step ahead. If that was the case, things could get tricky and Dominic didn't want to have to get Morton to interject his bulk.

He took a deep breath in and let a heavily laden sigh out.

Who else knew?

CHAPTER 57

True to his word, Dean, the pathologist, rang back a couple of hours later. They arranged to meet up at the same pub again but, this time, chat over a decent bar snack and a pint or two. After the day Alan had had searching through other people's belongings in a dark and draughty hangar, he'd been grateful for a hot shower and a change of clothes before heading back out. It hadn't gone unnoticed by Alan that Dean had something he'd rather not say over an unsecure line and wondering what it could be was making Alan's brain matter turn to froth. He was perched at a corner table, halfway down his first pint, when Dean entered, head searching. Alan waved him over with as relaxed a grin as he could muster and waited for him to sit down. Dean glanced at the waiting pint, nodded his appreciation and took a long swig. It could have rivalled Alan's own Olympic guzzle.

"I'm intrigued," Alan said, keen to get his answer and avoiding preamble. He wanted to rub his hands together in anticipation but refrained. The wait was killing him.

"You know I told you about Chief Superintendent Morton dropping by?"

Alan nodded a 'get on with it', his head bobbing furiously, eyes wide.

"Well, he wouldn't confirm that he knew the woman or not, kind of avoided my direct question, and I thought nothing of it. The poor woman could do with a confirmed name and next of kin, mind, but I guess she'll have to wait. Anyway, as I say, I didn't think much of it, but then it dawned on me when you asked about her tattoo." He stopped to take a much smaller mouthful of beer.

Alan waited patiently but couldn't help the "And?" that urgently wanted to leave his mouth.

"And that was what Morton wanted to see too. The inside of her thigh. Now, answer me this: if he didn't know her, how did he know she had a tattoo in such a place? It wasn't like he picked her arm up to look underneath on the off chance. He was *checking* whether it was there or not. And when he saw it, he left almost immediately, without another word."

This was getting deeper and deeper with each day dawning. "And did you check if the tattoo was real?" Alan had to know.

"I did, and yes, it is. Can I ask why you thought it might not be?"

"Because the other missing woman, Susan Smith, had the exact same tattoo, as a temporary transfer, in her luggage. All ready to be applied at some point." Alan sat back and watched Dean's reaction. It was genuine, and similar to what his own had been. And since Dean had come to him for help originally, Alan felt comfortable he could be trusted with such information.

"So those two *are* connected somehow. Yet we know they are not related. That leaves one option," Dean said.

"I agree. They had something planned. And I need to find out what because Susan Smith is gallivanting across France pretending to be Tabitha Child, a woman in the protected-persons programme."

"Shit, you have been busy. And I gather you think Susan could be in danger?"

"I do, yes. But, and here's the tricky part, I think she may be in danger from Tabitha Child's handler too, or at the very least Morton, since you've told me of his reaction. Now they know Tabitha is dead, I'm wondering if they'll figure out Susan and go after her." Alan downed another quarter glass and wiped foam off his upper lip while Dean thought about the situation.

"I doubt it and here's why: they don't know of the tattoo transfer, I'm guessing?"

"No, and they won't. But they might somehow know of Tabitha's passport being used. It's easy enough to check the footage and see a woman who looks a lot like their woman."

"Yeah, but I doubt any officer would use a fake person in a court case, simply because she looked like their protected one, now deceased. She wouldn't have the knowledge to pull it off." He sat thoughtfully for a moment before continuing. "Though the medical evidence would already be on file so no need for further checks, I suppose." He pondered for a moment, "Could it really be pulled off with coaching?"

"Anything's possible. But what's in it for Susan Smith?"

"That's easy. They'll offer her something she can't refuse. Everyone's got a weak spot when the pressure is on. Children, sick parents needing treatment, it's easy enough to find something painful in most people's lives. No matter how ordinary and suburban they might seem."

"You watch too many movies."

Dean shrugged. Both men chewed over what they'd spoken about: could it be done? Was Susan Smith really in danger? It wasn't the first time it had crossed Alan's mind.

"They'd have to be more than dirty to attempt it if that's their viable plan. And proving it, suggesting it even, that's massive. It's career suicide if you go down that track." Dean's voice was full of concern for his friend and colleague.

"I know, and I have no proof, only an inkling at the moment. It fits a theory."

Alan could see two plates of food heading their way. Changing the subject for a moment, he said, "I took the liberty of ordering fish and chips each," as plates piled high with food were placed in front of them. Fat chips sent tiny trails of steam into the air and Dean reached in a picked one up, biting into the end and instantly dropping it back on his plate.

"Damn, that's hot," he said, tossing the small amount he'd bitten off around his mouth to try and cool it. "Thanks, though, I'm ravenous."

"So, what should we do next?"

"We?"

"All right, me. Because the fewer people that know about this the better. I don't trust Morton in the least, and he won't be doing this on his own, there'll be a fall guy in between."

"Don't you think you're reaching a little too far? You've only got my word that he was *looking* for a tattoo. It's not much to go on."

Alan picked up his fork and stabbed a chip, ready. "I hear you. But I've got to take a closer look, because if I'm right, Susan Smith could be in bother. And I've got to try and find her. Though I'm struggling how."

"You're a detective, you'll find a way."

"Thanks for the vote of confidence. But let's keep this between you and me, okay?"

"Fine by me. I wonder who she really was, Tabitha Child. What's her story, do you think?" Dean tucked into his cod, crispy batter crumbling on his plate as he scooped up peas for a tasty forkful. "I'm assuming the tattoo is important then?"

"Oh yes. If you look closely at the centre of it, there's a distinctive first tat that has since been inked around to disguise it – it's been added to. The rose was tastefully done whoever did it. But the original tat? It was the signature of something really rather ugly and I don't want to put you off your meal."

"I'm a pathologist, remember? There's not much I haven't seen mankind do to another human being. My stomach is solid. So, tell me, if you don't mind, what it signified?"

There was no point hiding what had gone on. The supposed ringleaders were in prison, and Tabitha Child had been a remaining victim. He'd helped put them away some years ago. But, like any festering cyst, sometimes a modicum of infection stayed behind after its removal. It seemed that's what had happened here. He wondered if there were still others carrying the inky moniker.

"It was a sign of ownership. Tabitha, or whatever her real name was, had been kept as breeding stock for a time."

"Shit. That explains her pregnancies and no one missing her."

"Quite."

CHAPTER 58

Tabby watched the world whizz by as the car sped out of Paris and down through rural France. Albert had graciously suggested she try Albi, though she knew virtually nothing of the place. He'd said it was a small medieval town; though with its own rather grand cathedral, it was perhaps officially a tiny city. Not on as grand a scale as Paris, but more akin to a picturesque town in Devon. Since they'd made brief introductions, she'd not said another word, choosing instead to relish the gentle hum of the engine. It was making her eyelids droop uncontrollably. Tiredness was catching up with her and being constantly on the move was exhausting. She needed to find a base for a while so she could readjust to her newfound lifestyle and start to relax a little. Her shoulders were constantly taut, like cling film covering salad greens in a bowl at home.

The mere mention of home, even in her mind, sent her recoiling and she moved away from the window slightly, resting her head back as if the motion of doing so would reset the images in her mind. It didn't work. Marcus's face swam in front of her eyes and he wasn't smiling. She wondered what he was doing right then. At work and back in Hong Kong? Drinking red wine and getting drunk at her absence? She doubted it. She doubted he'd understand the reason she'd fled the scene of the accident. She doubted anyone would.

Tabby desperately needed more belongings – the few pieces of clothing she did have needed washing, or tossing – but her funds were running low. Though she'd ditched the phone after Dominic's last call, she still had the credit cards – for a dire emergency, she'd told herself. But looking down at herself and feeling the need to tidy up and eat a decent meal, she was tormented by the thought of a hotel room. Could it do any harm? How would anyone know it was her using the dead woman's card? And, since she'd pay on departure, so what if someone was alerted to the expenditure? She'd be long gone by the time they got there. It was tempting.

Last night, she and the others in the car had stayed north of Toulouse, tiredness overcoming the trio and stopping them from driving on any longer. It had been a long way down. Since Tabby was tagging along, she'd chosen to stick with the group rather than find another way on her own, her options limited. The cheap backpackers' place had been the worst yet, her mattress lumpy, the shower tepid at best. She certainly didn't look like the princess of *The Princess and the Pea*, but she did feel like she'd slept on something knobbly all night, her back voicing its discomfort.

Kirsty was in the back of the car alongside her. It was Will's turn to drive, with Jez riding in the passenger seat and doing directions. Each was quiet, busy in their own worlds, as they made their way south. Once they arrived in Toulouse, she knew she'd have to find another ride and, so far, she'd been lucky with who had picked her up. Kirsty yawned loudly and Tabby turned towards her and smiled a little. "I guess it won't be long until you're at your destination."

"I guess not," she answered, sounding uninterested, bored even, at the prospect. "I think I'd rather be going on further, like you, to Albi or even the coast. It sounds much more fun."

"So what's stopping you?"

"We agreed to go to Toulouse, find work. And Will has a mate there so we can crash with him for a few nights. It's all arranged. Do you have somewhere to stay when you get to Albi?"

"Nothing organised, no. More backpackers' lumpy mattresses and cold showers, I expect, though I've got to get there first."

"You'll be fine. You've got this far," Kirsty said, drifting off a little. Tabby thought the young woman had finished and had turned her gaze out of the window when she added, "You know, I'm sure whatever it is that's bothering you will work its way out in the end. It always does."

Tabby turned quickly at the young woman's observation. Her green eyes held hope and kindness as they connected with her own. The redhead meant well.

"I think it already is," she said, forcing a smile.

Already the time away was starting to have an impact on how she felt, how she viewed things and decided on what was important to her. Life's luxuries that she'd been used to didn't matter so much any more, though a soft bed and hot shower would still be delightful and hard to turn down. But it was the fleeting friendships she'd had over recent days that mattered more, and Tabby wondered about Albert, the older man. He'd been so wise, a delight to travel with, a lot like her grandfather. She thought of the nice lorry driver on her first day alone on the road, and the three that surrounded her now. Each with their own story to tell. What about her own? And the real reason she'd set off to Paris that day. It seemed almost silly now, immature of her. And now Tabitha Child was dead. Her life now in stark contrast to her life only last week.

And next week? It could well be different again.

Tabby opened her mouth and words she wasn't planning on using came tumbling out. "Why don't you come with me, to Albi? Leave the boys to their mate in Toulouse, and tag along with me. I can't promise you bright lights and excitement, but I can offer you female company, if you'd prefer. My schedule is fairly loose at this stage." Tabby smiled, immediately wondering where the hell that had come from. When she'd recovered from the shock of what she'd just suggested, she realised it no longer mattered. No one knew her real name, no one knew where she was and she was hardly leaving any kind of trail if someone was indeed looking for her. France, in fact, Europe, was a big place to get and stay lost in. The time away was healing her.

Until she was ready to go back. And deal with her issue.

Green eyes searched Tabby's as Kirsty's mind ticked over.

"Why not!"

CHAPTER 59

Alan Davies left the pub deep in thought. The case seemed to be getting murkier and murkier, and the more he found out, the more it disturbed him. The knowledge that Tabitha Child been part of some macabre baby-breeding idealism was hard to imagine. But she'd had several pregnancies, had the distinctive tattoo, and was in the protected-persons programme. It was likely the reason nobody had come forward and claimed her – she was in this world totally on her own.

Alan sat in his car but failed to start the engine. His head was spinning with so many unanswered questions.

"What the hell was Tabitha going to Paris for in the first place?" he asked himself out loud. "And add to that, what was Susan Smith going to do in Paris? Because they quite clearly knew one another and were up to something together. And maybe Susan is *still* planning to do whatever it was that they'd arranged between them. Where had they arranged to stay in Paris? What was nearby to interest them? There must be something, some way I can figure it out." Alan had always found it easier to say his questions out loud to himself, but a young couple must have overheard him as they walked by, because the woman glanced back over her shoulder and smiled his way. Even though it was dark outside, the lights in the pub car park made it easy to be seen. Suddenly he was self-conscious about having a one-sided conversation where he sat and decided to do so while he drove. The engine caught and he pulled out of the car park.

"I need someone to bounce ideas off, preferably right now," he said to the dark road ahead of him. He'd been alone in this case since it started because really Susan Smith was just another missing person. And with the crash, other officers and detectives were tied up with much bigger issues needing their attention. He wondered about Bridget. She was always a night owl; would she mind some company? He asked Siri to dial her number and a moment later Bridget's voice filled the car in her normal welcoming manner.

"What's up?" She said brightly. He wondered if she took uppers to stay awake as much as she did. He'd never seen any signs that she used them.

"I'm sorry to ring you, I know it's a bit late, but I could do with a hand on something. Are you busy?" Alan asked, hoping that she'd say she wasn't.

"I don't have a social life – well, not your idea of social, you know that," Bridget said abruptly, and Alan could understand why that was. She could be scary if you didn't know her and she didn't allow men to get to know her very well. She favoured the one-night stand more. No ties.

"I need to bounce ideas around and after what I've just found out from the pathologist I need to get moving somehow. But quietly."

"Well, you've got my attention now. If you need to do it quietly, you'd better come over."

"I'm not far away," he said. "I'll be there shortly. And Bridget? This is between you and me, okay?" But she was gone already, as was customary with Bridget: to the point if it would suffice. Alan smiled to himself. Bridget was one woman you wanted on your side, particularly when you needed something done without raising any eyebrows. Or flags.

Bridget lived in a flat on the third floor, though there were only three floors. By the time he'd walked up the stairs, she was waiting for him in the doorway, or her foot was in the doorway. He pushed the door open and thanked her again for the seeing him at such a late hour.

"You've done that already. What is it you need?" Straight down to business.

"I need to talk it through with a bright set of ears. But you will need to put a different head on if we're going to find the answer."

"What's wrong with my current head?"

"Well, if I said you needed to think like a girl, you'd be offended, but I need you to think like a girl."

"You're right, I'm offended," she said flatly. "What do you think I am, a hermaphrodite?"

"Well, I can see you're all girl, Bridget, but sometimes you don't act like one. But anyway, can we skip all this and get down to it?" He realised the mistake in his words as soon as they'd slipped out of his mouth and Bridget wiggled her eyebrows. Alan hoped he wasn't blushing and ploughed on, ignoring his faux pas. "So here's the scenario," he said, making himself comfortable. "You're going to Paris and you have a liaison planned with another woman."

Her eyebrows wiggled again and Bridget almost cracked a smile. "Go on," she said.

"I'm not sure what kind of liaison, but two women arranged to meet in Paris. I say arranged to meet in Paris, and not before, because we now know that both Susan Smith and Tabitha Child knew one another. And whatever they were planning, they didn't do it on the train beforehand because they weren't sat together. I'm guessing when I say this, but I'd say it was part of keeping a low profile."

"Do we know which hotel they were headed to, then? Because that will give us an idea of what's in the surrounding area, where they could possibly be going, what they could be doing."

"That's a good start, and I'm hoping you've got an easy way of finding out because ringing every hotel in Paris is a massive job."

"I can help with that. Leave it to me." It was Alan's turn to wiggle eyebrows. Bridget had some unorthodox methods of finding information, and scraping websites to find out the hotel booking would probably take all of ten seconds to do. It was best not to ask about her methods in any detail. It was more of a hobby than authorised police work. She got her laptop and immediately started tapping the keys furiously while Alan watched on – not that it made any sense to him. A timer rotated as the information loaded. When it finally settled, there was the relevant information on the screen. It wasn't so much the name and address of the hotel that caught his eye, it was the name on the booking. And a booking for two separate rooms.

"Well, I'll be damned," said Alan.

CHAPTER 60

"So they really did know one another then," Bridget said. "You were right. What made you suspect, by the way?"

"It's just something I found in Susan's luggage that made me wonder. It seemed a bit too wild for them to be complete strangers."

"I guess you're not going to tell me what it is," said Bridget. Then, "Come on, you can trust me – otherwise you wouldn't be here now."

She had a point.

"There was a temporary tattoo transfer in an envelope in Susan's bag, identical to the one that Tabitha has on her upper thigh, and that's what made me think there was something going on, as you would. They were obviously planning on swapping, maybe each pretending to be the other person, and that tattoo was vital if she was going to pass as Tabitha. The problem I have now is that the original tattoo on Tabitha leads to a horrific set-up that I'd rather not go into right now. Trust me on that, it's not something either of us wants to get involved in."

Bridget nodded her understanding. "Well, I guess we should ring the hotel and find out who actually booked it and when, because Marcus Smith's name on the booking doesn't mean it was actually him.

"Let's hope they tell us without a warrant. Never mind it being way outside our jurisdiction."

Alan watched Bridget pick the phone up, dial and wait to be connected. He knew exactly when the call was answered because her whole stance changed and a huge bright smile appeared on her face. It would be a male on the line and Bridget was about to turn on her best charm. Alan listened as an eloquent and fluent French Bridget went to town and asked what he assumed would be relevant questions. He had no idea on the actual content of the conversation and was only able to pick up certain words. Studying French at school had been a long time ago. When the call came to an end and she hung up, he had never seen a smile as bright as the one facing him now.

"So?" he said, impatiently prodding her along.

"So, get this, Susan Smith herself booked the room. She booked both rooms actually, one for herself and the other for her friend Tabitha Child, which we kind of assumed. So we've got that confirmed. She specified two rooms that looked across to the Eiffel Tower, that's why there's a record it was Susan that booked it. She did the online transaction then called ahead. But – this is the beautiful part – the receptionist apologised at having to charge the credit card for a no-show as is customary with hotels. You hold your room with a credit card and since the two women never showed... So Marcus will know now as he'll have access to the credit-card account. He'll have seen where she was staying and that there were two rooms. So I wonder what he's been thinking and why he hasn't said anything to us. But that's immaterial. Because it gets better."

"How so?" asked Alan.

"Well, apparently there's a package still waiting for Tabitha Child that arrived a couple of days before she was due, and it's still sat in a pigeonhole waiting to be picked up. Now, I didn't think he would forward it on so I asked for it to be held and told him I'd pick it up."

"Bridget, you're a genius!" he said. "I wonder what's in it, and how the hell are we going to get hold of it now?"

"Fancy a trip to Paris?" Bridget questioned.

"We'll never get that authorised. So, while it's a wonderful idea, there's not a cat in hell's chance that you and I are going to France. But you know what?"

"Do tell," she said in a deflated tone.

"I know somebody in France already and I'm betting they would be happy to get on the train and pick up that package."

"Securely?"

"Of that, I couldn't be sure. But how else are we going to get it?"

"How about if we send in the local police?"

"No, I think that would raise too many questions. What did you say to the guy anyway? I assumed it was a guy?"

"I merely said that I was a friend of Susan's and I had been meant to join the two of them but couldn't. And since my friends wouldn't be heading back, I asked if it would it be okay to retrieve the package – he doesn't need to know that I'm a police officer, it makes things too complicated sometimes – and he said yes, he didn't see why not. So I'm kind of thinking we need to get that package picked up pronto before he changes his mind or someone else makes the decision for him."

"Agreed. We'll come back to that in a moment. So now we know where they were staying, what part of town, we just need to figure out what they could possibly have been doing. And the Eiffel Tower is significant. The tattoo must be involved because why else would Susan Smith have it?"

"Was there anything of interest in Tabitha's suitcase when you looked?"

"Not really, although both suitcases were identical. The one thing that Tabitha had was a wig, a short brown wig."

"What kind of style?" Bridget asked, intrigued.

"A bit like Coco Chanel, I suppose, a short bob."

Bridget cocked her head in question. "My sister is a hairdresser; I grew up having my hair done, being a guinea pig. What else?"

"Nothing, just a change of clothes or two, black stilettos, black dress in each, the tattoo and the wig. They were travelling light for two women going away for the weekend."

"I'm going to do some research on the dance halls. Call it gut instinct but since we have nothing else to go on... Those girls all wear wigs and look identical."

"You go with dance halls, but what else would a woman want to wear a wig for? Bridget, you're a woman, why would you possess a short-haired wig in your wardrobe? And, more importantly, why would you take a wig on your trip to Paris, in your luggage? Particularly if you're not a dancer."

Bridget thought for a moment. "Because I want to disguise myself, obviously," she said slowly. "Or maybe I don't want someone to see the real me while I do something out of *my* ordinary. When you wear a wig, it becomes almost like a mask, I suppose. Like certain clothes make you feel different: severe, flirty or powerful. Like Superman with his undies. Inhibitions dissolve. I wonder..." she said thoughtfully, furrowing two fine blonde eyebrows.

"What are you thinking?"

"That maybe we have one bored female that's gone off to Paris for a bit of razzle-dazzle of her own."

"But that won't work because you've got the wrong woman there with the wig. It was Tabitha that had the wig, Susan had the tattoo."

"Unless," said Bridget, something dawning on her, eyes opening wide with a smile spreading across her face, "these two women knew one another, yet they didn't sit together on the train to Paris. They stayed in the same hotel, paid for by the same woman, but in separate rooms. And they've each got something to disguise themselves with. Do you know what I'm thinking?"

"No clue," said Alan.

"I'm thinking these two women were swapping places for some reason. Or for a time. The tattoo was to make Susan more like Tabitha, and the wig because Tabitha *didn't* want to look like herself or Susan. Does that make sense?"

"I'm not sure it does entirely, but I see your line of thinking. It's not necessarily as straightforward as we might think. You're saying if Tabitha didn't want to be Tabitha and didn't want to be Susan, but wanted another disguise to be somebody else... Do you think there is a third person in this that we haven't come across yet?"

"I've no clue, I'm simply putting the notion out there. But it's obvious Susan was going to be Tabitha and we need to find out why. And Tabitha was going to be someone else, and if there isn't a third person involved, then how about this: Tabitha was going to be *something* important to Susan. But since Tabitha in now deceased, that tattoo is still in her Susan's luggage, and of course the train crashed so the swap never happened."

"What in heaven's name were the two of them up to? And with Susan out there, is she still trying to complete whatever it was they'd planned? Without the tattoo?"

"We need that package. Call your contact."

CHAPTER 61

It was nearly 1am when Chrissy's phone rang and, in the silence of the hotel bedroom, it shrilled like an air-raid siren going off. Chrissy heard it immediately, but then she didn't sleep with earplugs in and an eyemask over her face. Julie, on the other hand, did both of those things. Chrissy hoped it wasn't an emergency back home – it was her general ringtone, but who else would be calling so late? And if it was a spam call, they were going to get the wrath of Chrissy Livingstone tenfold. She hoped it was the latter. Sliding to open the call before the whole hotel woke up, she could see it wasn't Adam or one of the boys. Chrissy wasn't expecting Detective Alan Davies either – something was adrift.

"Hello," she said quietly. Julie still hadn't stirred. "This is Chrissy Livingstone. Is something wrong, detective?"

"No. And I'm sorry to disturb you so late, but I wanted to catch you. Are you still in France by chance?"

"Yes, why?"

"There's been a bit of a development in your case. It could well be linked to another as I've mentioned once before. I can't say anything about the other, but I wondered if you were heading to Paris by chance."

Chrissy couldn't help smiling: was Susan in Paris then?

"What's the development and what's in Paris? Susan?"

"A package actually. It's expecting to be picked up and quickly but..."

"You can't get authorisation, or too much tape, and while I'm here..." She let the words hang in the air. It was déjà vu, like the USB drive. And that had proved useful. "What's in it for my investigation? Apart from the expense." If he needed a favour, she needed something back.

Alan had been prepared for the question, "Susan had been scheduled to check into a hotel for a couple of nights. There is a package at the hotel that is waiting to be picked up and I'm hoping it will give us another clue to follow.

Chrissy didn't need to think for long. "Deal. Text the address and who I need to ask for, and I'm on my way first thing."

"One more thing. Do you or your sister speak French fluently?"

"I speak four languages fluently, including French. Why do you ask?"

"Because my contact is expecting a gushing, French-speaking woman, and you're it."

"I've played worse parts. I'll call you when I have it. Can I open it before you actually receive it?"

"I'm afraid you can, yes, unfortunately for me. In fact, I'm relying on you to do the right thing here. Can you take some photos of the package and the contents, and email them to me?"

"Of course." She was checking the fastest way to get there on her laptop as they spoke. "There are a couple of trains around 6 am so we'll be in Paris around 8.30. I'll keep you posted."

"Excellent. And Chrissy?"

"Yes?"

"Keep your wits about you."

He rang off. Now that had her wondering.

Behind her, Julie finally stirred, mumbled something incoherently, then fell silent once more. A package intrigued Chrissy and as she climbed back into bed and set an early alarm call, she wondered how its contents might help them find Susan, now known as Tabby. She hoped it contained good news. Turning the lamp out, she slipped back under the covers. It would be another hour until sleep finally came and she could no longer hear the gentle snores of her sister in the bed beside her.

When the alarm went off just after 5 am, Chrissy was already awake, having spent a fitful night tossing and turning. She'd have felt better by not going back to sleep at all. The call had only been four hours ago. She rubbed the grit from her eyes and padded across to awaken Julie, who was still blissfully unaware of the adventure ahead of them both. Shaking her gently wasn't enough, it appeared, so she upped the pressure to firm. Finally, there was breakthrough. A slender, well-looked-after hand slipped the eyemask up to her forehead and Chrissy couldn't help but wonder how her sister still looked so immaculate lying in bed in her nightdress. She didn't have a hair out of place.

"Do you sleep in a hairnet?" Chrissy asked, looking closer though there was nothing visible.

"Why are you up so early, what's happened?" Julie enquired, stretching and glancing at the clock.

"Get up and I'll tell you as we go. But we're booked on the 6.15 am train to Paris so get a move on. Throw your things back in your case and we'll leave it at left luggage in Gare du Nord. I'm not sure if we're coming back today or not." Julie stared without a word. It didn't appear to be computing. "Julie! Come on, get up!"

"All right, I heard you the first time," she moaned, heading for the bathroom where she splashed water on her face and brushed her teeth.

"You'll have to do your make-up on the train. The taxi will be here soon, though without your big bag we could have walked it." It wasn't a dig, merely an observation. Chrissy threw her own belongings into her bag and made a start on Julie's, pulling out clean underwear, trousers and a blouse for her to wear. They'd have to do and would go with her newly acquired walking sandals. The rest she packed up ready to go. No doubt there'd be complaints, having her clothes chosen for her like a child would have had, but there wasn't time to work by Julie's schedule. Not if they were to catch the early train.

Twenty minutes later they were on the platform waiting. As Chrissy recited the conversation between herself and DS Alan Davies, Julie's eyes lit up with excitement.

"How exciting!" she exclaimed.

Chrissy hoped it would, in fact, be so. Maybe she'd been wrong about Susan staying in the city after all.

CHAPTER 62

It was significantly easier for two attractive women to get a lift than it was for two guys and they struck lucky within minutes of trying. Even if it was a tight squeeze in the lorry's cab. Kirsty opted for the middle seat, sitting close to the driver, who, in this case, also turned out to be a woman. Somewhat big and butch with close-cropped grey hair and tattoos around each wrist, she seemed pleasant enough, welcoming the two aboard with a broad, toothy grin.

"Can't leave you two girls out there all alone. You'll be safer with me," she'd quipped as they settled in and fastened seatbelts. "Who smacked your face, love?" she asked Tabby. The sudden and direct question threw her off balance a little – she'd only just met the woman. Instinctively, she touched her brow area, the lump had gone down but she knew it was still a rainbow of colours, mainly purple and yellow. "A man was it?" the woman prodded.

"No, it wasn't a man actually. A bit of an accident in a vehicle. I banged my head."

The driver flicked her chin at her as if to say 'whatever', then introduced herself as Maureen.

"I'm Kirsty and this is Tabby," Kirsty replied by way of their own introduction. Would there be a cat comment coming?

"Tabby. I had a tabby cat once, called it Henry, though she was a girl." At least the name Susan hadn't brought up everybody's 'Susan' experience like her new name did. But then that was then and this was now, and she didn't much feel like a Susan any more. Maureen carried on, "What's in Albi for you both, then?" Maureen had pulled back on to the road and they rumbled along, gaining speed.

"Work and a room. For the rest of the summer, we're hoping." Tabby let Kirsty do the talking.

"Sounds great. I did that one time, many summers ago. It wasn't Albi, it was Paris and I had an absolute ball. Heck of a time actually. I made ice creams for the whole summer." Was there a reason for this or was she making polite conversation? "I was a whole lot younger then," she said. There was something sad in the way she spoke that Tabby picked up on. Intrigued, she probed with a question of her own.

"And what happened?" she asked.

"I got in a spot of bother," Maureen offered, face focused on the road ahead. "But that's history, so keep yourselves out of mischief is my advice," she added hurriedly.

"You can't tell us half a story," Kirsty whined. "What was the spot of bother?"

Maureen must have been considering what or how much to tell, because it was a long moment before she spoke again. Tabby was about to change the subject with something mundane but didn't get the chance.

"Ah, what the bother. I've long past cared what people think of me and you might learn from it, though at your age you should know better anyway. I was still in my twenties when I did what I did."

"I'm still in my twenties," Kirsty announced. "Twenty-nine in fact."

Maureen rolled her eyes in a 'doesn't really count' kind of way and smiled at Tabby, who was still quiet.

"So, what was it?" Kirsty seemed to be pushing it a little but there was intrigue for Tabby also.

"I had a great body back then, you understand. None of the soft covering of my duvet body you see before you now. So I did some pole dancing to make ends meet. And, well, I didn't stick to the poles." Her mouth folded in a tight smile as if to say, 'there, I've told you and I'm not proud.'

"And what was the bother, then? Plenty of women do stuff like that, particularly students at uni."

"The crowd I worked for. They weren't the sweetest of individuals and could be pushy. I'm a strong-minded woman and didn't appreciate being told what I could and couldn't do so when things got a bit heated one day and one of them took a swing at me, I defended myself. He smacked a couple of my teeth out so I stuck my penknife in his groin. It was a shame I missed his main artery – the pig."

That shut the two women up and the cab fell quiet for a time as they processed the scenario.

"I'm guessing he lived?" from Kirsty.

"Yes, he did. But I had to leave town in a hurry so I've spent a bit of time on the run I suppose you could say. At least there was no prison time. I dare say if I'd killed him, it would have been a different outcome. And I went straight from then on. No more toilet walls or car seats for me."

"How long did you survive? On the run, I mean?" asked Tabby. Maureen looked across at her and for a moment Tabby felt like the woman was searching inside her soul. Could Maureen sense she too was on the run? Had she noticed the signs?

"All of a month. I remember being both terrified and thrilled all at the same time, but I was low on funds and wasn't about to go back to selling myself. My options were limited and well, after the initial thrill and excitement, I figured I should head back home and start again. So back to Leeds I went – that was one hell of a culture shock after what I'd been doing in Paris, let me tell you!" Maureen's laugh sounded like she'd smoked far too many unfiltered cigarettes in her time, and the rough gravelly sound finished with a throat-clearing cough.

"And did you settle in? At Leeds, I mean?"

"We all adjust to our surroundings easier than we think we might and before long, it was as if I'd always been there. Take your old slippers. They were new once, felt a little stiff for a while, but a week later, they fit your feet perfectly. Life isn't much different really."

Tabby thought about that. Had she had enough of life sleeping in lumpy beds and missing out on proper meals and hot showers? And for what? A crazy notion that she could be someone else for a while, take another woman's identity and do her own thing, be someone more exciting? And how was that working out?

But her old life held no appeal.

No, if she ever went back, it would be for a different life. It had to be, for her own sanity.

CHAPTER 63

Maureen's words were still ringing in her ears as they approached yet another backpackers' accommodation. Tabby hoped the water would be hot and the bed soft. How difficult could it be?

"She was a hard case, wasn't she?" Kirsty said as they headed through the main entrance and pressed the buzzer at the tiny reception area. A wooden interior that had been stained somewhere between dark oak and rotting tree bark, it felt like a dungeon before they'd even got both feet inside. An older woman, who wore an old-fashioned housedress apron and was almost bent double, shuffled into the tiny room and did her best to look up at them both. The act looked awkward, but her voice was strong and clear.

"*Bonjour.*"

The girls greeted her back and Kirsty ordered two bunks for one night only. Until they'd sampled the accommodation, there was little point in committing themselves. Tabby knew she'd be staying, come what may. There was little choice. Kirsty might feel comfortable crashing on a stranger's sofa, but that was not on Tabby's agenda. Not until she got desperate. After each had paid for their own bed, Tabby announced she was taking a shower and then would be off job hunting. There must be at least one café that required some casual labour and didn't mind paying cash in hand. Since she only had a passport and credit card, and didn't have any of Tabitha Child's documents with tax details on, working legitimately was not an option. There was time to figure that out later. But right now, she needed an income.

"Great, good idea. You go first, and I'll follow." The two girls headed towards their allocated dorm-style room and threw themselves down on their bunks to test them. To Tabby's surprise and delight, hers was considerably more comfortable than anything she'd occupied previously – since she'd started with her new life anyway. She closed her eyes and was tempted to take a nap but sat straight back up again. If she was going to get earning, it wasn't going to happen lying on her back. Tabby smiled at her own words: many women, Maureen included, had indeed earned their keep from lying on their backs, though it wasn't something she could see herself doing. She thought about Maureen's tale of woe earlier, and how the woman had ended up stabbing her boss in the groin. Why had she had a penknife on her at that time? Tabby wondered. Did she carry it all the time? Should Tabby get one herself, for self-defence? Perhaps when she'd got an income. It seemed sensible. Grabbing a few toiletries and clothes from her bag, Tabby said she could be taking a long shower if it was as good as the bed.

"Take your time," called Kirsty, settling back on her own bunk. "I might be asleep when you get back, I'm as tired as you are." And Tabby was gone.

As soon as the coast was clear, Kirsty wriggled off her bunk and moved straight for Tabby's bag. Keeping an eye on the door in case her friend had forgotten something and came back, she deftly rummaged with one hand until she found what she was looking for. With the wallet in her hand, she scurried back to her own bed to examine the contents, ready at a moment's notice to stuff it rapidly under her pillow if the need arose. The sound of water running told her Tabby was now otherwise occupied.

Kirsty checked how much cash it contained and then examined the rest of the contents. Inside the zipped-up change pouch was a gold bracelet and Kirsty felt the weight of it in her hand. It would have cost a fortune. Turning it over, she strained to read the inscription: *Susan and Melanie Marchment. Forever always.* She tossed it back inside. There were two credit cards, both in the name of Tabitha Child, and apart from a couple of other loyalty cards, there was nothing else of interest. But either credit card was. Kirsty sat thoughtful for a moment. A woman hitchhiking through France on her own, with a story to tell, wouldn't necessarily travel with credit cards, that she's not using. She'd carry more cash. In Kirsty's mind, that answered one of the questions she had about her new friend: she wasn't on the run from the law.

"Maybe she's on some sort of digital detox or something," she said under her breath. "Living on as few basics as possible. Another bored snowflake trying to 'find herself'. Give me strength," she finished, shaking her head in disappointment. Kirsty slipped the wallet back into Tabby's bag, but only after she'd removed one of the credit cards. The signature on the back looked simple enough, a 'T' and 'Child'. It couldn't have been any easier. And if the transactions were low enough, she might not even need that. Hopefully, by the time Tabby realised there were charges other than her own, she'd be back home, her boring life resumed. Kirsty smiled at her own idea. If Tabby was refraining from using the card, she'd have no reason to suspect anything was amiss. But who were Susan and Melanie Marchment? They sounded like lovers.

On impulse, she slipped out of their room and headed swiftly towards the town centre. Her plan was simple: a decent meal. If that went without a hitch, there'd be a purchase for herself, something she could hide easily under her own clothes if she needed to, until she was back in the safety of the shower room. There was no need for Tabby to know.

Finding the card was a godsend. It meant that, given the opportunity, Kirsty now had access to funds for small luxuries, like fresh undies and a burger here and there, all without spending a penny of her own. For her first outing, she didn't have much time to spare so she slipped inside the first café she came to and placed her order: a simple steak and fries.

"May I pay now? Only I'm in a bit of a rush," she explained to the young waiter. There was no attempt at even the tiniest bit of French, but it wasn't a problem. He understood perfectly.

"Certainly," he said, and presented her with a mobile payment machine. Kirsty tapped the card and waited, not daring to breathe. It couldn't have gone any better. There was no need for a PIN or signature. Knowing it worked, there was no need to be greedy all in one day. Tomorrow, there would be some alone time she could make productive use of.

Kirsty could never have known just what she'd started rolling in the background.

CHAPTER 64

The train from Calais to Paris was as crowded as any other commuter train headed into a major city for morning rush hour. Chrissy and Julie managed to get a seat each and, with the journey being long enough, Chrissy was glad of being able to rest a little, having hardly slept the night before. There was nothing more she could do now until they got to their destination. But her nerves felt like sharp razor blades in her body and the caffeine she'd consumed was already making her jingle. If she fell asleep for an hour, she knew she'd feel worse when she woke up.

Detective Alan Davies had not mentioned anything other than picking up a package and the name of the person to ask for. She hoped the man would be on duty. It was a long way to come to be refused what they were so anxious to see the contents of. Chrissy glanced across at Julie who was artfully putting on her make-up. A natural beauty, she attracted glances from various men as she applied pink to her beautifully shaped lips. Chrissy smiled inwardly. Wearing more casual make-up than usual actually made her sister look more youthful and less formal, less rigid, if that was the right word. Perhaps Chrissy could encourage her to relax a little more before they headed home. Subconsciously she rubbed her own lips together. They needed moisturising.

By the time they arrived at Gare du Nord the place was heaving. Commuters from all parts of France were descending on the one spot. Chrissy helped her sister pull her bag off the train and they headed to find a place where they could store it for the day – until they knew what their plans were. They could well be staying in town overnight or they might find themselves moving on to somewhere else, following the trail that the next clue gave them. She made a mental note to ring Adam later. She hadn't spoken to him for a day or two, only exchanged texts, and she was missing both him and the boys. If she was staying away much longer, she'd have to make plans for her boys back home. She couldn't just leave them all to fend for themselves. Since Adam had a stressful job too, she needed to make sure she pulled her own weight, even if she was absent. She hoped they were eating healthily and not living on junk food.

After dropping the bag at 'left luggage' they headed out towards the taxi rank and joined the queue, which, thankfully, was moving relatively fast. When their turn finally arrived, she gave the taxi driver the address of the hotel and they both sat back to watch the streets of Paris fly by the window. It was non-stop hustle and bustle, and Chrissy admired how the local women dressed stylishly no matter where they were going for the day. Smart yet relaxed, not rigid navy as many of their British counterparts would have been, they looked glamorous, tanned, and in good shape.

It wasn't far to the hotel and as Julie paid the driver, Chrissy stood on the pavement and took in the surroundings. It was an older part of town and the architecture was beautiful, like many of the European cities she'd visited. The Eiffel Tower stood majestically in the near distance – not that there would be time for sightseeing. They were on a mission and the longer they left it, the further away Susan Smith was likely to be. Whatever was in the package to be picked up, Chrissy hoped it would provide another clue as to what had happened and where Susan was headed. They'd both assumed that she had simply been going on a shopping trip while Marcus was away, but they had no evidence that that was indeed the case. It was only an assumption. Perhaps she'd been attending to something else and that something had led her to run. There was so much they didn't know.

Chrissy glanced at her watch and hoped the person they needed was on duty already and that there wouldn't be any fuss handing the package over. As the taxi pulled away and Julie joined Chrissy on the pavement, she turned to her sister and said, "We need to find the ladies room first so you can work some of your make-up magic on me and I don't look like your ugly sister," Chrissy said with a half-smile.

"You don't look like my ugly sister, you look like *my* sister and you're beautiful just like I am," she said, fluttering eyelashes comically. Chrissy had played many parts in her time and spoke French perfectly, but the glamour side she didn't possess. They needed that package so she was going to have to turn on the charm tenfold.

In the ladies room, Julie took out a hairbrush and handed it to Chrissy so she could pull her hair into better shape. If she was going to be a flirty, Parisian-looking lady with a somewhat English accent, there was work to do. Having earlier found the largest garment she could from Julie's bag, she now dressed somewhat more smartly than she had for the journey down. Being more accustomed to cotton trousers and a T-shirt, she felt claustrophobic in the rather formal dress.

"Don't put too much make-up on, I don't want to look like a clown," Chrissy had said before Julie had even started applying the light foundation to her face.

"I know what I'm doing, sweetie," she said. "I do my own every day and I look nice, don't I?"

"I'm just saying."

"It would have been easier if I'd just done the acting part," Julie said. "Then you wouldn't need to feel so uncomfortable. I can see already that you hate it."

"But you don't speak French," Chrissy said.

"I don't need French to get what I need when I've got eyelashes like these," Julie said adamantly, demonstrating that they were in fact perfect.

"We can't take any chances. We're in France and he's expecting someone French-speaking, and that's me." Chrissy was matter of fact; she didn't want to mess this up, it was too important.

"Still, my lashes might come in useful as a fall-back plan."

Chrissy left the comment as the last word to Julie. It wasn't worth bugging her for.

Two minutes later, Chrissy was unrecognisable after the expert makeover. She looked at herself in the huge gilt mirror, turning from side to side, checking out Julie's handiwork and marvelling at how it transformed her own face. Now she looked a lot like one of the stylish women she had seen on the taxi ride in: stylish, glamorous and ready for her day ahead. Playing a part was all about getting your head in the right space and she rubbed her pink lips together then ran her hand down her front to remove imaginary creases and loose hair. Chrissy Livingstone was ready to go.

"Wish me luck," she said.

"I'll be right behind you."

CHAPTER 65

Chrissy approached the front desk, asked to speak to the contact she'd been given and waited. A moment later an older man, smartly dressed in a black suit and shiny silver tie, smiled graciously as he made his way across to Chrissy Livingstone.

"*Bonjour madame*," he said in a voice as smooth as old-fashioned velvet. It held a certain richness and he suited his surroundings perfectly.

"*Bonjour, je suis ici pour prendre un colis au nom de Tabitha Child.*"

Chrissy quickly introduced herself and told the man what it was that she was picking up. She was a friend of Tabitha Child, who sadly hadn't made it after being involved in a train crash, and Chrissy was here to pick up the package that was waiting for her.

"One moment please," the man said with a gracious smile and a slight bow as he returned back to the office that he'd come from only moments ago. A few seconds later he returned with the package, which was nothing more than an A4-size Jiffy envelope. It was hardly going to be the Crown jewels inside, but Chrissy and Julie both glanced at the small package with interest. Julie kept her distance, not saying a word. With Chrissy's performance, it seemed that Julie wouldn't be needed after all.

"*Merci beaucoup*," said Chrissy. She too could be gracious and, without wanting to appear in a rush or to engage in further conversation after she'd got what she'd come for, smiled pleasantly. The two ladies slowly made their way back to the main entrance. Neither of them said a word. Once out on the pavement, Chrissy sucked city air into her lungs like a smoker before exhaling, closing her eyes almost in pleasure. It couldn't have gone any smoother.

"Let's find somewhere to sit down and have a coffee," said Chrissy matter-of-factly. The two women turned left and entered the first café they came to. It was perfectly Parisian, a place for the locals. Adrenaline was circulating fast in Chrissy's veins and the spike of caffeine to come would send her into another orbit, but she was excited that the package would contain something of use. A waitress took their order.

"Are you going to open it or sit and stare at it?" Julie asked. "Because if you don't, we'll never know what's inside it."

"I know Alan Davies said we could open it, but I'm thinking if there's something in here that can be used in a court case, say, we shouldn't contaminate it."

"Whatever are you talking about? We're looking for Susan, a missing friend, not drug smuggling. There won't be a court case."

"I know but it all seems a little more sinister now. And look at the name on the front: Tabitha Child. Who is this woman and how on earth does she know Susan?" she said, reaching into her bag for the spare pair of latex gloves she always carried. She slipped them on.

"Just open the package and you'll soon see whatever it is," Julie said, sounding impatient. Chrissy flipped it over and carefully peeled away the seal. She could feel bubble wrap from the outside squishiness in her hand, suggesting there was something fragile that needed protecting. Something that needed more than just a regular paper envelope. With the seal fully open, Chrissy pressed both creased-edge sides together slightly so that she could create a larger hole to view what was inside.

"Come on," said Julie, drumming her fingers.

Chrissy tipped the contents carefully on to the table in front of them. Both women gasped out loud at the same time at the realisation of what they were looking at. Chrissy picked up each item for closer examination.

"I wasn't expecting that," said Chrissy. "I don't know quite what I was expecting, but I certainly wasn't expecting that."

"Neither was I," said Julie. "Who the hell is Tabitha Child and what does she want with this lot? What are we going to do?"

"I think this takes things up another level, don't you? And I think Detective Davies needs to get himself a bit more involved, because this is a lot more than a woman going missing."

"I agree. We're out of our depth."

"Well, if he's got any sense, he'll get straight on a plane and meet us because finding Susan just got a whole lot more important. But I won't tell him over the telephone what we found. There could be someone listening. I'll email him, like he suggested."

Julie was about to roll her eyes at the suggestion but considered what her sister had said and thought it plausible. Under the circumstances. The two women stared at the contents laid out on the table. Chrissy prepared to take photos. The package contained a complete set of personal documents: passport, credit cards, birth certificate. And all in the name of Susan Smith – but with Tabitha Child's photo.

She'd been planning on taking another woman's identity.

CHAPTER 66

Detective Alan Davies was buried in paperwork, trying to play catch-up with other cases on his workload. It seemed endless, but each new case created piles of it and every day brought fresh victims of crime. A sad fact. His phone ringing was a welcome distraction. It was Chrissy Livingstone and he swiped to accept the call. He couldn't resist smiling, even though she couldn't see him. He was warming to the woman.

"DS Alan Davies," he announced in a sing-song voice.

"Detective, it's Chrissy."

"And good afternoon to you," he said jovially. "Early afternoon at least," he added, glancing at his computer screen. "Are you in Paris still?"

"We are, yes. And we have the package." She wasn't giving anything away, not over the phone.

"And, what is it?"

"I can't tell you over the phone, I'm afraid. Or should I say, I'm not willing to say over the phone."

Alan readjusted himself in his chair. The fake leather squeaked unhelpfully beneath him. He hoped Julie hadn't heard it and thought him rude.

"And why is that?"

"Because of what Tabitha Child had, or was having, should I say, delivered. And on that, who is this woman? I gather you already know of her?"

There was no way Alan was going to say who Tabitha was at this point, if ever. But he was now intrigued as to what the woman had sent or had organised to be sent. Lots of people addressed and posted items to themselves, considering it a safer option than carrying it, if that's what she'd done. Alternatively, without seeing what was inside the package or the package itself, anyone could have dropped it off for delivery. Even Susan Smith herself. But he couldn't help the intrigue building in his gut.

"I don't know much about her, save for she's part of another case for another colleague." It wasn't a lie. Should he mention she'd been on the train? He searched his head for the answer – would it be helpful or be more harmful than good? Maybe they already knew?

"Since she was meeting Susan," Chrissy said. "I'm thinking Tabitha might have been on the same train. I'm pretty certain they were travelling together."

Damn it. Alan wondered how she could have figured that out, got confirmation of what he already knew. Private investigators didn't play by the same set of rules as police did, but then they also didn't have access to the same tools. If Chrissy had a contact at the police that was divulging information, they could lose their job searching databases for unrelated cases. An officer couldn't do a background check on a Tinder date any more – it was considered a violation of the person's privacy and a waste of police resources – so how could they find out?

Chrissy let out an exaggerated sigh. He wasn't going to confirm or deny. She moved on: "I'll email the photos now. Stand by."

Alan waited, listening for the faint whoosh sound at her end, notification the email was sent. He refreshed his inbox and the email landed almost immediately. He quickly scanned each image. It was his turn for a heavy sigh.

"Text me where to meet you," he said. "I'm on my way." Then hung up.

He tossed his phone to his desktop and it clattered loudly before hurling itself on to the floor. "Damn and damn again!" he yelled, reaching to retrieve it.

"What's got your undies in a twist?" Bridget called his way. Her glasses perched on the end of her nose and green eyes peered over the upper rim at him. She'd make an excellent school headmistress in a TV sketch.

"I've got to get to Paris. This case is getting heavy."

"Well, I'm going to add to it," she said, rising and strolling over to his desk. "Because Tabitha Child's credit card has just pinged in a town called Albi. Your nearest airport is Toulouse so I suspect you'll want to meet Chrissy there instead?"

Alan stood excitedly and wrapped his hands around Bridget's head, pulling it forward to plant a kiss on her forehead.

"I think I love you!" he exclaimed as she wiped the damp spot with her sleeve.

"Do that again, and I'll swat you like a fly."

At least she was smiling.

"Toulouse. I'll meet the two of them there. They can get there easy enough, I'm sure," he said, making a grab for his jacket. "Let's hope Morton doesn't find me before the plane takes off."

CHAPTER 67

It didn't take long for the CCTV link to come through and Dominic was able to have a quick look before the flight attendant told him, for the final time, to put his laptop away for take-off. Begrudgingly, he did so. But what he'd seen had given him hope that his idea could work. Even though it was a grainy image, the woman pretending to be Tabitha Child had faced the camera head-on and Dominic had been surprised at the uncanny resemblance. But then passport control hadn't been hard for her to convince either.

By the time he landed back in England there was a text waiting for him from Morton. One that surprised him even more. It appeared that somebody had used Tabitha Child's credit card and the ping had come through, Morton had let him know. The card had been used at a café in Albi, not far from Toulouse. Dominic hoped it wasn't going to turn out to be like his trip to Paris, following her phone when a spotty youth had picked up. Had someone stolen her credit card, or was it actually the lookalike woman using it? There was only one way to find out for sure and that was to follow the trail. He'd be nuts not to. He needed to get back there. And fast.

Pulling his overnight case behind him, Dominic headed straight for ticketing to book a flight to a destination not far from where he'd just come from. It could be the breakthrough he needed. Now all he had to do was hope that she returned to the same café or that she got slack again; after all, it was the first time she'd used the card since disappearing.

"Sit tight, I'm coming to find you," he muttered as he headed for the departure gate again.

He had plenty of time before his flight back, which didn't go until 6.40 pm, so he wandered aimlessly around the airport, hoping that the act of walking would stir something useful in his mind. If you had an issue with something, had a problem to sort, the best thing to do was to do something mundane that allowed your brain to work on the issue or problem in the background as you performed something entirely different. Taking your focus off it worked wonders. It had worked in the past and he hoped it would work now. He had an hour or two to kill. But nothing was going happen when he got to Toulouse and then on to Albi later in the evening, it would be too late, around midnight local time. All he could hope for was an early start in the morning and the woman making another mistake. Yes, he could go to the café and interview the person that had taken her payment, show them a photograph, and confirm it had been the lookalike and not another spotty youth thief. It would be a start. But after that? It was back to the waiting game with his eyes wide open.

Albi is a beautiful place, a tourist attraction, with a majestic cathedral at its centre. Cathedral Basilica of Saint Cecilia, also known as Albi Cathedral, is home to nearly 200,000 square feet of Renaissance frescoes, but Dominic would have no time for sightseeing – he'd have to return another day and in a different frame of mind to explore. But the many steps that lay at the foot of the cathedral gave him the opportunity to sit and watch without looking out of place for long periods of time. He wasn't the only person doing so now, though he'd been the only one at seven o'clock that morning. The café, where the card had been used, opened early so Dominic had eaten his croissant and lingered over coffee before casually asking the waiter if he'd seen the woman in his photo. Had she been in for lunch the previous day?

"*Non, désolé je ne sais pas,*" the young man said and Dominic managed to decipher that he didn't know. In his own broken French, he asked if the waiter that had served her yesterday was in today. The reply came back the same. He didn't know. At that point, an older man, that Dominic assumed to be the owner, entered the café from a back room, wisps of hair floating on an otherwise bald head, large red-and-white broad-striped apron stretched around his ample girth. Dominic stood and caught his attention before he disappeared again. He asked if the man had seen the woman, but the man shook his head.

"I'm out in the back most of the time," he said in perfect English, though with a strong French accent. He reminded Dominic of René Artois on the TV show *'Allo, 'Allo!* He would have smiled and enjoyed the man's manner more if he wasn't on such an important mission.

"The waiter from lunch yesterday," – there was no point struggling with his French efforts – "will he be in today?"

"Louis? Yes, he will be. He starts at ten. Come back then." And then he disappeared, back to the kitchen presumably, leaving Dominic with nothing left to do but return later. And that's how he'd found himself sat on the cathedral steps, again, watching and waiting. It was useful the cathedral held such a central spot in the town, with shops and cafés all around its base, some in full sun and some covered in shade from nearby buildings. By lunchtime the temperature would be in the mid-thirties and a shaded table would be in huge demand.

When 10 am finally came around, Dominic ventured back to the café where he'd eaten breakfast and spoke to Louis who graciously shook his head – no, he hadn't seen her.

Agitated by this negative response, Dominic tried a different approach. Who had he then served at 1.13 pm, the time of the transaction?

"I will need to see the receipts, to remind me. Lunch is a busy time, you see."

"Please, can you take a look? It's important."

"I'll have to ask. Please wait here," and he vanished out the back, probably to check in with the owner. A minute or two later the young man appeared again, credit card slips in his hand. Dominic waited while he cross-checked with the written orders for the same amount, allowing him to see what she'd ordered.

"I remember her!" Louis said, excitedly, as if he had figured out the murderer in a game of Cluedo. Dominic's pulse quickened, the smile on the man's face giving him hope of a breakthrough in his case.

But that hope was about to be dashed. "But she's not the lady in your picture."

Dominic's heart sank again. It wasn't the news he'd hoped for. It seemed someone had in fact taken her credit card, just like someone had taken her phone.

"Are you positive?" Dominic was desperate.

"Yes. The lady at lunch had long red hair."

Dominic raised his fist as if to smash it through the counter but refrained at the last moment.

Could it be as simple as the woman wearing a wig? He doubted it.

CHAPTER 68

Kirsty Peters was used to taking what wasn't rightfully hers. She'd had to for most of her life. With parents who had shown early on they didn't give a damn, Kirsty had been brought up by her older brother in a large family of seven kids. Money had always been scarce during her childhood. Her parents spent most of it spent on booze and cigarettes for the two of them. Putting food on the table had been an afterthought. As long as their own stomachs were full, usually from the chip shop, there was never a thought spared for the rest of the family. Her brother Billy, only a couple of years older than her, had taken on the responsibility of feeding them, taking money from both their parents' wallets while they slept off their hangovers. They'd assumed they'd spent it before passing out, no doubt. Billy had used the money to fill a secret store cupboard in the disused outhouse at the bottom of the garden. Even though the old toilet wasn't the most salubrious place for a makeshift kitchen, it was all they had available. A hastily made jam sandwich from the cold, damp brick structure was better than going hungry, and at least on weekdays they could get a hot meal from school at lunchtime. The children weren't too proud to accept the state's charity; it was the only proper meal they got. And so Billy had continued to look after the smaller kids as he grew up, nicking money where he could and hiding it for rations. He had learned early on, and out of necessity, how to budget and keep seven mouths from having rumbling tums when they went to bed. But when Billy left home at the age of fifteen after yet another violent argument with their father, he'd told Kirsty she had to fill his shoes and carry their secret on, for the sake of the younger ones. And he'd left them to it. The last she'd heard of Billy was he was sleeping rough around London – somewhere. It was a big place.

And so Kirsty had carried on until her siblings had grown wild enough to look after themselves or be taken into care after offending, then reoffending. Both parents had washed their hands of them all and moved further up north. Where to, she'd no clue and didn't much care. But her survival instincts had stayed with her through her formative years, having to make do and make the best of what was available.

Tabby had seemed nice enough – naïve, maybe – and when she'd offered companionship without excitement travelling across to Albi and beyond, Kirsty had been willing to tag along. The free meal from the woman's credit card had been an extravagance but worth every euro, and Kirsty had then felt bad about doing it and told herself it would be a one off. But she had no self-control and was used to hoarding like a squirrel. When Tabby had announced the following morning she was taking a shower, Kirsty slipped out, card in her pocket, and found another café, down a cobbled side street, that was serving eggs for breakfast. There she sat quietly, watching the early risers go about their morning business, the market stall-holders preparing their produce and other goods for sale throughout the day. Judging by the already clear blue sky, it was going to be another hot one. Sitting there relaxing, she felt like the cat with the cream pot.

An hour later, Kirsty ventured back to wait for the opportunity to slip the credit card back into Tabby's wallet without raising suspicion. Entering the small room that the women slept in, she found Tabby lying stretched out on her bunk, a borrowed book in her hands.

"Nice walk?" she enquired, not taking her eyes off the page she was finishing.

"It's so pretty this town. I could quite happily live here for a while," she said and flopped on to her own bunk with a heavy sigh.

"Well, if we manage to get jobs each today, we can stay for a while. Unless you have other plans?"

Remembering and suddenly feeling a little uneasy that sometime soon Tabby would see the charges, she made her excuses. "I'm not sure I'd want to stay too long, mind. Itchy feet, me."

"Well, there's no point looking for a job just for a week if you're planning on leaving," Tabby ventured in a sing-song voice.

"True. It is pretty though."

Tabby reared up and swung her legs over the side. "Well, you decide. I'm going to see what's on offer job-wise, so up to you." Slithering off the bed, she applied a little lipstick and fluffed her hair up in the small mirror hanging on the wall. "I'll have to do."

"Where will you head first? Clothes shops or cafés?"

"Cafés. The tips will be a bonus."

"Good thinking. Anyway, I'm staying here, I'll take a shower myself so if you want to leave your bag, I'll take care of it. No sense in carting it with you if you don't need to." Kirsty had a plan for everything.

"Well, if you're sure... I'll pop back at lunchtime then, shall I? You'll be wanting to get out yourself."

"Perfect," she said, stifling a yawn after her big breakfast. "I might still be lying here when you get back."

"How do I look?" Tabby asked, smiling.

"Great. I'd employ you. Go get 'em."

If Susan had done some dumb things in her life, they were nothing compared to letting Kirsty look after Tabby's things.

CHAPTER 69

Much to his annoyance, Alan Davies had had to wait until the following morning to grab the first flight out to Toulouse and was getting into a hire car with Chrissy and Julie when he received further notification from Bridget. It was a simple text telling him the bare details of another transaction at a café in Albi – the time it occurred and the amount spent. The smile he couldn't keep from his face was noticed instantly by Chrissy and she enquired after it.

"Good news?" she asked hopefully, shutting the boot lid. Julie and Chrissy had grabbed a flight down to Toulouse where they'd stayed overnight and waited for Alan's arrival. The nice hotel, which Julie had sprung for, was an excuse to wear one of the more formal outfits she'd brought with her and Chrissy had enjoyed the luxury in the bargain. They'd both slept and eaten well and felt re-energised for the trip ahead.

"You could say that," Alan said, sending a quick thumbs-up emoji back to Bridget. "It looks like another transaction at another café in Albi – how convenient."

"Sounds like we might be getting closer. I hope it is her."

"What makes you think it's not?"

"Well, anybody could have stolen her purse. And after everything we've managed to wheedle out of you – and I suspect you're still hiding some of it – it sounds like this Tabitha Child woman was up to no good. I mean, now you've seen what's in that package, does it make more sense to you?"

"I'm still short on a lot of the details of exactly who she is, but yes, it does. The protected-person's scheme is just that and I'm not allowed access to her file, for obvious reasons. I can't find anything out, not without raising more red flags. Quite honestly, I can do without somebody else's superintendent asking what my interest is in a case that I'd rather have nothing to do with."

"So why are you here then, detective?" Julie asked.

"Because I work with my gut *and* I work with facts. So when my gut tells me something is adrift, it's generally right. And when the first transaction came through, I thought it odd after all this time of radio silence. Like you, I'm hoping it is in fact Susan at the end of this trail."

"I am," said Chrissy. "It's costing me a fortune."

"It's costing *me* a fortune actually," said Julie. "*I'm* your client, remember. But if it brings Susan home that's all that matters. It's not like Richard can't afford this."

"Speaking of your husband, when did you last speak to him? I've not heard you mention him. Or the shop."

"Couple of days ago," said Julie. "I suppose I ought to give him a call, make sure he's all right and not fallen into the dishwasher trying to put the soap in." She looked off into the distance as if actually imagining the scene with disappointment.

"He's not that bad," said Chrissy with a smirk on her face. Richard might be a bore, but he wasn't stupid.

"His heart is in the right place and that's all that matters."

It wasn't the reason most women stayed married, but Chrissy wasn't about to say so. She'd better give Adam a call later on; they didn't go for long without chatting on the phone. And the college had called again.

With Alan in the back seat and Julie as passenger, they were ready to go. Once they were out of the airport complex and on the open road, heading towards Albi, Chrissy brought up the subject of the package at the hotel again.

"So, who do you think organised the fake IDs?" she asked. "What are your thoughts on it?"

Since Alan had discovered the contents, he'd barely thought of much else. The obvious answer was the woman, Tabitha Child, had planned all along to swap her identification and likely take off with it. The question was, had that same woman had designs on taking Susan Smith's place permanently? And if so, why? And what was the plan then for Susan? Make her disappear? It didn't bear thinking about. Tabitha, the poor individual they thought her to be, placed in a protected-persons scheme, the victim of a heinous crime in a case that was still to be fully wrapped up, had desires to break free from it all. The tattoo on her inner thigh was a stamp of ownership and since Susan had the identical tattoo in her luggage, ready to be applied, the two of them had intended to swap places – certainly for a time. With only a couple of spare changes of clothes in their cases, it seemed they were swapping for a short period of time and then would go back home to their normal lives. At least that's what Alan was hoping they'd planned. But now he wondered if Tabitha had other ideas, though as yet he'd no proof other than the fake IDs. Maybe, when they found her, Susan would be able to throw some light on what they were up to, where they were headed and what the outcome was to be. Or, of course, he could be barking up the wrong tree again. He hoped he didn't need to find yet another new one.

Alan had told Chrissy and Julie as much in a rushed conversation on his arrival, but they were still unaware of the tattoo in Susan's luggage. That added the sinister element for Alan, and he didn't want to unnerve or worry the two women unnecessarily. The wig he'd found in Tabitha's case also added to the puzzle. After throwing ideas about with Bridget, they'd come to the conclusion that Tabitha was adding a disguise of her own, not solely taking another ID. Why though? But neither of the women had arrived in Paris as planned, the unexpected train crash seeing to that.

Somehow Susan had survived it and had gone on as Tabitha Child, not wanting to be found. Again, why?

When disasters happened – like an earthquake, or a building blowing up, or a floods ripping through a town and washing people away – they offered a way out for anyone caught up in them who'd been thinking about changing their lives and disappearing forever. It gave them a way to leave, be presumed dead. The trouble was there had been no flood, no earthquake, no bomb going off. The flaw in Susan's plan was that her disappearance could be explained: she could have left on foot. To be presumed dead, there had to be no other explanation, no way of surviving the catastrophe, and, preferably, there had to be a body as proof.

And now suddenly there were two transactions to chase. Could it be Susan? Were they close to putting an end to the mystery and taking her home?

Alan suspected there was yet more to come.

CHAPTER 70

Dominic had been sat on the cathedral steps for far too long and his bum was turning numb. He stretched his legs out in front of him to try and relieve some of the pressure as he focused his eyes on as many faces as he possibly could, scanning his near environment, scanning in the distance. He didn't want to think about needles and haystacks. He knew the person he was looking for had used the credit card in the town already, and he was hoping that they'd hung around for a while longer and that they would make another slip-up and lead him to his mystery woman. His plan after that was simply to approach her and have a conversation about how he could wreak havoc in her life. She'd have no choice but to speak with him. As the chief super had said, everybody has a price. It was just a matter of finding out what that was. Needs must: Tabitha Child was no longer able to give evidence and he wasn't going to let the case collapse around him, and if the woman could fill that space, it was the only way to resolve his own problem.

Then his own debt would be paid.

He was bored, not to mention desperate for a coffee. Dominic scrambled to his feet and sauntered off, moving around the edge of the town square, looking for a café he fancied. While it was still reasonably early in the day the temperature was already cranking up. Still, to sit in the shade seemed a waste of sunshine. He chose a sunny spot and made himself comfortable with his back against a stone wall. From his vantage point, he could see a good proportion of the area around him, though both locals and tourist numbers had picked up, making it more difficult to peruse each and every face that passed by. At least the few redheads were a little easier to see, though none looked like his mystery woman. Maybe the redhead never would appear? And how could he possibly know which one had used the card?

A young waiter took his order and vanished back inside, leaving Dominic to stare out from behind his sunglasses at every passing female face he could. When his phone buzzed in his pocket with an incoming text, he read it and smiled, shaking his head slightly, almost in disbelief.

"You are getting desperate or getting stupid, one of the two," he said to himself quietly. He read the message again to make doubly sure he'd understood it correctly, but there was no mistaking it. Tabitha Child's credit card had been used yet again. It was another café in Albi, as it had been previously, and, because of the early hour of the transaction, it must've been breakfast, not that it mattered. Yet another clue, another pointer to finding the woman he needed so desperately, had landed in his lap, or his back pocket to be precise. He headed straight for the café the transaction had come from and pulled out the photograph of his mystery woman ready. Since the last transaction had not been her in person, he expected the result to be the same though was hoping not. As he approached the counter, a young woman smiled a greeting and offered him "*Bonjour monsieur.*" Not attempting French past the first word, he pointed to the photograph. "*Bonjour.* Have you seen this woman today, for breakfast, perhaps? Has she been in the morning?" He flashed his detective ID at the same time; the authority of it, even without jurisdiction, always helped with those not in the know.

"No, sorry, *monsieur*," she said, "I have not seen this lady."

"If you find her order, you might remember who it was?" he offered hopefully. A quick search and she knew exactly who she had served. Dominic snatched the attached credit card receipt and made a mental note of the last four digits.

"A woman, yes, but with long red hair and green eyes." The waitress pointed halfway down her own back to indicate the length. "I remember her so because she ordered eggs, not a traditional French breakfast. Most tourists enjoy fresh croissants, unlike this lady."

"Was anyone with her, nearby, perhaps?"

"I did not notice, no."

Long red hair and green eyes narrowed it down further – it was better than nothing. Figuring there was nothing more to ask the young woman, he left without another word. The woman with long red hair was most likely the same person from yesterday lunchtime. And chances were she'd spend again later.

He needed to find her – today. Perhaps she could lead him to the woman he really needed.

CHAPTER 71

By the time Chrissy, Julie and Detective Alan Davies finally arrived in Albi it was almost lunchtime. Chrissy got out to stretch and could feel the hot sun searing into the bare skin of her shoulders. It must have been about 40°C; one of the hottest days of the summer, no doubt. But that didn't seem to stop the swarms of tourists that still filled the medieval and picturesque town. Chrissy had managed to park in one of the few small car parks. From there they'd planned to find the café where the transaction had taken place earlier that morning and get something to eat at the same time. Together the trio walked up the steep incline towards the town square, Julie taking a moment to be in awe of the beauty of the cathedral building itself – it seemed too large for the area in which it stood. Built of light red brick, it gleamed in the sunlight.

"Maybe we can go in when we've finished our enquiry here? I'd love to go inside and take a closer look," she cooed. Chrissy wasn't planning on sightseeing on this trip, it was work after all, and Richard could easily bring her back for a longer visit. Alan had Google Maps open and was directing them to the café.

"There should be a left turn on the other side of the square," he said, pointing. The whole area looked ancient, the cobbles smooth and shiny under foot, and Chrissy was glad Julie was still wearing her flat sandals. A sprained ankle they could do without. Like the other turns they had passed, this led to nothing more than a cobbled alleyway, not much wider than a single small car and not somewhere you'd want to meet oncoming traffic if you were driving. The alley sloped downwards and an array of tables and chairs outside several cafés and restaurants all mixed in together, border-lines for each boundary blurred. The colour of the tablecloths or napkins seemed the way to differentiate one establishment from another. When they arrived at the right one, the three sunk on to a wooden chair each. At least the hot sun had moved over behind the buildings and the space was gloriously cool. A young woman approached their table with menus in hand, passing them out with a bright smile.

"*Bonjour*. Hello," she said, covering both languages and receiving a chorus from three voices in return. Quickly scanning the menu, Chrissy ordered sparkling water, a filled crêpe and another coffee, all in perfect French.

"Make that two," chimed Julie.

"Three then," added Alan and the waitress nodded and disap-peared to prepare their order. "As soon as I've had a drink, I'll ask her," Alan announced.

"Why don't I go first, woman to woman?" Chrissy offered. "She might open up a bit more. You're a big guy after all; we don't want to intimidate her." It was a fact not a criticism.

"My size has stood me in good stead over the years, I'll have you know," Alan said, though he wasn't offended. "But as you like. Maybe I'll take the next stop."

Chrissy removed the photo she had of Susan and laid it on the table as the waitress returned with three glasses and the distinctive green of a bottle of Perrier. As she placed the glasses in front of each of them, Chrissy spotted her reaction as she caught sight of the photo. Her pause was ever so slight, but it was there, though she never said a word. When she'd left the group, Chrissy leaned in excitedly and said, "She's seen her. For sure. Susan has been here."

"Then go and talk to her," Alan said. "She may be alerting Susan that we're here looking for her. We don't know what the set-up is yet – if and how they know one another." Alan was anxious to get a result too.

Chrissy stood and entered the café building itself, heading for the counter where their waitress was making coffee. "Hello again," she said, smiling at Chrissy.

"*Le Français est plus facile pour vous?*" Is French easier for you?

"I speak English. How can I help?"

Chrissy placed the photo on the wooden countertop and waited a moment before asking, "She was here this morning? Only she's been missing for a few days and we are worried about her. Maybe she came for breakfast, early?"

The young woman shook her head, "No, she didn't come for breakfast."

"Well, that's odd because her credit card says differently. Are you sure?"

"I am sure. I told the other man, the woman at breakfast had long red hair. This is not her."

That stumped Chrissy for a moment, she felt sure their waitress had recognised Susan in the photo. "What other man?"

"The dark man, he was asking this morning. About the woman and breakfast. But she had long red hair, not like this," she said, pointing to photo again.

"What did the dark man look like, was he English?"

"Yes. Not friendly. He came this morning asking. He had a police card with him."

"He was an English policeman?"

"Yes, I think so."

Another cop was looking for her too, yet they didn't know about it. Odd, why not?

"Is she in trouble?" the woman asked nervously.

"Not from us, no. But if we don't find her soon, she may be. Why do you ask?"

"She was here earlier but looking for work, not eating breakfast."

"Really? And?"

"She starts here tomorrow morning."

CHAPTER 72

Dominic had moved out of the square early afternoon and wandered the narrow streets, watching for a woman with long red hair. There couldn't be many of them and if she was still in town, he'd follow her, hopefully back to her accommodation so he could see where she was staying. He hoped she was staying with the woman he actually needed.

The narrow streets filled with small fashionable boutiques gave him cover, and their windows allowed him to see inside a shop and scan behind him if the light was just right for the reflection. Since both women needed to eat, and dinner time was fast approaching, there could be another chance for a hit on the credit card. He'd alerted his colleague back home and asked them to inform him of the details as soon as they came through, no matter what time of day or night they happened. Waiting was boring work, and hard on his feet, and his stomach churned acid from too many cups of coffee, which in turn made him edgy.

Finally, his luck changed, and he spotted a red-headed woman that fitted the description. She looked about thirty years old, slim, tanned and relaxed in her shorts and T-shirt, casually browsing in shop windows with not a care in the world. Her auburn hair gleamed in the sunshine. He waited until she'd passed by and carried on his surveillance from a few feet back, slipping into doorways as she slowed up ahead or entered a shop herself. The last thing he wanted was for her to notice him, though it appeared she was intent on making a purchase. He could see her sifting through a rail of clothes in a store. Window reflections were a useful tool and the light in the narrow alleyway was perfect for him to watch in the opposite direction. Once she was satisfied with what she'd chosen, she made the purchase and then, on leaving the shop, she removed the item from the shopkeeper's bag and stuffed it inside her own. Dominic grinned to himself. It was classic behaviour of someone that was hiding their purchase and he bet she'd used the stolen credit card. When the woman had sauntered on, he dashed across and grabbed the credit-card receipt from the hands of a startled cashier. He looked for the last four digits he'd noted from the last transaction — they were the same. Dominic dashed back out without any explanation, leaving the cashier calling after him. He was tailing the right woman. Now all he had to do was see where she returned to and approach her there. He hoped it would lead him to the woman he desperately sought — nothing else mattered to him now. He'd got himself into this mess and she was his ticket out of it.

The redhead slipped inside another shop and he waited patiently for her to complete her purchase and transfer it from one bag to her own, as before. He wondered how much more she was planning on spending; he needed her to head back, and the sooner the better. He picked up his pace a little so he didn't lose her and was hopeful that she might be done this time. Dominic, only a couple of metres behind her and conscious she'd slowed her pace, was about to dart into a nearby doorway when she showed her hand. Flipping round quickly, she locked eyes with him immediately.

His game was up.

But she didn't run. Instead, the redhead moved towards him,

never dropping her eyes, and boldly asked, "Why are you following me?"

"I wasn't," he lied. It sounded lame because it was.

"Cut the crap. Now, before I knee you in the nuts and scream, why are you following me?"

Dominic didn't doubt she would use her knee if he didn't say something plausible. "Okay, you win. But not here." He scanned the area and noticed a bench off to the right. "Over there. We can talk out in public."

She raised an eyebrow at him and said, "But it's not safe in private, eh?"

It wasn't worth getting into. When they were sitting down, green eyes turned his way again and they were filled with energy, like a fox before it ran for its life. Was Dominic the hound then?

"The credit card you've been using. Where did you get it?" He flashed his warrant card briefly, long enough for her to see he was with the police.

"So that's what this is about? Since when did they start sending dodgy surveillance out for credit-card fraud?"

"They don't. Now please, answer the question."

"What's it worth, for me?"

"Nothing, but I won't report the usage either."

She stood to leave. "No can do."

He couldn't afford for her to go. He had to know more.

"Okay, fine. What do you want?"

"Money. Then I'll tell." Defiant.

"Really? This isn't the movies, you know," he said, exasperated. "How much?"

"What can you lay your hands on?"

Dominic had about £2,000 in his current account, but he'd be damned if she was going to get it all. But what was she worth to him, in the long run?

"I can get you the equivalent of £200 but obviously in euros. We're in France after all. Take it or leave it, but I want the full story, yes?"

"That's not enough."

"Well, until I know if the answer is what I need, there's no more. You could have found that card on the street for all I know."

Kirsty nodded her agreement and sat back down. "I have the right answer. Make it £800."

"What?" He had no choice. "Okay, okay, £800."

"Before I tell you, I want half as a down payment, though you may as well get it all while you're there. I'll wait here." This woman was stubborn and used to dealing with thugs, Dominic thought. Not many women her age would be giving him the same attitude and ball-threatening behaviour she was. He wondered why: what was her history to make her so? He glanced around for the nearest ATM; it was visible from where they sat.

"I'll be a moment," he said, pointing to it. "If you want your money, you'll wait here, understood?"

Nodding her acceptance, Kirsty wondered how much to tell the man, how much information on her new friend was £800's worth. In her gut, she knew it was a low trick, but it was easy money and she wasn't about to turn that away. Anyway, she'd only known Tabby for all of five minutes so what was the harm? By the time he returned, she'd finished caring.

Out came the story of what she knew, along with the names on the bracelet she'd found in Tabby's bag. It had explained a few things to Kirsty. Like why her friend hadn't used the credit card herself.

She wasn't really Tabby. She was Susan or Melanie Marchment.

Kirsty left nothing out – how they'd come to meet, her suspicions that Tabby was really someone else, everything. It was a low trick and Dominic handed over her reward. Wanting her out of the way, he drove her to collect her things then dropped her at Gare d'Albi-Ville, the train station at Albi, destination of her choice. He didn't want her to spoil his plan.

For Kirsty, it was back to doing what she did best: looking out for herself.

CHAPTER 73

Susan had taken herself for a well-deserved ice cream and a walk
down by the river to celebrate. Kirsty hadn't wanted to come. She'd
said she wanted to do some window shopping, which Susan wasn't
interested in herself, not having the budget – hence why she was
only having an ice cream is a treat. A couple of new blouses would
have been nice, especially since she started work the following
morning, but she was chuffed that she'd got a job waitressing. It
didn't pay much but at least it paid something, and she'd find somewhere else to stay as soon as she could gather enough rent money.
The backpackers' place wasn't suitable for longer-term living.

Once back at their room, she was surprised to find that Kirsty's
belongings had all gone and so it appeared had she. No note. Kirsty
the free spirit had simply left. She checked with the owner, the
bent-over-double older lady, who said that Kirsty had paid her bill,
paid for Susan's couple of nights and left. So it appeared Susan was
all alone once again, and she'd just begun to enjoy the woman's
company. Not that they talked about their past lives much; she
knew nothing of Kirsty herself. Still, Susan couldn't help but feel a
little dejected. She was only just getting used to being out in the
big, wide world on her own and wasn't entirely sure that she liked

it. Not for the first time, she wondered about home and, in particular, her tiny garden room. She loved spending time in there when the sun was out. It reminded her of playing 'house' with her younger sister – before the accident.

"I miss you, Melanie," she said to the empty room. "Every damn day." Dipping her head, she stood in the empty room and held back the tears that were fighting to flow.

Maybe being on her own again would force her to think of what she should do next. Travelling around France illegally, using someone else's ID, was not the bright thing to do going forward. How was she ever going to get official papers, a proper job even? And what would happen if she got sick, what would she do then? All these things had been playing on her mind as time wore on. They had not been at the forefront of her mind, not things she'd contemplated when she'd first left the train with another woman's life in her hands.

But something had prompted her to do so. Something had triggered her reaction. At the time of an event or crisis, no one thought about consequences, you just did what felt right, or what somebody else encouraged you to do, and figured it out from there. Her actions on leaving the train were all her own. She reached into her purse and took out the bracelet, turning it to read the inscription she knew was engraved there.

"What next, Susan Smith? Or are you Tabby Child? Who do you want to be? What would *Melanie* want you to be?" she asked, looking at her reflection in the mirror, waiting for an answer that never came.

CHAPTER 74

Chrissy, Julie and Alan sat in a bar on the edge of the cathedral square, feeling like the Three Amigos. They looked an odd trio: Alan, big, built like a gorilla; Julie so dainty, pale-skinned, looking demure; and Chrissy, casual in shorts and shirt, looking confident.

"I don't think I'm going to sleep much tonight," Julie said. "I'm all nerves at the thought that we could be bringing Susan home tomorrow. It's just thrilling, and I want to thank you both for putting in so much hard work because without you it would never have got this far. And in particular, thanks to you, Alan, for flying across here, to France."

"It's been my pleasure," said Alan. "I'm just glad Susan is alive and well. How she survived that crash, I've no clue. And who knows what the plan in Paris was to be." He took a sip of his drink before adding, "I've enjoyed working with you both. Maybe I should consider a switch of career and join forces with Chrissy here, because the both of you have been pretty persuasive in this whole deal." He was joking, of course. Or was he? Chrissy took his comment lightly, but his eyes shone in her direction.

"It doesn't bear thinking about," said Chrissy, referring to the plan in Paris. If she had got to her destination, I wonder what

Tabitha Child's plan was. To run off with Susan's ID is ironic considering what has actually happened, don't you think?"

"We don't know for sure that that's what was going to happen, but it does seem plausible at this stage," Alan added. "I know I'm certainly looking forward to talking more with Susan and finding out why they were meeting, what the plan was. Just out of interest."

"I wish she was here now and we could ask her," said Julie.

"It won't be long till the morning," Alan said. "And if I may suggest the plan for the morning?" The two women nodded for him to carry on with his thoughts. "I'll stay outside since Chrissy thinks I'm intimidating," he said, smiling. "I suggest Julie goes in on her own since Susan is her friend – it will be less emotional and less of a surprise than everyone walking in together."

"I agree, that's sensible," said Chrissy. "I'll keep myself scarce with you, Alan, until needed." She glanced across the table at him and he nodded back in agreement.

"What if she doesn't want to go home with us?" Julie asked.

"I guess that's where I come in. Since she's committed offences and I've got no jurisdiction in France, I'm obliged to let the French police know and they'll take care of it. Apart from credit-card fraud, she's been using somebody's ID to get in and out of the country, and there are probably other crimes that we can add to the list so she will find herself in trouble when she gets back for sure. But I daresay she'll find a decent lawyer and, it being a first offence, she'll be fine."

"Do you really have to do that?" Julie whined. "It seems so mean after all this time. You've come out here to help us and take her back, and then she'd be in trouble with the law here or at home. She loses either way, whether she agrees to come back or not."

"I can't just sweep her actions under a rock, I'm sorry. But it's her first offence so she won't go down, I'm sure. A community order, perhaps."

"Let's hope she comes willingly, and she turns up for work as planned," said Chrissy. "She's just as likely to change her mind and carry on running because we don't know if she's seen us here already. We've no idea where she is."

"I hadn't thought about that," said Julie. "Do you think we should go back to the hotel and hide out there, just in case she's nearby and can see us?"

"Well, I'm going to head back now anyway," Chrissy said. "I'm beat on my feet and you must be too, Julie. It's been a long day Have you even checked in to a hotel yet, Alan?"

"With all the day's events, I haven't given it much thought to be honest. Maybe I'll stroll back to your hotel with you two and hope they've got a room free."

"I'm sure they will have and anyway, if they don't, Julie and I will bunk in together and you can take her room." Chrissy gave her sister a friendly prod in the arm with her finger before swallowing the remaining contents of her glass. She stood to leave. The other two followed suit. It had been a long day for everybody and as they walked slowly back through the narrow streets, across to the other side of the river, Julie asked, "Who do you think the dark-haired man was then, the other policeman, and what you think he is doing here? Why hasn't he made himself known to us, particularly you, Alan?" she enquired.

"I wasn't aware anybody else was working on the case, and to be fair he probably doesn't know we're here looking either. But I've no idea who he is. Pity, a name would have been useful." They walked in silence for a couple of beats, then, "Actually, I'll ask Bridget, see if she can find out," he said as an afterthought and pulled out his phone to give her a call. "You girls go on ahead and I'll follow a few steps behind you." He found Bridget's number and held back for the girls to pull ahead while he waited for it to connect.

"*Bonjour*," she said with a fake French accent. Alan couldn't help smiling at the phone.

"Hello yourself. Look, I need another favour. Can you find out who the other detective is that's here in France? Who else has got an interest in Susan Smith or Tabitha Child? The only description I've got is he's dark."

"Alan, that could be anybody," Bridget quipped.

"I wasn't aware anybody else was interested. Can you do some digging, quietly?

"Didn't you mention somebody else? Morton was his name, wasn't it? I'll see what I can find out."

"Thanks, Bridget, I appreciate it. If it's not Morton, I don't know who it is since I don't know the man. A close colleague, maybe, a dark one. I doubt a chief super would be here looking without telling me."

"Leave it to me. You go find your woman and I'll go find your man." Then she was gone, leaving Alan's smile on his face as he hurried to catch up the two women before he lost sight of them altogether.

He hoped there was, indeed, a bed for him.

CHAPTER 75

Bridget hadn't come through with much. It seemed Chief Superintendent Morton was still in Kent and kept himself to himself. There were no avenues for Bridget to work with to find out who he might have sent to follow Susan. But she wasn't going to give up that easily. She'd find some way of making the puzzle fit together, that's what she did best.

It was another beautifully warm day in the cathedral town of Albi. The sun was already climbing in the sky as Julie, Chrissy and Alan rose with the larks, anxious of what lay ahead. So as the three walked from their hotel, across the river and back up towards the cathedral and the café, there was a tingling of excitement in the air, along with nerves and a tiny bit of worry. At 8 am they split up. Chrissy stood on one side of the square, Alan on the other, while Julie headed to the café alone, bats circling in her flat stomach. The two were a little way off but from their vantage points could clearly see anyone coming or going. Each of them in turn was to saunter past the café several times to monitor what was happening. They had to trust Julie and her method, they had to leave her to it, but neither of them was far away should she need help. It wasn't like Julie was going to throw a bag over Susan then wrestle her friend to the ground in a dramatic capture. It would be a conversation to encourage Susan to come home, and Julie hoped with all her heart that it would work out as planned. Dressed in a pale linen shift dress and kitten heels, she looked her usual stunning self, though a little more relaxed. The light dusting of sunshine had done her the world of good. She took a seat in a sunny spot, an umbrella overhead giving her some dappled shade, and ordered coffee and a croissant. She looked every bit the French local. Her large sunglasses shielded a good proportion of her face as well as allowing her to monitor her surroundings without giving the game away. She didn't want to be easily noticeable. Shocking Susan was the last thing she wanted to do.

As Julie sipped her coffee and nibbled on half her croissant, she was somewhat surprised to see a gentleman approach a table nearby, pull out a newspaper and make himself comfortable. She wouldn't normally have given him a second glance except that he was dark. His skin had a European 'oliveness' about it, his hair cropped short and styled. A handsome individual. But it was the newspaper that gave him away. The *Daily Telegraph* was not a newspaper normally found in a small French town at eight in the morning. It could only mean one thing: he was the dark man the waitress had referred to and he too had an interest in finding Susan that morning. Cold dread filled Julie's stomach and mixed with the coffee. She stifled the urge to vomit. There was nothing she could do without revealing she was there for Susan too. In an effort to steady her nerves, she took a couple of deep breaths and mumbled to herself, "No matter, Julie. You can do this. You can do this." She wished she had a newspaper of her own to hide behind, but the sunglasses would have to do. Since he wouldn't be expecting anyone else after the same prize, he'd likely concentrate on his own intentions anyway.

Julie watched the waitress from yesterday make her way across and take his order. It wouldn't be long until Susan showed up and Julie was nervous of what would happen now there was somebody else in the game. What was *his* plan? How would *he* handle things?

Had he got backup? She sipped on her glass of water and finished the croissant, all the while watching the man periodically peer over the top of his newspaper. If he was a police detective, he wasn't particularly good at surveillance, Julie mused, trying to find lightness in the situation and steady her nerves. Out the corner of her eye, she could see Alan walking towards her casually, trying not to take an interest in the surroundings, and she took the chance to alert him. She slipped her sunglasses down her nose and tried desperately to point with her eyes. Alan could see that another player had arrived. When she was confident he'd received her message, she slid the sunglasses back up her nose, glad now that somebody else knew – she wasn't on her own. He'd likely tell Chrissy and between them they would come up with a revised proposition.

She willed Susan to arrive, her nerves starting to jangle as the caffeine circulated around her bloodstream, and she tried to stay calm, the pressure getting to her somewhat. In her own mind, she tried to work out how this was going to pan out now the dark man had joined in. If she approached Susan first, they would never find out so she decided to let the man have his way, feeling sure he wasn't going to make a grab for her either. How could he? He was a British cop and since she had seen no French equivalent hovering anywhere nearby, he was a lone wolf just like she was.

At that moment Susan entered the picture. Julie restrained herself from calling out to her, desperate to talk, to warn her even. Instead, Julie watched as she casually put on her apron and approached a table of two obvious tourists that had arrived around the same time. With their order taken, the dark man raised his hand in her direction to call her attention and she made her way over. Julie could only watch, trying her best and failing to lip-read. Whatever he was saying, he was barely moving his mouth, but judging by the look on Susan's face it wasn't good news. She seemed to pale. Blood left her cheeks and a hand shot to her mouth in obvious horror. Whatever the man had said had upset her deeply and she stood frozen to the spot. Julie wondered what she should do now. She didn't want to let on why she too was there, and she didn't want to see her friend slip away again.

She waited it out.

When Susan had gone back inside, Julie stood up and pretended she was heading in to pay for her breakfast, even though it wasn't the custom in France. The young waitress from yesterday looked at her puzzled, her eyes flicking around, seemingly scared. But Julie couldn't contain herself any longer and asked in a hurried whisper "Where did she go?" With a flick of her eyes, the waitress indicated that Susan had gone through to the back room and Julie followed, hoping she was still there and hadn't been scared away.

Susan Smith, Tabby, was sat on a chair with her head bowed, wiping her face, silently trying to stop the flow of tears.

"Susan," Julie said quietly and gently, and watched as her friend raised her head and registered who it was stood in front of her. Half expecting her to flee she was surprised then when Susan stood and wrapped her arms around her, sobbing into her shoulder. All Julie could do was rub the woman's back and calm her.

And wait.

CHAPTER 76

Both Alan and Chrissy had seen what had happened from their vantage points. As the dark-haired man had risen and slid euros under his coffee cup for payment, he sauntered off, pulling his phone out at the same time. Alan decided immediately to follow him. Although Alan had no idea what had taken place, he was intrigued to know how this man fitted in and who he was talking to. He assumed the dark man was the other police detective. Alan strained to hear his words, albeit a one-sided conversation, but as he passed by, pretending he wasn't interested in the slightest, he was able to hear, "I think it's done the trick. I'll be back with her soon." While those words on their own didn't sound sinister, if the man *was* intending something with Susan they certainly did. But Alan had to carry on past and pull into a shop, pretending he was on a mission for something else entirely. He had no intention of going inside but stood in the doorway with his back pressed against the wall, waiting for the man to pass by, hoping to catch more of the conversation. It seemed there was nothing more to be said, the man was silent, but Alan observed him turn around and slowly head back where he'd just come from. Alan quickly pressed himself against the opposite wall so as not to be seen and peered out to watch the man walk back towards the café and Susan Smith. He slipped in behind him, keeping his distance, watching and waiting to see if there was anybody else in the surrounding area that could be part of whatever this man had planned. He half expected to see the French police but got the vibe the man was up to no good on his own. He had to find out.

Alan needed Bridget's help. He dialled her number and hoped she wasn't too busy.

"Have you found him?" she said, opening the conversation.

"I think I have," Alan said, "but I don't know who he is. Is there any way that you can see via my GPS location who has just received a call to a British mobile? I need to know who he's talking to. All police phones are tracked, aren't they?"

"You don't want much, do you?" Bridget said. "That's not going to be easy or quick, if I can even do it. Do you know how many mobile phones there will be where you are?"

"Well, can you think of another way?"

"Hang on a minute," she said. "Let me get your coordinates and see what I can do. But you owe me big time if I manage to pull this off without pesky flags being raised. I'll call you shortly."

Before she hung up on him, Alan managed to add, "Text me, don't call."

"Will do." And then she was gone. Alan didn't want his phone ringing in an inopportune moment, but he needed the information, like, yesterday. He needed to know who he was dealing with and how they fitted in.

He sauntered back into the café, but instead of sitting at a table, he headed straight inside, figuring that's where the women were. He was right. In the back room, Chrissy, Julie and Susan all sat together with an overriding sense of foreboding.

"What's happened?" Alan enquired.

"You'd better sit down," Chrissy instructed, and Alan pulled up a plastic crate to perch on. They were in a back storeroom. There was barely room for four people and it was not the ideal place for a conversation, but at least it was out of the way of prying eyes.

Chrissy introduced Alan to Susan so she knew who else had joined the party – not that she was celebrating.

"What's happened?" asked Alan again.

"We're not the only ones looking for Susan as we suspected," Chrissy said. "And whoever that guy is, he's got some dirt on Susan and he's threatening to go to Marcus with it if she doesn't go back with him. He's coming to pick her up in an hour and if she doesn't go, her life as she knows it will be over. She's got to decide what she wants. Oh, and he knows where she's staying and has her few belongings with him. He's giving her no choice at the moment. She can't exactly run again, she has nothing."

"That's a pretty broad threat. What is it about, have you any idea?" Alan asked gently.

Susan raised her head and said, "He knows about my past, and if it comes out, Marcus will suffer the embarrassment of it all. And he doesn't deserve that." She started sobbing again. Whatever her secret was, it was obviously going to be a painful event for them both. Through the sobs she added, "I can't bear it, not now, after all this time, and Marcus doesn't deserve the messy publicity it would create. I might not love him any more, but I care about him, and I can't do this to him." Her sobs carried on quietly, tears dropping from her jawline.

"But that's not all," said Chrissy. "He wants her to do something and if she agrees to do it, he won't tell."

Blackmail. "What does he want you to do?" Alan asked. He waited for her to calm a little, anxious for the answer.

"He wants me to be a witness to an event for him. An event I've no idea about, but he'll coach me. If I do this, if I go to court and pretend I'm somebody else, it will be over. And my past won't come out."

"Who is this man? Do you know him, did he give his name?" Alan asked.

Susan shook her head. "He just said he had the power to do it and he was part of the police and I had no choice." She bowed her head again and carried on sobbing, tears streaming down her face and trickling to the floor in front of her. Julie continued to rub Susan's back to comfort her; it was all she could do. Alan was the only one with professional experience in such a matter. He was, after all, police.

"Here's what we do," he said matter-of-factly. "Susan," he said, catching her attention, "you say yes, agree to do this." She glared at him in a 'have you gone mad?' kind of way and Alan put his hand up in order to silence her. "Let me carry on. No one's got the right to blackmail you and if this guy is a copper as he says he is, he's certainly got no right to ask you to do any of this. I need to get some backup to sort this out once and for all. This is much bigger than you sauntering off taking someone's identity for a few days. It's much too dangerous by the sounds of it and we can't have that. So I need you to say yes and pull yourself together. I know that's hard, but you need to do it to carry this through."

Susan stared, wet-eyed, at Alan. He carried on.

"Arrange to meet him later on today and you have to be adamant about that. We need as much time as possible to get things organised so if you can delay him until, say, one o'clock that gives us about four hours to organise something. Better still, if you can get him to agree to meet you at, say, five o'clock this afternoon that gives us plenty of time."

It was a lot to ask. With a faint nod she accepted the terms.

"I can't let this out. I can't ruin Marcus like this," she said.

"And you won't have to," said Alan. "So pull yourself together and when he comes back, tell him your terms. One o'clock and no sooner. And, in the meantime, I'll liaise with the local police and find out what's going on, who this guy really is, and then we need to get you to the embassy because you don't have any travelling documents to go home with."

"Can't I use the passport as I came with?"

Alan shook his head in disbelief.

"No. Not on my watch."

CHAPTER 77

Alan had left the three women in the back room of the café and asked the owner to give them some space and certainly not to let anybody else in. Begrudgingly, he had agreed. There was still no news from Bridget with a name for the other man and Alan figured he was unlikely to find out. But cop or no cop, it was an offence to blackmail somebody and since Alan had no jurisdiction in France himself, he needed the local police to take over for him. The other detective was coming back shortly to get Susan's decision and presumably take her with him. Alan wondered how he was planning on getting Susan back into the UK without using Tabitha Child's passport again. If he knew she was travelling on false documents that was an offence all on its own. Alan knew the man's intentions couldn't be legitimate; this had nothing to do with police work and everything to do with corruption. When he eventually found out the man's name, he'd be interested to know just what he'd got himself into because his career as a police detective would be over.

Unless whoever had sent him was in on it too.

Just before Alan entered the local police station, he called Bridget one more time for an update. He was disappointed that even Bridget, with her unorthodox computer talents, couldn't figure out the identity of someone who'd made a phone call while standing so close to him. He needed more. But how? His phone immediately vibrated again and looking down at the screen realised it was his boss – he sent him straight to voicemail. He'd call in when this was all over and he could report a positive outcome. He stepped inside the station and asked to speak to a detective on duty, explaining who he was and that it was a matter of some urgency. Then he sat down to wait.

Back in the café storeroom, the three women sat huddled together on makeshift chairs, waiting. Susan had said very little since Alan left, though Julie and Chrissy were both anxious to find out more. Sensing that she was in a delicate space, worrying about what was going to happen and how she was going to get out of this mess, Chrissy hadn't pushed it. Julie had tried coaxing her and had got nowhere, but as time wore on Chrissy began to feel more and more impatient. If the man blackmailing her was involved in something bigger, who knew what else he could be planning right now. Chrissy needed to find out what had happened to put Susan in the spot she was in now. Just what had she been planning, meeting up with Tabitha Child in Paris? And why weren't they sitting together if they knew one another? And that was just for starters. Chrissy needed to know in case there was something looming that could blindside them.

"Susan?" she said gently. "We really need to talk some more because time is marching on and we need to know what we're dealing with. Do you feel strong enough to tell us?"

"I'll try," she said weakly. She'd cried so hard Chrissy doubted there were any tears left to spill. Her shoulders had rocked with pain and hurt – the realisation of the trouble she was now in.

"So why don't you take your time, start at the very beginning and tell us everything you can remember," Chrissy said. "And if it's okay with you, I'm going to record it on my iPhone, just so we've got everything and Alan can hear it too. Is that okay?"

"Yes," Susan said, barely audible.

Chrissy pressed on. "Let's start with how you came to be going to Paris in the first place. Where or how did you meet the woman you were then to join in Paris?"

Susan raised her head and looked directly at Chrissy. She must have realised at that moment they knew so much already. She started slowly and the story came out.

"I miss my sister," she said. "It's the anniversary of her death. *Was* the anniversary," she corrected, looking at her friend Julie who nodded encouragingly. "I found a website that promised they could find someone to do pretty much anything on your behalf. Nothing bad like murdering someone," she added rapidly. "But other stuff, something that might be important to you personally. It sounded fun." Susan paused and Chrissy caught Julie's eye. They were both thinking the same thing: it sounded odd. For Chrissy though, it sounded all too familiar. The college.

"And what was to happen?" Chrissy pressed.

"I found a woman who looked a lot like my sister, Melanie, and she wanted to do a swap. She'd do something for me, and I'd do something for her. And we agreed to meet in Paris where we'd each carry out our role for the other." Susan's voice faded a little at the memory. Chrissy could sense embarrassment coming.

"You can tell us, Susan, what it was. It really doesn't matter to anyone what you had planned, but it's important we know."

Susan wiped her nose – it looked sore. She took a deep breath and carried on. "I wanted to spend the day with Melanie – go shopping, have tea together, chase fairies – that's all. Like we used to. Nothing weird. And the woman agreed, it was all set up and then..." The words tumbled out and fresh tears fell in torrents as Susan shared her somewhat awkward situation – to an onlooker anyway. To Susan, it had been quite natural, the chance to play 'dress-up' with her sister as the two girls had done before Melanie's death.

"So Tabitha Child was to spend the day with you, dressed as your sister, a role play experience?"

Susan nodded, embarrassment halting her words. Chrissy continued, "And what were you to do for her, Susan?"

"I was to meet a man for dinner, and pretend I was her. She said I'd have a ball, be taken out for the evening. It sounded intriguing."

"How so?"

"I was to meet him at the top of the Eiffel Tower, just before it closed at midnight. She even sent me a dress to wear. She said it was important the man saw my thigh."

Chrissy opened her mouth to speak but let it close again.

"It was only dinner and dancing, nothing more," Susan added hurriedly. "I've always been faithful to Marcus."

"Did you meet each other before? Did you have photographs of each other?" asked Chrissy. "How did you manage to find somebody that looked so much like you?"

"I don't know, that was a bit of a fluke. Tabitha approached me first. I didn't go looking for it, I just got an email one day that asked if I wanted to swap my life with someone else and, after a couple of messages, I thought actually that sounds like fun. It all looked professional and above board – I had Marcus to think about. I don't know how they got my details, spam, I expect. And one day after Marcus had left for the day, I was sat in the garden room and another email came through and I thought sod it, why not, let's have some fun. I arranged everything for Melanie's anniversary date."

Julie and Chrissy caught each other's eyes. It sounded like Susan had been targeted – it wasn't a fluke – but neither of them said anything and Chrissy prompted her to carry on. "What happened then?"

"I clicked on the link and went through to a chat room, and I could see there were so many different conversations going on involving other people. I thought this looks real enough and no harm, so when a message came through that a woman wanted to trade, it was like my short-term prayers had been answered, and Paris sounded ideal."

"Was it her idea to meet in Paris?"

"Yes, it was all set and then we had the train crash. We were travelling on the same train, though we'd both said we wouldn't let on that we knew each other so we didn't sit together. I booked the hotel rooms, one for me and one for her."

"Did you know who to look for when you reached the top of the Eiffel Tower?" Chrissy asked.

Susan shook her head, no. "I just knew that when I got there I had to show my inner thigh. She had given me a tattoo transfer, like what you had when you were young. It was quite an elaborate one and I was to apply it to my thigh and wear a dress with a high slit in it to make it visible. I guess it was a sign, like a password, though I don't suppose there'd be many women at the top of the tower just before midnight. And wearing a dress with a slit in it."

The tattoo was news to Chrissy. Alan had obviously kept it from her, unless he didn't know himself. "And when you met him, what was to happen next?"

"He was to escort me down and take me off for an evening of grandeur, a spot of romance that was to go nowhere if I didn't want it to, and just generally have a nice evening out with a lovely gentleman. Show me the town."

"Do you, by chance, know the name of the person you were meeting?" Chrissy asked, not expecting Susan to know.

"Yes, his name was Charles. Lovely name, don't you think? He sounded like a real gentleman."

"Did you catch a surname or was it first names only?"

"Yes. It was Morton, Charles Morton. He was travelling in from Europe somewhere."

CHAPTER 78

Chrissy knew she'd heard the name Morton. From Alan.

"Let's take a break for a minute, Susan," Chrissy said. "Give yourself a rest. I know how draining this must be."

"And embarrassing," Susan said. "It sounds so sordid now I repeat it all."

"Don't worry about that now, and don't be hard on yourself. I need to make a phone call, so sit tight here with Julie then we'll carry on, okay?"

Susan nodded gratefully.

"I'll get you a glass of water," Julie said helpfully.

Chrissy composed a text to Alan. Knowing full well that he could be deep in conversation with the local police, she didn't want to disturb him with a call. Still, she needed her own question answering. The text asked, *do you know Charles Morton?* She clicked send and hoped he'd reply soon.

Alan was still in the waiting area when he saw the message and put two and two together. There was only one way that Chrissy could have heard of Charles Morton and that was from Susan – that meant *he* was involved too. He hoped there weren't going to be any more surprises, that the colleagues he worked with, trusted, were all bona fide. He texted back:

Yes I know Morton or should I say I know of him. Okay to call?

Chrissy replied *yes* and waited for the phone to ring.

"Susan mentioned she was meeting Charles Morton. I assume, if you know of him, he's also with the police? This gets worse if he is," she said wearily.

"You're telling me it gets worse. I've got to report this up the chain somehow, and that puts me right in the shit. Not that I have any evidence, only one woman's word and a name, and we all know how that might play out. Senior brass don't like this kind of mess – goings on with one of their own, especially a top-ranking officer. The publicity this accusation could generate would be the commissioner's worst nightmare. Not to mention my own tarnished reputation. Not that I'm particularly thinking of myself too much right now." He let out a deep sigh.

"He would never have used his real name unless he was planning on her not surviving this," Chrissy said. "From what I've learnt so far, the girls were to change places, but I'm figuring, with what we know already, that for Tabitha at least it was a permanent thing. It was Tabitha that was going to make a run for it, leaving Susan behind to take her place and, I suspect, not as a protected person. More likely, she would be disposed of by those that were looking for Tabitha in the first place. Am I right?"

She didn't need Alan to say anything to the contrary. His silence told her all she needed to know. He'd figured similar, but now things had fallen into place, it only made the suggestion stronger.

"And Susan got embroiled in a huge mess that could have got her killed," Chrissy said.

"How's she doing?" he asked.

"She's feeling rather embarrassed, rather gullible right now, and I don't blame her. By the way, I assume you knew about the fake tattoo?"

"Yes, sorry about not telling you. I had to keep something back just in case. What did she say about it?"

"Only that she had to wear it as proof of who she was when they rendezvoused up the top of the Eiffel Tower. She was destined for a night of luxury, intrigue and excitement – or so she thought. And look how it's all turned out. I've recorded everything so far for you so you can listen when you get back."

"Good thinking."

"The more I stew on this, the more I'm certain of what was to happen. They were trading places and Charles Morton knew all about it. And that stinks. Why his interest, I wonder?"

"I've no idea. This is getting way above my pay grade now. I've not even spoken to a local detective yet and time's marching on..." But his phone vibrating stopped him going any further. It was a message from Bridget. "Hang on a minute, Chrissy," he said, reading what it said.

I've found your man. It's Dominic Berger, French for Shepherd actually, and he's French born. Worked in vice but PP now. Protected persons. Another piece slotted into place.

Any idea of his particular interest? He hit send and waited. It was only a moment before the reply came back.

I was getting to that, works for protected persons and he's got a reputation for pushing boundaries. Been in trouble in the past. He's likely her contact. Handler?

Alan wasn't surprised to read the reputation part. Detectives that worked in vice were often well placed for corruption. It was easy money to turn a blind eye. Or get a freebie. No harm done. And if they were involved in something corrupt, invariably lines could be blurred on their non-vice job too. He sent *thanks* and returned to Chrissy. "Are you still there?" he enquired.

"Yes, what's happening?"

"It seems our man's Dominic Berger, French born, protected persons back in the UK and has a record for not being straight up."

"Makes sense then. It also makes sense why Tabitha Child wanted to swap the life she had – and permanently. She *was* going to run away and leave Susan behind. What a bloody mess. And ironically that's exactly what Susan has been doing all week, running in someone else's shoes."

"I'd say your friend Susan's had a lucky escape. Naïve, yes, but a lucky escape for sure."

"I think that's going to be too much to tell her right now, she's pretty frail. I just hope she can go through with this when she has to meet Berger again. It's best that she doesn't know that aspect at this stage."

"I agree. We can tell her afterwards. Right now, I need to go banging on some doors and find somebody we can trust because I really can't do this single-handedly now. I don't want the wheels to fall off or any other clichés you might hear me say."

Chrissy smiled at that. Even stressed, Alan kept his wit.

"Well, if you can't get any joy with the local police, the only thing left to do is to create a disturbance, a distraction of sorts. I can get Julie to scream that he touched her inappropriately or something and the local cops can take him away. It will buy us some time." It was Alan's turn to smile. Julie would love the part of damsel in distress, he was sure.

"Let's hope it doesn't come to that, we don't want any more hassle. Take care of Susan and if there's anything else, let me know. Just don't pass any information back to her, not yet anyway. There's plenty time when we get back to the UK to tell her the full story of how close she came to being abducted."

"Go get some local help then, we'll be waiting."

Alan decided he'd been sitting there long enough and slipping his phone back into a pocket, went to bang on a door or two.

He then made a call to the National Crime Agency, which covered corruption, kidnapping and a whole raft of other crimes in the UK, to start the ball rolling on Berger and Morton. It was far from ideal, but it would have to do for now.

CHAPTER 79

There had to be another way to solve this mess and get Susan home safely. Chrissy checked her watch; it was almost time for Dominic Berger to return and he'd be expecting to take Susan with him. Before she headed back inside the café, she took a moment and sat on a nearby stone wall dappled by sunlight. The morning was turning out to be full of events, and the warm sunshine calmed her a little and she turned her face up to catch a few rays on her cheeks. Her shoulders ached; her nerves felt frayed at their edges. This case hadn't been her average PI job. Snooping on an errant spouse might be boring, but it was a lot easier than gallivanting across France chasing a ghost. It was Dominic Berger that was bothering her. Why hadn't he arrested her on the spot for travelling under a fake identity and committing credit-card fraud? Why the cloak and dagger, the threats and blackmail? The original proposed switch sprang to mind: could it be that simple?

"Hell, really? Is that it?" she said out loud at the incredulity of her thought. "Susan as Tabitha in a court of law?" Tabitha had been in protected persons after all. And since she'd been killed on that train...

That was his main driver, it had to be. But to what end?

He has a reputation of not being straight up.

What was in it for him? Promotion, perhaps? Pay off?

Chrissy's head was in turmoil as she attempted to filter what was relevant and put it in some sort of order. They had a runaway woman, plenty of hearsay and speculation, and a whole lot of nothing else. The more she thought it through, the more she realised Alan had no chance getting help this side of the Channel. Once Dominic— if Dominic ever reached a French police station interview room, their accusation would be dropped in an instant. Had Alan arrived at the same conclusion? she wondered. She dialled his number and listened as it rang out. If he was in fact speaking with the local police, he wasn't going to pick up, not when time was of the essence, so she quickly tapped out a text with her own proposal explained. Reading it back to herself, it seemed the only option to get the job done. It was a risk, but one she was willing to take under the unusual circumstances. The whole saga needed handing over to his colleagues back in the UK, who had the motivation and the tools to see it through.

She clicked send and hoped he read it before Dominic arrived back to pick Susan up. Just because Susan had said she would put him off didn't mean that's what would actually happen when it came down to it. She was sinking fast and her resolve to stand up to him could end up going down like a pile of falling bricks. Surely Dominic wouldn't be stupid enough to forcefully drag her out of the café and risk her squealing like a two-year-old. He couldn't have that, not in a town full of onlookers. Everyone had a camera with them these days and the scene would be up on YouTube before the next coffee was poured. Susan had to delay him until lunchtime at least. Chrissy's phone vibrated; it was Alan calling back.

"It's risky, but it would work," was his opening line.

"They didn't want to get involved, I'm guessing?"

"Correct. Hearsay and too much for a local team. Let's discuss option two. I'm fifteen minutes out. Has he been back yet?"

"No, but he won't be too much longer."

Alan was silent as he hurried back, having told Chrissy he

needed to think for a moment. When he was ready, he said, "Maybe not. Look, when he shows, you or Julie need to eavesdrop. Be a damn waitress yourself if you have to, but we have to know how he's planning to leave the country with her. Toulouse airport is the nearest and flies directly to London so unless he's planning on a ferry, which would be the long way home, it would have to be a flight. We can plan from there. Remember, he's no idea we're on to him or even that we're here."

"I need to get back inside then and brief them both. See you shortly," she said before hanging up. Quickly checking her surroundings from behind her dark shades, she casually sauntered into the café as if she were about to use the toilet. Once inside, she slipped into the rear store cupboard where Susan and Julie were waiting. A pink, blotchy face and a near-perfectly made-up one greeted her. Susan looked beat. All the energy had been sucked out of her and she resembled an airport windsock on a still day. Julie looked somewhat frazzled but eager to know what was to happen next. Chrissy needed to force some energy into the situation and, rubbing her hands together, excitedly announced, "Change of plan ladies. Here's what we're going to do."

When she'd relayed the details, it didn't sound the least bit exciting at all. In fact, it sounded incredibly stupid and dangerous, but what other choice did they have? Chrissy felt sure it was the only way. All she had to do was hope Susan was mentally capable and strong enough to carry it through.

There was no time to lose.

CHAPTER 80

Alan knew it was risky but couldn't come up with a better solution in time. It wasn't simply a case of getting Susan Smith back home. There was so much more at stake now: a corrupt police officer ready to commit yet another crime to add on to his already substantial list, and a chief superintendent with corruption links that would likely go nowhere. With no evidence to back the story up, a defence lawyer would laugh them out of a holding cell. And unless any proof did come to light, there was hardly any point Alan even bringing it up for the grief it would cause. That didn't make it right though. There had to be retribution of some kind. As he turned the final corner, heading back towards the café, he could see Dominic was already seated at the same table where he'd spoken to Susan earlier on. His body language looked relaxed and in control, and confidence oozed off his broad shoulders. One leg crossed the other casually, and he appeared to be talking and laughing into his phone.

"Who are you chatting to, arsehole?" he said quietly to himself, as he watched from a distance, before slipping into a nearby glacier for an ice cream, all the time watching the man. Blending in as a tourist was a safe bet, and he was glad of the cover of his sunglasses. None of the three women appeared to be there, and he assumed they were still out back in the storeroom. He sent Chrissy a text telling her where he was.

I'm in the glacier across the way, what's happening at your end? He ordered a double scoop of chocolate and waited for her reply. She called him straight back.

"All set. Saunter over and sit near his table when you see Julie, who'll be wearing a large hat. Don't let on you know her," she said. She was an organised, gutsy woman and Alan couldn't help rolling his eyes at the last part. Did she think he hadn't been a detective long?

"We're monitoring airline bookings, assuming that's his plan – it's the obvious choice. She'll have to travel as Tabitha Child so that's easily found. How's Susan holding up?"

"Scared witless. She'll be fine. Now she knows the plan. Okay, here comes Julie. Ready?"

"Ready," he said, hanging up and heading over to the café. Dominic had the majority of his face turned away from him so it made Alan's approach that bit easier. He hoped Dominic hadn't noticed him following earlier, but he couldn't worry about it now. He pulled out a chair to the side and rear of the man and made himself comfortable. Julie was at a table on the other side, looking as stunning as ever, half hidden behind a huge straw hat and sunglasses that almost swallowed her whole face. Bright red lips were about all he could see. Alan assumed Chrissy was inside, still coaching Susan. She hadn't looked particularly strong earlier, but then an experience like this would turn the staunchest into quivering jelly. A moment later, Susan came out into the sunlight, looking reasonably upbeat, ready to play her part. Alan watched as she headed straight for Dominic's table and pretended to take his order.

"And what's it to be?" he asked, as if he were ordering his lunch. He sounded casual about it.

"How do we get back?" Not a quiver in her voice. Alan was impressed.

"We fly of course. Why?"

"I get seasick. I was hoping we'd fly. Toulouse, I assume. What time?"

"Flight leaves at two," he said, standing. "You'll be home before you know it." There was a definite smile in his voice and Alan was tempted to rear up and punch it away, but that would have been tantamount to operational suicide. Taking a deep breath quietly, he refocused on the conversation going on to the side of him. Julie had also stood, though she had her back to Dominic so he couldn't see her face at all.

"Ready?"

"Not really, but I don't have a choice, do I? Have you got my belongings?"

"In the hire car, ready to go." And the two slowly made their way back towards the cathedral square and on to his vehicle. When they were both out of earshot, Chrissy joined Julie and Alan.

"Let's hope this works," he said dubiously. "Or else I'll be looking for a waitressing job when I get back."

"Waitering," Julie corrected. "You're a male."

"Either or. If they chop my balls off, I could be the former," he said, glancing around out of habit. "Check your phone tracker before she gets much further away, make sure it's working." The women had connected via *Find My iPhone*, which had been the quickest way to sort out a tracking device at short notice. The phone was set on silent though Airplane Mode would have to sing for it. Chrissy was sure people forgot to turn their phones off on flights all the time. This was no time to worry about it.

"We already did, and it's fine. I'll never see my phone again though," Julie said.

"You can afford a new one, I'm sure. Okay, let's get ourselves to the airport and changed," Chrissy added, taking charge and heading for their own hire car. She'd tipped the concierge at the hotel for organising their bags to be packed and their car brought around ready.

"And I'll get Bridget to allocate seats on that flight," Alan said. "And I think we're done bar the waiting to set off." His smile was there to add encouragement to the others as well as make himself feel better about what would happen next.

He only hoped Susan was safe. He'd made some unorthodox moves in his time, but nothing like this. His intentions and motives were always for the good and he hoped this one would be no different.

A little over an hour and a half later, they were in the departure hall of Toulouse Airport.

"And another charge added to his list," Alan said happily as they watched Dominic and Susan pass successfully through passport control. This had been Alan's main worry about the whole set-up, but it had gone as smoothly as any other passenger interaction with the officers. The ticket had been issued in Tabitha Child's name so Dominic had intended to use her passport too. A silent tick filled a box in Alan's head. At least Dominic Berger would be investigated for his part in all this, and if he had any sense, he'd add Charles Morton into the mix, if only as leverage in the face of his own punishment.

Everyone has a price.

Filing through passport control themselves, safe in the knowledge that Susan and Dominic were now airside in the small airport, they settled themselves separately around the various nearby departure gates.

There was nothing left to do until they touched down back in the UK.

CHAPTER 81

Alan had worked with Bridget for many years and trusted her implicitly. So when their plane finally landed and he read her text, he knew everything was going to work out just fine. Still, it would be good to see her plan in full swing. All through the flight, Alan, Chrissy and Julie had watched the two heads further up the front of the plane – Susan's and Dominic's. They were safe and sound and blissfully unaware of what was to happen once they arrived at Heathrow.

The plane taxied to its designated spot and, as usual, impatient people clambered to get their luggage from the overhead lockers long before the seatbelt sign had been switched off. It was distracting and none of the three could see their targets clearly, but since the cabin door hadn't yet been opened, it didn't much matter. Susan still had Julie's phone as a tracking device anyway. Just in case. As people finally filed out and headed towards passport control, the three hung back together just to be sure Susan's passport in particular went through smoothly, which it did. Regardless of whether Bridget had had a hand in making the transition at both ends so, they were grateful for no hiccups.

Then, all at once, they were through customs and out into the arrivals hall. Alan scanned the area nervously, as did Chrissy. But there was no sign of any police officers waiting. And they couldn't see Susan and Dominic either.

Alan's stomach dropped and Chrissy started to feel frantic. Had they just allowed Susan to be abducted by Dominic after all? Had he in fact managed successfully to get her back to England and then had someone else take over without them noticing? It didn't bear thinking about, but none of them could see Susan or Dominic anywhere.

"Check the app," screamed Alan and Chrissy pulled her phone out. The blue blob of Susan flashed nearby.

"This way!" she urged and the three darted towards one of the exit doors, not sure what they would eventually see on the other side. They needn't have worried. A small swarm of officers had surrounded both Susan and Dominic, and Chrissy could see the surprise and frustration in Dominic's eyes as they neared them. Susan, on the other hand, looked relieved it was all finally over, save for her own misdemeanours. She'd have some explaining to do to Marcus, but there was a limit to what he needed to know. Her past could stay buried a good while longer; there was no need to upset him. Alan scanned for Bridget, her blonde hair settling about shoulder height to one of the officers, and he idled over.

"Nice work, Bridget," he said. Chrissy and Julie sidled up alongside and nodded to the petit woman.

"Thanks, big man."

Chrissy and Julie exchanged amused glances.

"I had to involve the boss man, sorry," she said as Alan's DI joined the four of them. Not really sure how the man was going to react, Alan kept it businesslike.

"It's much bigger than this," he said, waving at the two now in cuffs. People had started to gather. Several had their phones out and were filming the scene ready for YouTube.

"Relax, Alan. Bridget's filled me in with the most part, though we still need to have a formal chat, obviously." He made it sound like they were going to share coffee and cake. Alan rather doubted they would. But at least his tone was civil and there'd be no public bollocking for the crowd to witness, which was a saving grace in that respect. "Come on. You can start explaining on the way." He turned to Chrissy and Julie. "And don't you two be going far. We'll need your formal statements soon enough."

"I'll be in touch," Alan said to them both before shaking their hands and heading off with his boss. "Thanks again. It's sort of been a pleasure."

Chrissy and Julie were aware they were spare parts now; there was nothing more for them to do as the authorities took over. Watching as Susan and Dominic were escorted away, the two women waved lightly at Susan for a moral boost and she smiled weakly. Julie yelled, "See you soon!"

"I doubt that, Julie," Chrissy said. "Not for a while at least. There's a lot to get sorted yet."

"I know, but she's not feeling so strong, not at the moment, and she needs hope."

"She won't go unpunished, of that I'm sure. Fingers crossed for a community order, eh? Marcus will know a smart lawyer, and on that note, you should call him. Or do you want me to speak to him?"

Julie looked at her watch. It wasn't late in Hong Kong. "Damn, Susan still has my phone. You've got his number?"

Chrissy nodded. "I'll call him then," she said and waited to be connected to break the news.

If he was thrilled, he wasn't showing it in his voice or word choice. Chrissy hung up after a brief and rather one-sided conversation.

"He's just odd, that man, but he's on his way back. I wonder what his deal is?"

"What do you mean 'deal'?"

"Well, I know Susan said it's been over between them for a while, but still, she is his wife, he can't dislike her that much, can he?"

"Who knows what goes on behind closed doors, Chrissy. Some marriages are like that," Julie said. Sadness tinged her words. Was

Julie trying to tell Chrissy that her own marriage to Richard was 'like that'? It wasn't the time or the place to dig further into that one.

"Come on. Let's get your bag back and go home to our own lives. I know I'm looking forward to my own bed tonight. Preferably with Adam in it," she said, winking at her sister.

CHAPTER 82

The following day Susan was sitting in an interview room along with her lawyer. Alan was also there, as was his DI, making it a typical interview foursome. Having already covered much of the ins and outs of what had happened, there was still one burning question that Alan was anxious to know the answer to: why? Why had she run? What had driven her to take off with another person's identity? These weren't the actions of a rational individual. Whatever Alan had been expecting it to be it certainly wasn't what she was about to say.

"When I was young, eight years old," Susan started quietly, "my sister, Melanie, was seven, and we'd go for walks together in the local fields near where we lived. We'd pretend to see fairies and play hide and seek with them. Fantasy, like young girls do, I guess. We'd give them names and hide out with them behind walls and in bushes. It was fun." She smiled at the memory and Alan could only guess the fairies filled her mind now as she reminisced. But her face began to darken, her smile fading as she spoke, eyes focusing on a spot somewhere in the near distance. "But it was spoiled. And I couldn't help her. The fairies couldn't help her, and neither could I."

A single tear made its way from her right eye and it tumbled down her cheek. Alan couldn't see where it landed, but it didn't matter.

"What happened?" he prodded gently. "What was spoiled, what couldn't you help her with?"

"She lost her footing in the long grass. She was reaching for one of the fairies – they were at arm's length, she'd said. But she stumbled and fell. I ran towards her, but she rolled away on her side and couldn't stop herself," she said, her words gathering urgency as she relived that day out loud. "And then I couldn't see her, the grass was too long, but I could hear her calling, screaming as she tumbled down the steep banking towards the tracks and I couldn't help her." Tears flowed freely as she turned and her wet eyes locked with Alan's. He could only guess what would happen next. "The train came so fast, so fast... the noise..." She covered her ears with her hands and squeezed, trying to block it out.

The interview room was silent, nobody spoke as they digested what they assumed must have happened. But Susan wasn't finished. She had to cleanse her soul, cleanse her heart, and finish what she'd finally started. Not even her parents knew the truth of what had actually happened that day. "The brakes screamed, the driver tried to stop, but there was no time. Melanie was..." She dropped her eyes again, something on the floor attracting her attention. She couldn't bring herself to say it.

Decapitated.

"And all I could do was lie there, hidden by the same tall grass, and cry for her. I can still smell it, what the brakes made. Hot. Ammonia. I'll never forget." She lifted her gaze directly to Alan again, as if remembering something, and added, "I remember the same smell, on the train, when it crashed," she said hurriedly. "I could smell ammonia!" For Susan, something had clicked into place and the three of them understood. The smell of ammonia had been the trigger, the one thing that had made her return to that day, then run.

She'd run as a child. She'd run as an adult.

"I've never told anyone I was there," she said, looking around the room at the three of them, her eyes willing compassion, a sign that they each understood her pain. "I ran off."

Alan reached out, "It wasn't your fault Melanie fell. It was an accident. You weren't to blame, Susan."

But she shook her head, no. "If we hadn't been playing with the fairies, we wouldn't have been in those fields. It had been my idea to go. I'm to blame! Mum blamed me too, for not keeping Melanie safe, and she's gone too." Her eyes were wide, pupils dilated as she fixated on Alan. "It's my fault she's dead, they're both dead!" she screamed, standing up, her chair scraping back noisily as the room filled with her raw and concentrated emotion. Her lawyer stood, anxious to help. Susan was visibly distraught.

Melanie Marchment had been killed. And Susan had carried the raw guilt for nearly twenty-five years.

Alan understood. *That's* what Dominic Berger had threatened to tell, to blackmail her with. The death of her sister that she'd run away from. Finally, he now had a reason for it all.

"My client needs a break," Susan's lawyer said, and Alan agreed with a nod. Seeing the state she was in, he wondered if to call the doctor. The woman had been through enough stress and anguish to last her a lifetime. Losing a sister would have been bad enough on its own, but to then lose your mother and carry that guilt for so long? And not tell anyone? He hoped, now she'd finally let it all out, she'd be able to heal and gain her emotional strength back. She'd likely need the help of a professional as well as the support of her friends. Alan wondered about where Marcus might fit – did he even have a role in her life from this point on? He doubted it. Not needing any further information for the time being, they decided to hold off on any more questions for the day. The doctor had been called, just to be safe, and had recommended a light sedation. Susan needed to rest.

Alan had contacted Julie who picked her friend up and took her back to her place for the night. Julie didn't want to leave her alone and thought it was the best thing – a quiet place for Susan to start her recovery in. She could stay as long as she'd like. Marcus was on his way back from Hong Kong and from there, it depended on how strong Susan felt as to what would happen next. But at least Susan Smith was home.

CHAPTER 83

A week later

It was always enjoyable to go away but lovely to get home again. Chrissy and Julie's trip to France hadn't exactly been a holiday, though it had been an experience to remember. One for the memoir and one Chrissy would enjoy reciting to her grandchildren one day. Wrapping the whole thing up with Susan had simultaneously brought answers for Chrissy's other case at the college. While it had been a rather specialist website that Susan had visited and committed herself to, digital forensics had found fine tentacles and similarities to several other sites that targeted a wide range of demographics encouraging unusual behaviour. From auction sites where you could bid for someone to take your driver's test on your behalf, to sites offering fake employment medicals. Or maybe you wanted to swap your life with someone else for forty-eight hours. It was all available. It seemed no one was spared – teenager to old-age pensioner, they had an angle and sales pitch for all. The problem was how to deal with it. It was way beyond the capabilities of Chrissy and her techy contact so they'd handed over to the police. Bridget had pricked her ears up with interest, though she also knew the site's creators would have covered their tracks well, employing proxy servers all over the world to keep names and locations hidden. It would be a tough one to unravel, if ever they could. Still, the publicity Chrissy's college case had generated was hot news. It was one way of making sure vulnerable individuals were aware of the dangers out there.

Dominic Berger still faced charges, and he'd done his best to drop his boss, Morton, in it too. But as Alan had voiced, there was little to no evidence. Phone conversations were not enough – one word against another. And with no digital trace of the rendezvous that night between Susan and Morton, the case would go nowhere. Morton's alibi for that night was simple. He had been asleep with his wife in bed at their hotel and it had been verified. The fact that he'd been in Paris himself that night? Pure coincidence. Morton had declared any suggestion of his involvement utterly preposterous. That would likely be the end of it. According to Dominic, he himself had been promised a passage back to vice. That would never happen now, and he still had his own disciplinary and punishment to get through. His future as a detective was likely over.

In Susan's small garden studio, Chrissy, Julie, Alan, Susan and Bridget raised their glasses in a toast.

"To a new life!" they cheered in unison, five smiling faces sipping on an expensive bottle of champagne. It would likely be Susan's last for a while. She and Marcus had agreed to go their separate ways and finally get divorced. Having spent so much time without him around, Susan was used to living on her own and, after her solo trip, it really didn't bother her at all. In fact, she was looking forward to being herself again and getting back to work. New opportunities were on the horizon and Julie had mooted an idea concerning Jooles, Jooles. A franchise, perhaps.

"Where will you move to?" Alan asked Susan.

"I've no clue. But I've got a court appearance to get through first and I can't leave the country. So France is out of the question, which is a shame. I quite liked Albi," she quipped, smiling. "Another boutique shoe business would work well there."

"We'll go back for a visit together," offered Julie. "I missed out on seeing the inside of the cathedral. Something more pressing about a lost woman we were tracking down," she said, laughing, and the others joined in.

"You're on!" Susan shouted, eyes wide. "And I love those flats on you, by the way. So pretty," Susan added, catching Chrissy's knowing eye and winking.

"My footwear has yet again been the topic of conversation, I see." Julie said with mock disdain.

"If you'd stuck to wearing your heels, we'd still be pecking about in Calais," Chrissy said, laughing along with her sister.

But it was good to see Susan relax a little. She was feeling a good deal better about herself and her future and gained more emotional strength each day. Her expedition had taught her a lot about herself and even though she'd never recommend running away, particularly with virtually no belongings to your name and having stolen another's identity in the process, she was glad she'd done it.

"One thing that still puzzles me," Chrissy said. "If you knew Marcus was tracking your phone and your emails, how did he not know about your rendezvous in Paris?"

Alan and Bridget exchanged a glance.

"He did know, I expect. He'd have to have had."

"Yet he never mentioned it to us when we asked about the tracker," Chrissy said thoughtfully.

Susan shrugged. "It'll have slipped his mind. He's a busy man," she added soundly. "Anyway, it's almost over now, I don't much care. And we're getting divorced." Susan had drawn a line under the question; she didn't want to discuss it any further. It would have to do for Chrissy. "I'm just happy to be back home." She raised her glass and shouted another toast. "Here's to getting a community order."

"To community orders," they chimed in unison.

And to Melanie... Susan added in her head, silently.

But Bridget and Alan knew a little more. They'd debated whether to mention their news to Susan or not and had decided against it since it would serve no purpose and she was mentally getting herself back on her feet. There was a long journey ahead yet.

It seemed both Chief Superintendent Charles Morton and Marcus Smith had attended the same boarding school.

Another coincidence?

ACKNOWLEDGMENTS

This book is a work of fiction, though some physical places featured are indeed real. The characters, however, are most definitely figments of my imagination.

I'd like to thank Graham Bartlett, a police procedural advisor who makes sure the correct process is followed when it comes to the technical stuff. That said, any variation from actual procedure is for creative purposes because in reality it takes weeks to get the results back from some tests and that would mess with the story's timelines too much, and we'd be all day waiting.

Thanks to Darren Attwood, a real-life PI at Belso Investigations, for your valuable input. If I'm ever missing, I'll call you! And not forgetting my local area police commander, who shall remain nameless. You know who you are though. I wouldn't want to ever spend a night in a cell.

And thanks to you, the reader, because if you didn't buy my books, there would be little point in me writing any more.

The hunt is on…

They kill wild animals for sport. She's about to return the favour. A spate
of distressing big-game hunter posts are clogging up her newsfeed. As
hunters brag about the exotic animals they've murdered and the followers
they've gained along the way, a passionate veterinarian can no longer sit
back and do nothing. To stop the killings, she creates her own endangered
list of hunters. By stalking their online profiles and infiltrating their inner
circles, she vows to take them out one-by-one. How far will she go to add
the guilty to her own trophy collection?

Dark Service

**The dark web can satisfy any perversion, but two detectives
might just pull the plug…**

Taylor never felt the blade pressed to her scalp. She wakes frightened and
alone in an unfamiliar hotel room with a near shaved head and a warning…
tell no one.

As detectives Amanda Lacey and Jack Rutherford investigate, they venture
deep into the fetish-fueled underbelly of the dark web. The traumatized
woman is only the latest victim in a decade-long string of disturbing—and
intensely personal—thefts.

To take down a perverted black market, they'll go undercover. But just
when justice seems within reach, an unexpected event sends their sting
operation spiraling out of control. Their only chance at catching the
culprits lies with a local reporter… and a sex scandal that could ruin
them all.

One Last Hit

The greatest danger may come from inside his own home.

Detective Duncan Riley has always worked hard to maintain order on the
streets of Manchester. But when a series of incidents at home cause him to
worry about his wife's behaviour, he finds himself pulled in too many
directions at once.

After a colleague Amanda Lacey asks for his help with a local drug epidemic, he never expected the case would infiltrate his own family...And a situation that spirals out of control...

Hey You, Pretty Face

An abandoned infant. Three girls stolen in the night. Can one overworked detective find the connection to save them all?

London, 1999. Short-staffed during a holiday week, Detective Jack Rutherford can't afford to spend time on the couch with his beloved wife. With a skeleton staff, he's forced to handle a deserted infant and a trio of missing girls almost single-handedly. Despite the overload, Jack has a sneaking suspicion that the baby and the abductions are somehow connected...

As he fights to reunite the girls with their families, the clues point to a dark secret that sends chills down his spine. With evidence revealing a detestable crime ring, can Jack catch the criminals before the girls go missing forever?

Scream Blue Murder

Two cold cases are about to turn red hot...

Detective Jack Rutherford's instincts have only sharpened with age. So when a violent road fatality reminds him of a near-identical crime from 15 years earlier, he digs up the past to investigate both. But with one case already closed, he fears the wrong man still festers behind bars while the real killer roams free...

For Detective Amanda Lacey, family always comes first. But when she unearths a skeleton in her father-in-law's garden, she has to balance her heart with her desire for justice. And with darkness lurking just beneath the surface, DS Lacey must push her feelings to one side to discover the chilling truth.

As the sins of the past haunt both detectives, will solving the crimes have consequences that echo for the rest of their lives?

The Chrissy Livingstone series:

Tin Men

She thought she knew her father. But what she doesn't know could fill a mortuary...

Chrissy Livingstone grieves over her dad's sudden death. While she cleans out his old things, she discovers something she can't explain: seven photos of schoolboys with the year 1987 stamped on the back. Unable to turn off her desire for the truth, she hunts down the boys in the photos only to find out that three of the seven have committed suicide...

Tracing the clues from Surrey to Santa Monica, Chrissy unearths disturbing ties between her father's work as a financier and the victims. As each new connection raises more sinister questions about her family, she fears she should've left the secrets buried with the dead.

Will Chrissy put the past to rest, or will the sins of the father destroy her?

Walk Like You

When a major railway accident turns into a bizarre case of a missing body, will this PI's hunt for the truth take her way off track?

London. Private investigator Chrissy Livingstone's dirty work has taken her down a different path to her family. But when her upper-class sister begs her to locate a friend missing after a horrific train crash, she feels duty-bound to assist. Though when the two dig deeper, all the evidence seems to lead to one mysterious conclusion: the woman doesn't want to be found.

Still with no idea why the woman was on the train, and an unidentified body uncannily resembling the missing person lying unclaimed in the mortuary, the sisters follow a trail of cryptic clues through France. The mystery deepens when they learn someone else is searching, and their motive could be murder...

Can Chrissy find the woman before she meets a terrible fate?

ABOUT THE AUTHOR

Hi, I'm Linda Coles. Thanks for choosing this book, I really hope you enjoyed it and collect the following ones in the series. Great characters make a great read and I hope I've managed to create that for you.

Originally from the UK, I now live and work in beautiful New Zealand along with my hubby, 2 cats and 6 goats. My office sits by the edge of my vegetable garden, and apart from reading and writing, I get to run by the beach for pleasure.

If you find a moment, please do write an honest online review of my work, they really do make such a difference to those choosing what book to buy next.

If you'd like to keep in touch via my newsletter, use this link to leave your details:

http://eepurl.com/gwfVqL

Enjoy! And tell your friends.

Thanks, Linda

Follow me on BookBub

ALSO BY LINDA COLES

Jack Rutherford and Amanda Lacey Series:

The Controller

Hot to Kill

The Hunted

Dark Service

One Last Hit

Hey You, Pretty Face

Scream Blue Murder

Chrissy Livingstone:

Tin Men

Walk Like You

Manufactured by Amazon.ca
Bolton, ON